"I shall then make known to you something of the history of this man, which has been ascertained for me."

Abraham **VAN HELSING**

An Abaddon Books™ Publication
www.abaddonbooks.com
abaddon@rebellion.co.uk

First published in 2018 by Abaddon Books™,
Rebellion Publishing Limited,
Riverside House, Osney Mead, Oxford, OX2 0ES, UK.

10 9 8 7 6 5 4 3 2 1

Design: Sam Gretton, Oz Osborne and Maz Smith
Marketing and PR: Remy Njambi
Commissioning Editor: David Thomas Moore
Editor-in-Chief: Jonathan Oliver
Head of Books and Comics Publishing: Ben Smith
Creative Director and CEO: Jason Kingsley
Chief Technical Officer: Chris Kingsley

Cover design by Sam Gretton, based on
a 15th-century painting of Vlad Dracula and
the cover of the 1916 edition of Bram Stoker's *Dracula*.

UK ISBN: 978-1-78108-666-7

Printed in Denmark

DRACULA
RISE OF THE BEAST

Bogi **TAKÁCS**
Adrian **TCHAIKOVSKY**
Milena **BENINI**
Emil **MINCHEV**
Caren **GUSSOFF SUMPTION**

Edited by David Thomas **MOORE**

ABADDON
BOOKS

PROLOGUE

From: Jonathan Holmwood (jwlh1947@amol.com)
To: Dani Văduvă (bornwithteeth@webmail.com)
Date: January 11, 2018
Subject: Re: Mina Harker?

Hi Dani,

I must admit to being a bit surprised by your contact; I haven't thought much about all this for years! Yes, I am that Jonathan Holmwood—Wilhelmina Harker was my great-grandmother on my mother's side.

I can't actually tell you a lot about her: she died before I was born. Grandad Quincey talked about her a lot, but never about the business with D—. Mum apparently asked him about it once, after she married, and he said he'd "seen enough evil in the trenches without going chasing after ghosts and goblins." We only actually found Mina's letter when we sorted through his house, after he passed on.

That said, I may be of some help anyway. Dad had his own copy of Mina's file—*his* grandfather, Arthur, was another one of the hunters—and even added to it, after digging up some of D—'s history. I guess he wanted to understand the *why* of it all, in a way Van Helsing never bothered. I added to it myself as a young man, and again twenty years or so later when the Soviet Union collapsed; but I lost interest in it not long after that.

I'll see if I can dig up the old journal and scan it over the weekend; look out for more emails in the next few days.

And Dani? Good luck. I'm honestly not sure if what you're doing is the most sensible thing, although I appreciate you feel like you don't have a choice. I looked at /r/fanghunters like you asked, and a lot of it seems legitimate, from what I know, but be careful about exposing yourself there. If nothing else, there's no reason *they* couldn't be lurking there too.

Thank you,

JH

ONE

THE SOULS OF THOSE
GONE ASTRAY FROM THE PATH

INTERLUDE

From: Jonathan Holmwood (jwlh1947@amol.com)
To: Dani Văduvă (bornwithteeth@webmail.com)
Date: January 13, 2018
Subject: Re: Mina Harker?

Hi Dani,

Okay, part one. This is the oldest source, although it was nearly the last I got my hands on, back in 1992.

You're too young to remember life before the internet. (A lot of chaps my age grumble on about the good old days before iPhones and computers, but blow all that for a game of soldiers, the internet's great.) But back when I was your age, if you wanted to find anything out, you had to go to a library—and if it was in any way obscure or unusual, often a *particular* library, somewhere bloody miles away, even in another country.

And then, of course, this was before the Wall came down; I suppose your mother could tell you more about that time. What my father and I both struggled with, in our researches, was that most of the best, oldest sources on D— and his career were stuck in the Eastern Bloc, and all but impossible to get at, even with money and connections. Austria was open, of course, and I had some luck with Yugoslavia in the 'sixties, but Hungary and Romania were right out. Any number of lines of enquiry cut off, doors slammed in our faces, as we hit that invisible line across Central Europe.

And then we watched on the telly as soldiers broke down the Berlin Wall, and it all changed. I started making some phone calls that evening, as I recall, half-cut on whiskey and goodwill.

It took me a couple of years, but I ended up making contact with Mózes Mendel, a professor at the Rabbiképző in Budapest, who'd written a couple of papers about the treatment of Jews in the Kingdom of Hungary around the time of D—'s career, and who—it had been strongly hinted to me—might be able to answer some of my questions.

Rabbi Mendel was a lovely chap, and spoke better English than I did, thank heaven; but it took me three meetings with him before he eventually came up with this: a collection of letters and papers passed down from an ancestor of his. He wouldn't be drawn on the implications, even after I explained who I was, and about my family's history with D—, but it's clear his family treated the threat very seriously, or why would they have held them so close, for so long?

At any rate, here they are.

Thanks,

JH x

THE SOULS OF THOSE GONE ASTRAY FROM THE PATH

Bogi Takács

Letter from Jakab Mendel the Elder to Rabbi Izsák the Scribe

With the Aid of the Heavens
The 21st of Av, the year 5235 since Creation
July 25, 1475

Esteemed Rabbi Izsák,

I hope this letter finds you well, and the weather in Provence brings a speedy recovery for you. The winter here has been difficult, and the Court is all aflutter and restless.

I would like to ask your advice, for it is said that the one who understands shall know. Nothing is new under the Sun, and yet I find myself concerned about a situation developing in Pest-Buda. Everyone from maids to courtiers is gossiping about the King's former captive, Vlad of Wallachia the Third—also known as Drakulya after his father, who was a member of the knightly Order of the Dragonists.

The King released Vlad after fourteen years of imprisonment and recognized his claim to Wallachia, and no one understands the reasons to this change. Vlad settled down on the Pest side of the river and has been avoiding social events, mostly staying in his house. The word is, he even attacked a young messenger sent to invite him to a ball in the Buda castle.

Ever since Vlad has been released, King Mátyás seems distraught. Whenever I talk to the King in my capacity as prefect of all Jews in the Kingdom of Hungary, he moans and groans, his eyes tired and his face worn. Last week before Shabbes I suggested to him that it would elevate his mood to remarry, which suggestion he took with the utmost animosity. I know well that he no longer mourns poor young Katalin, may she rest in peace. So I could not understand his abrupt anger and shouting. You of all people understand I do not wish to alienate the King; the safety of the entire nation of Israel in Hungarian exile depends on his continued goodwill. I did manage to calm him, but sometimes he has the ferocity of a lion.

Yet this is not what most concerns me. We are all familiar with the stories of how he wanders the countryside, disguised as a simple peasant, determined to uncover the true state of his kingdom. He remains well-respected for it despite his occasional cruelty and the high taxes he imposes upon his subjects. And yet I have always wondered how he can hide his identity; his portraits are widely dispersed across the land, and he has a distinctive profile.

This past week I believe I have come closer to understanding this mystery. After I had left the audience-room and gone down the stairs, I realized with alarm that I had forgotten to ask the King for his royal signature and seal on an important document concerning the planned reconstruction of the Main Synagogue. I hastened to return and ask the guards for readmittance, and seeing that they had already left their posts, I pushed open the heavy door. I hoped that the King would forgive my impertinence based on our longstanding good relations, despite his recent capricious mood.

In the room, I saw a thin, reedy youngster in the King's royal garb, the Crown of Hungary in his hands. He gazed upon the crown, shook his head and murmured "Vlad, Vlad..."—at least, that was what I could make out.

Now, you should understand that I do not hold by the Magyars' beliefs about the Crown, and especially not its sanctity stemming from the Papal dispensation. But I felt that if I were to preempt this blatant lèse-majesté, the King might reward me, and through me all Jews of the kingdom.

I yelled at the unknown stranger to stop, and called upon the guards. He looked up at me, tearing his gaze from the Crown with palpable difficulty—and as he turned his head, I saw his visage change like water rippling in a pond. His nose sharpened and his brow thickened, the reddish-blond curls of his hair fell on his shoulders as if someone had pulled them out of his skull. His shoulders broadened and his form filled out his limply hanging garb.

The King, having regained his usual leonine appearance, spoke to me with much aggravation. He berated me for having disturbed his peace, and he barely deigned to sign the document, telling me to ask his majordomo for the royal seal. Knowing I had overstayed my welcome, I hurried out.

On our next meeting, he acted as if nothing had happened, and certainly gave no indication that I had seen him change his shape. Yet I am certain my eyes did not betray me. This was not a vision like the Prophets speak of, an appearance of a likeness, hard for the mind to fathom; but rather, something plain as day.

This is why I ask you for your advice, as you have a reputation for being a Master of the Name, and knowing about all that is revealed as well as all that has been hidden. Do you think the King is consorting with forces of the Other Side, and if so, what steps should I take to safeguard my soul and protect the people I lead? I would be glad for your guidance. As I have said above, the safety of the entire community depends on my continued good relations with the King.

Please answer with the returning courier if possible; I have instructed him to wait a day or two while you compose your answer, if necessary. You can make use of the enclosed funds for his room and board—I know you would not accept compensation for teaching Torah, but I hope you accept this small kindness from one who has been blessed with earthly abundance.

I have paid one of the few Magyar youths not hostile to us to observe the actions of Vlad of Wallachia, but the lord has not left his house in over a week now, and so my knowledge is limited. I have also asked one of my nephews to keep an eye on King Mátyás and his disguised excursions, and I will send you his report as soon as I have it. Please excuse his brusque language and his lack of facility with the written word; what he lacks in Torah learning and scholarship, he makes up for in physical ability and discretion.

I look forward to receiving your answer—G-d willing, hopefully soon.

In peace,

Jakab Mendel the Elder

Letter from Jakab Mendel the Elder to Rabbi Izsák the Scribe

With the Aid of the Heavens
The 27th of Av, the year 5235 since Creation
July 31, 1475

Esteemed Rabbi Izsák, my good friend and respected teacher,

I have not heard from you, but the courier is not expected to return so soon. Provence is a great distance away even with horse-swapping, and one cannot ride all day and night. Yet I do not dare entrust these missives to strangers.

I have received the report I mentioned in my previous letter. My young nephew has observed some truly startling events. I am sending this report to you with another of my trusted men, hoping that this will enable you to provide more advice—for I follow the Sages' advice that it is only by wise counsel that one should wage war. If you think "war" is too belligerent a word, please reserve your judgment until you have finished reading the report.

All the best,

Jakab Mendel the Elder

The following report was enclosed with the letter:

<u>To the Rabbi</u>.

This is an accurate account of all that I have seen while I was walking in quest of the Jewish Prefect—that is, <u>spying</u>. I swear by G-d it is all accurate. It is all just as I have seen it!

First I <u>interrogated</u> the Prefect about the King's disguised appearance. He said, "the King is thin, tall, his hair is shorter and straight. His nose is ordinary, his face is smoother and he is not so ugly!!"

I would not even <u>imagine</u> to be able to shadow the King Himself, in his shape as King of the Kingdom, guarded by many guards wherever he goes. But I thought I could start to follow him once he has changed to his <u>hidden</u> shape!!

Of course you say "What if he can take three shapes, four shapes, any shape?" But I think what a man is accustomed to, a man likes to repeat. For instance I like to drink beer.

When night began to fall, I deposited myself in a place where many servants like to come and go, a courtyard of some kind. I thought, "He can change his shape but he probably does not disguise the way he walks." So I was looking for a man built like a reed who walks with the girth of a lion. Or maybe a bear, but truly <u>everyone</u> compares the King to a lion. They also say he is Just, but then why do both the nobles and the peasants grumble about taxes constantly??

<u>Then</u> I saw a young very <u>angry</u> man: thin, tall, his hair shorter and straight, his nose ordinary, his face smooth and well he was not all that appealing, but not ugly after all. He strode across the courtyard like a bull and as if he was twice the width that he was. He bumped into people and swore at them imperiously like a King. They laughed and mocked him, but he just brushed past them and into the shadows he went!!

I followed him and it was <u>hard</u> so the Prefect should pay me well, please Rabbi put in a good word for me. He (<u>not</u> the Prefect) has a very keen sense of hearing and also possibly smell. Though I did wash. Smell can betray you. It made me think maybe he can smell my freshly washed clothes!! As strange as that sounds.

He made his way across the river and to Pest!! What on earth would one want to do in Pest. Well he went to see the Lord Vlad of Wallachia who is now supposedly the rightful ruler of his land but with <u>no</u> army and thus he spends his time moping in his many rooms. Though I did not actually see that. I was waiting outside and waiting, it was <u>very</u> boring.

Eventually he came out looking very frustrated. If I had not known he had gone to see Lord Vlad I would have thought him a lover thwarted. Alas! I needed to find a further explanation.

I followed him from a safe distance and he turned toward the orchards on the eastern side. I was perplexed and got even more perplexed as his demeanour changed and he now seemed like a man on the <u>hunt</u>! Even from the distance I could see him lean forward and stalk ahead, looking more like a hunting dog in this twig-thin shape than a lion. I was getting much concerned because I do not like to think of my King as some kind of predatory animal and yet this was <u>exactly</u> the impression he was making!

Of course if he is some kind of monster from the Other Side that would explain everything and yet isn't he supposed to be not just King Mátyás but King Mátyás the Just?!

What I saw next made me rethink the whole part about "Just" for I witnessed with my own two eyes him stalking up to a young maiden who had been waiting outside. King or no King I was ready to interfere.

Yet the maiden seemed <u>friendly</u> to him and this gave me pause!! But she also looked dazed and as if asleep on her feet. I know peasants have so much hard labor especially with these "Just" taxes and all. But this seemed like something else—for it was at the King's sight she got moon-charmed and wavery! <u>And then the King bit her</u> on the neck and made a loud slurping sound and ran off just as fast as he had come!!!!

I gathered my courage and went up to the maiden but I could hardly get a word out of her!! She was completely dazed and could not say anything!! I returned to my abode and swore to come back the next day.

The next day she was nowhere to be found. I spoke with her mother whose eyes were red from crying. She said her daughter was ailing and that morning they had decided to finally send her to one of the Northwestern villages to her aunt to recuperate. It must be the closeness of the City she said. I was trying to cautiously inquire about a possible suitor and oh yes she was worried about a possible suitor. But above all she was concerned for her health for she had become weak and anaemic.

I thought to myself of course she is anaemic, for she has the King sucking out her blood and this time I do not mean the taxes.

I present my report for the learned Rabbi to handle as you see fit.

In peace,

<u>Majsi</u> son of József, the short one.

Letter from Rabbi Izsák the Scribe to Jakab Mendel the Elder

With the Aid of the Heavens
The 8th of Elul, the year 5235 since Creation

Esteemed Jakab Mendel,

I have received your letter by courier and read it with much concern. I believe the situation is grave, and would appreciate the report you mentioned. I had the courier wait and dined him well from the sum you have provided, for almost two weeks—yet in the end I had to send him back, for your nephew's report failed to arrive.

Based on what you describe, I believe that it is not that the King is consorting with forces of the Other Side—rather, the King's place has been taken by an infernal creature. Here we do not speak of a summoning of Other forces by a human being, but rather of a being who might have arrived in our lands from the Other Side. Not a human, but an evil creature altogether. How, do you say, is such a thing possible? All is possible if the Almighty allows it, and who are we to explain and justify a Divine decree? More pressing is the question of what to do—I will briefly explain a few actions you might wish to take below, and urge you to re-send your nephew's report so that we can all see clearly.

I have consulted with the local circle of scholars—without providing details of your case, of course. Even with such impoverished information I did manage to obtain a few pointers.

I have located a manuscript from the Rhineland titled *The Book of the Pious*, by a certain R' Júda ben Semuél. This esteemed Rabbi, who seems to have lived in Regensburg, described certain beings called "estrie" commonly with the appearance of women, but with the behaviour of evil spirits. They would derive sustenance from human blood, especially preferring children's blood—and as it is said in the Torah, the soul of the flesh is in the blood, making this a truly vile act. One way of defending against the estrie lies in the secret of their hair. They have long flowing hair, and if it is loosened, they are able to fly and escape freely. You must contrive to have the demon-King's hair bound, and then he will be vulnerable and at your disposal. It is not for naught that his hair is frequently compared to a lion's mane.

Do tell me about the appearance of this noble Vlad, how does he wear his hair? Has he changed it recently? You must be cautious and safeguard your soul against the Other Side—but you are aware of all this and more. I hope the advice of Rabbi Júda, which will hopefully reach you soon, G-d willing, will be helpful to you and to the peace of the Kingdom. I have copied the relevant paragraphs for you, but what is most important is what I have humbly ventured to summarize above.

Peace and blessings,

Izsák the Scribe son of Selomó

Letter from Jakab Mendel the Elder to Rabbi Izsák the Scribe

With the Aid of the Heavens
The 29th of Elul, the year 5235 since Creation
September 1, 1475

Esteemed Rabbi Izsák,

I have received your kind advice and made efforts to re-send the report, although I have been busy with the holiday preparations throughout Elul. I have further information for you that I am attaching to this missive—Majsi has been his usual daring self and managed to get himself hired as a courier. He intercepted a letter entrusted to him, while people assumed him to be an ignorant, illiterate courier running back and forth between the two cities facing each other by the Danube. These Gentiles truly do not understand that our children learn Hebrew letters by the time they are three, and Latin letters soon after!

Majsi is skilled with opening seals and closing them with nary a sign—thank G-d, for this letter was sent to the courtier Galeotto Marzio with the Lord Vlad's personal seal, and expected to reach its destination in the Buda hills intact. He managed to copy it without giving any sign the letter had been opened.

I do believe the malady Vlad mentions is connected to what we have learned about the King. The King might have recruited the Wallachian lord to the Other Side, if my suspicions are correct. I will try to approach Galeotto Marzio if I can get a word in with him, but it will take time—he's just arrived from Italy and has many courtiers flitting around him as usual. He knows all about the goings-on of the court and he is always willing to share a few anecdotes with me. I might need to inquire of his wellbeing in a brief missive, for I know he enjoys his voluminous correspondence. It would be ideal to secure a private meeting with him, but I am not sure how to best to go about it—his attention is famously capricious.

Do you suppose there is any chance you could return earlier from the lands of Provence? I know the weather here is hard on your joints, but your knowledge and mastery of the Name might help the entire community. I implore you to consider this invitation.

All the best,

Jakab Mendel the Elder

The following letter was enclosed with the above:

September 1, 1475

Dearest Galeotto,

I heard with such relief and joy that you had returned to Hungary. I still miss Janus sorely, and I think out of all people, you might hear me out.

I know you're still on good terms with Mátyás. I will not hold this against you, but after all that has happened, I think you will understand my hesitation. Yes, he has given me my freedom back after these long years in his prison, but at what price? No one will truly understand the magnitude of the sacrifice I had to make to assure him of my loyalty. And my feelings... my feelings have only served to complicate the matter at hand.

I still talk to him, on a fairly regular basis; and he pays me a visit every once in a while. Yet I am not presently able to appear in court, and thus must confess ignorance of the royal goings-on. Even when Mátyás is in Buda Castle and not in Visegrád or elsewhere, only shreds of rumours reach me, and I have no independent source besides him.

I am ailing; with a malady of the body and the soul. Would you be willing to keep me company with your letters? If you could just share with me some of your courtly anecdotes once in a while, they could serve as a balm for my spirit.

With greatest appreciation,

Vlad

Letter from Majsi son of József to Jakab Mendel the Elder

To the Prefect. For his eyes only!!

I seem to have just missed you! I am writing this note and your housekeeper will hopefully keep it for you, alongside your house. G-d willing.

I have copied two more letters! With a few sums of gratitude to the servants of these nobles, I have become a permanent envoy.

Also I utterly believe what you told me about this Galeoto Martzio and that he gets to go into the private chambers of the King. But I don't think his stories about the King's Just behaviour are true!! I think the two of them make those tales up together. Maybe even when they are sitting in those private chambers. And then Galeoto spreads the stories among the common folk or maybe even the King himself spreads them when he is in a different shape. You always tell me those stories <u>before</u> I hear them on the marketplace and I certainly do not spread them myself!!

What does the Torah say is it allowed to say that possibly the King is not so Just?? And this Lord Vlad even though he is called the Impaler might actually be a nice fellow?? He even seems to have defended me, without his knowledge, as you can see in the second letter!

<u>Blessings</u>!!!

Majsi

The following letters were enclosed with the above:

September 4, 1475

My dear Vlad,

I am always glad to hear from you, and my soul gladdens that you haven't forgotten the memory of our mutual friend Janus, even after he'd so sorely fallen out of favour with the King. I appreciate that you have forgiven him that one poem written before either of us had truly known you. May the Eternal Light shine upon him, snatched away from us in his prime by cruel illness.

I find the court fascinating as usual. You and I, we both look upon the Magyars as outsiders, and are able to reflect on their nature. I am confident you will agree that their food is exquisite, and I am sure you also know that they have a tendency to mock people in their presence, assuming everyone is ignorant of their convoluted language. This way I hear much that was not intended for my ears.

People also talk about you, and it pains me to say that these rumours are not the most flattering. I assume the story of the thief and the city guardsmen is untrue, though I can definitely see you defending your privacy voraciously. Yet people are again reminded of your warlike nature, and even whisper that it might be time for you to return to the battlefield. The border regions in the South are threatened by the Ottoman Turks again, and while the King would probably never say this to your face, he believes you still owe him a favour for your release. I must stress that I do not know what conversations the two of you have had, but I understand many feel animosity toward Mátyás right now. I assure you that your feelings about the King will not impact our friendship in any way.

Rumours also fly about the reasons for your release from prison. Some say that you have converted to Catholicism, and these people seem satisfied in their belief, though I know you do not hold the Papists in high regard.

Yet others claim that the King has allied himself with István of Moldavia after much strife, in face of a yet larger enemy, the Turks. According to this theory, István also made a pact with *you*, and interceded with the King for your release. I believe this could be beneficial for you—you may wish to send an envoy to István as soon as you can. I know that the two of you haven't always been on the most friendly terms, but István is growing desperate in his war, and is growing low on both resources and allies. While Mátyás dithers about giving you an army to retake Wallachia, you might build a beneficial relationship with István.

I am just a simple scholar, but if you need my support, I will be by your side. I look forward to your timely response,

Galeotto

September 5, 1475

Dearest Galeotto,

Thank you for your delightful summary. I do believe I must keep a few details straight.

First, whatever you may have heard about the thief and the head of the guardsmen is likely incorrect. What happened was this: Late at night I was relaxing in my private chambers, where these days I prefer even my servants not to attend on me. I also had a highly important guest. Suddenly there was a great ruckus and banging on the front gate, that I could hear all the way from my chambers despite the thick stone walls.

I had scarcely dressed to venture downstairs when the town guards committed the unimaginable offence of breaking my mansion's gates open with a small battering ram. They provided some rambling explanation that they were looking for a thief, or in any case a suspicious youngster, hunched over and possibly dressed like one of those Jewish boys from Buda. I immediately suspected this to be a bogus explanation, for I know the locals harbour significant animosity toward Jews. I explained that my staff had recently hired a young Jewish boy as a messenger, but it was not like him to show up at this late hour.

Of course there was no thief to be found in my mansion; I have my own guards. I said as much. I could hardly have had the intruders arrested—who would arrest the representatives of the law?—but my important guest was a high-ranking court official and he had the forthrightness to make a stand for me. Needless to say, the head of the guards received a most appropriate punishment. That is all I can tell you about this story.

I have definitely not converted to Catholicism, but I put little coin in piety and more in the power of iron and steel. If you ever hear me swear such an oath, you will certainly know it to be as bogus as these rumours are.

I will take into consideration your advice about István. I am regaining my physical and spiritual strength after my long stay in prison, and I am eager to retake the lands that are my right to rule. If Mátyás wants me to participate in another campaign before that, to assure him of my loyalty and fortitude, that will be a small price compared with many others I have already paid.

I will let you know if I need you to get in a word for me. How has your work been? I believe with so many rumours and stories, you have ample material for your literary works depicting the life of the court. I would very much enjoy reading your manuscripts if you would be willing to share.

Wishing you sustained good health,

Vlad.

Letter from Majsi son of József to Jakab Mendel the Elder

To the Prefect and No one else, very important!!!

I obtained a letter that was <u>not</u> supposed to go through my hands. Magyars don't like us but they are happy to take our money. I don't understand what's going on. Between the King and this Lord Vlad. Do they hate each other, do they like each other, or???

<u>Please</u> advise.

Majsi.

The following letter was enclosed with the above:

September 12, 1475

Vlad,

I miss you—surely the difficulties of the change could not have been that hard. I am sorry that my previous visit did not go well and we were interrupted at such an inopportune time. I do believe the consequences were more to your taste, but I still feel this damaged our connection, which used to be as strong as iron links in a chain.

I heard from Galeotto Marzio that you are regaining your strength, and I would like this to be true. Please do not ignore my missives—I will not order you to respond, but I still ask, not as a king, but as someone concerned for you.

This state of living has many advantages, as you are no doubt beginning to see. The trade-offs are slight and surely not so devastating to someone like you, who used to rule Wallachia with a strong hand and ample use of the various means of execution. Think of it as a way your subjects can support you in a more direct fashion than with tedious but necessary taxes.

I think of you. Please let me know when you would like to meet again.

[below and in a different hand]
It is not signed but it came closed with the Royal seal!!! You know what that means!!—Majsi. (I am good at opening these things.)

Letter from Rabbi Izsák the Scribe to Jakab Mendel the Elder

With the Aid of the Heavens
The 12th of Cheshvan, the year 5235 since Creation

Esteemed Jakab Mendel, my good friend,
I fear for your safety, and that of your young associate; G-d willing, this letter sent outside the usual channels will reach you unopened. I got your latest batch of correspondence, but the seal has been torn open in the most crude fashion. The courier professed ignorance, and I have no reason to disbelieve him; he is a G-d-fearing man and he was just as surprised as I had been. But he stayed at many inns, and at any one of them someone could have broken into his luggage.

We can no longer assume that our correspondence is private, but I must make sure you are sufficiently warned. Please consider that my words in this missive may be known by the King of Hungary, or by the rulers of other interested countries and further parties.

I do believe, based on your communications, that Vlad at least is aware of your nephew reading his letters. The fact that he has chosen to spare the youngster can be an act of defiance; Vlad's loyalties (and possibly the forces of the Other Side) bind him to the King, but he is conflicted and resentful. If the King turned him into a monster in exchange for his freedom, that affects their relationship even if otherwise it has been on good terms; and I believe this is exactly what has been happening.

You might say he already has been a monster, for the lord has a reputation for cruelty. But it is hard to draw a conclusion, for here in Provence there are many pamphlets and story-booklets being circulated about Vlad the Impaler's horrendous deeds—many so horrendous they were clearly invented for titillation, as a form of secular entertainment. The often anonymous writers of these pamphlets also profess a knowledge of the lord's prison years that they could scarcely have obtained—a knowledge that borders on the ridiculous. For who could believe that in the King's prison, Vlad of Wallachia having no access to enemy Turks, or rebellious peasants, turned to impaling rats on sticks? He had been living in house arrest in the Castle, not in a miserly dungeon.

Not to mention that some of these stories are clearly repurposed from other times, some even bearing a blasphemous familiarity to the lamentations and mournful songs most frequently heard on Tisha b'Av. (Understand that I am exposing myself to this shameful secular material for the sake of your safety only.)

Exactly how old is your nephew? I am assuming he must be at least of bar mitzvah age, which lessens the danger he is facing, but still I am very much concerned. Please keep in mind my advice about binding hair.

I have been praying for your nephew and you, and I am also sending both of you a selection of psalms and protective prayers to recite alongside your daily prayers, which I beg you not to neglect even in these trying times. (G-d forbid I should assume you have done so; I am stating this purely as a precaution.) Some of these quotations are also well-suited for engraving onto knives and daggers, as I've marked them in the appendix I attach to this letter. Stay safe.

I wish I could come visit, but my legs sadly continue to be in poor shape, and what little recovery the warm air has effected would be undone by a long carriage-ride; and riding a horse is out of the question entirely.

Wishing you all the best,

Izsák the Scribe son of Selomó

Letter from Galeotto Marzio to Jakab Mendel the Elder

December 7, 1475

To the Prefect of All Hungarian Jews, Jakab Mendel the Elder,

It is with great sadness and disappointment that I must inform you I will not be able to meet with you again this week, despite our prior arrangements. While our meeting last Thursday was most fruitful, I must return to my native lands as soon as possible due to family matters, and humbly ask for your understanding. We can continue our pleasant conversation in writing, and I do truly hope that I can keep you informed, and possibly in some measure also entertained. As you so rightly said, it is well within the domain of a Prefect to keep himself informed, to the greatest extent possible—and I am humbled that you sought me out to provide you with this honour.

But I do not wish to part from you without providing you with further news of the Court:

Vlad of Wallachia will be returning to fight the Turks in the South.

It is a very dangerous assignment, but the lord seems delighted, and when he finally reappeared from his self-imposed exile from courtly life, he seemed revivified, his cheeks bursting with fresh blood. He partook of the royal dinners he has been invited to with apparent delight, though he missed several of the lunches; I suppose he still needs those few daylight hours of additional rest.

I had been greatly worried about his health, as you know, but the news that he will be able to move forward with the campaign to retake Wallachia for himself has quite literally reanimated him. He has even taken to letting out his hair instead of braiding it in Transylvanian fashion. He looks most handsome with his long wavy hair, and standing next to King Mátyás, a resemblance between them struck me that went beyond the superficialities of physical appearance. I never dared ask the Wallachian lord if he had any Székely ancestry, feeling such a question to be importunate from a foreigner like me, but his command of the Magyar language is flawless. Then again, his Italian is also quite good, and his Latin shows a book learning surpassing that of any other noble who'd earned their reputation by the sword. It is no surprise that Mátyás appreciates him, even seeing that he held him in prison for so many years.

I do believe the upcoming campaigns bode well for all of us. But— and this should stay between us—I still dearly wish the King would marry, for he remains restless and agitated without a suitable Queen. I will see what I can organize in Italian lands.

Remaining truly yours,

Galeotto Marzio the Chronicler

Letter from Majsi son of József to Jakab Mendel the Elder

To the Prefect with great urgency!

I am going to be going South to fight in the King's new campaign!

Or rather to deliver more messages. I have joined Vlad's Personal Guard and I will be even allowed to have weapons and a <u>horse</u>!! It is amazing the King is now allowing all this for Jews and especially for me!

Father is very proud of me and financed the horse with much coin. I told him "I will make sure to feed it" but a lot of <u>my</u> coin will go to buying equipment, especially a suit of armour!! I am glad horses do not eat meat!!

I am trying to become Vlad's manservant or lance-bearer or I don't know all these military words! I remember what you told me about his hair but he never lets anyone touch his hair and he also only ventures out after dusk. It is very very frustrating. The armies will move under cover of darkness, people are saying.

I have already seen his <u>command tent</u> and I think he is hiding something under his beddings. <u>I will try to investigate!!!</u>

<u>Majsi, the Warrior</u> (And I would say "The Defender of the Christian Faith" like these people always say of themselves except that would not be so nice for a Jew like me to say. Am I still defending the Christian faith somehow!? <u>I think I am defending the world from a great evil.</u>)

Letter from Jakab Mendel the Elder to Rabbi Izsák the Scribe

With the Aid of the Heavens
The 13th of Teves, the year 5236 since Creation
December 11, 1475

Esteemed Rabbi Izsák,

I need your urgent advice. Against my judgment, but unfortunately with the support of his parents, my dear nephew has decided to join Mátyás' new southern campaign, led by Vlad of Wallachia.

I know very well what the Torah says about honouring one's parents and would not dare impose myself into this dispute—and the news Majsi will send home might ensure the safety of our community, and inform us in more detail about the lives of Jewish people under Turkish rule. But I am greatly concerned for him. I gifted him a dagger into which I had some of your protective sentences engraved, but it might not be sufficient. The Other Side can exert a strong pull and try to make us stray from the paths of the Law, and Vlad is a charismatic man; if anything, his transformation has no doubt made him stronger. I do not fear for my nephew's physical safety as much as I fear for his soul. He is by nature inquisitive, and might stumble on more than what would be good for him.

I also fear that if any of this secret knowledge were to come to light, surely the Gentiles would use it against us. They accuse us of kidnapping children and drinking their blood, although such acts are expressly forbidden in the Torah. Under the reign of King Mátyás, such libellous voices have received no royal support, but surely if the King had to choose between his most loyal commander and the Jewish community, he would not show us beneficence. I know you have been away and may be somewhat out of touch with our community, but I ask you to trust my judgment—any turn of events where the King and his loyal commander are revealed as these "estries" you spoke of would lead us to certain disaster.

I still do not know the identity of the thieves who stole our previous correspondence, but I suspect that they worked either for the King or Lord Vlad. I have taken steps to prevent this happening again, with the aid of the Heavens.

If in your studies you have come across any further weaknesses these creatures of the Other Side might have, I beseech you to inform me. Majsi will need all the help he can get.

I have heard that Galeotto Marzio has also decided to join the campaign, and he is certainly in Pest-Buda right now; but then, there are many rumours flying around about who might be joining Vlad of Wallachia. I will try to seek out Galeotto—I know he has been getting into gambling debts behind the King's back, and I might be able to use some of my discretionary expenses to motivate the chronicler to provide me with information.

I will strive to inform you—your knowledge, wisdom and learning are all that can help us in these times of danger and spiritual struggle.

All the best, and pray for us,

Jakab Mendel the Elder

Letter from Galeotto Marzio to Jakab Mendel the Elder

February 23, 1476

To the Prefect of All Hungarian Jews, Jakab Mendel the Elder—also my dear friend,

It pains me greatly that we had to part without one more of our fruitful and entertaining discussions. You know you are a natural-born storyteller, just like me? Tales will be sung of Galeotto Marzio, just as I am now singing the tales of others; and I trust your name shall also endure.

I will attempt to remedy my grave error by writing you a missive from camp. I have ample coin to ensure it reaches you speedily and safely; and in any case I need to repay you for the favours that you have generously bestowed upon me. I will not forget your intercession in the manner of the debts I had incurred with the nobles of the Court, and I hope this information proves useful to you in exchange.

Right now we mainly travel under cover of the night, and do our best not to light fires needlessly, so you will have to excuse my careless penmanship—I have but the smallest candle to cautiously light my tent for just a few minutes.

We have split from the armies of King Mátyás after our siege and conquest of Szabács, and our current goal is to retake Srebrenica and its rich silver mines. Vlad of Wallachia is leading the army, together with the Serbian lord Vuk Branković. The King is planning on returning to Buda soon, but our soldiers will push onward.

Vlad has designed a strategy that hinges on his great cunning. He has gathered to himself 150 horsemen bedecked in Turkish battle finery, and will ride into town with them tomorrow, on market day. They will mingle with the visitors to the great market, and then attack from within when our main force reaches the town. I am dubious of this plan's success, but Lord Vlad has spoken in council most persuasively, and has demonstrated his uncanny ability to disguise himself as a Turk. I do not know if the Magyar soldiers and the assorted foreign mercenaries of Mátyás will be capable of replicating his feat, but if Christ is with us, who's against us?

Pray for our souls, in your own way—it cannot hurt. And think of your dear friend,

Galeotto Marzio

Letter from Majsi son of József to Jakab Mendel the Elder

The 16 of Second Adar, the Year 5236

To the prefect!! You can also pass it along to the Rabbi.

I actually put a date this time!!

I hope you enjoyed my previous letter about the siege of Szabács! I hope it reached you speedily, I had to give it to someone who is not so used to couriering. I am still elated from our victory, and now I have <u>another</u> victory to report! <u>Today I dressed up as a Turk</u> and a mighty Turk to boot! We snuck into Srebrenica by posing as Turkish soldiers on a little bit of a leave and maybe slightly drunk too (a great excuse when you can't really speak Turkish). At first it was just me and the lord and a few more other people chosen from his most loyal soldiers. We split up to investigate and find weak points for the attack. I was with the lord and I get the impression he likes me a lot. He says Majsi you are cunning you know? And I say I am just a simple errand-boy. I am no scholar. He says we will find out today just how far my invincibility goes. Things will come to the light of day. I think he knows I'm reporting on him but <u>wants</u> me to report on him because he thinks he will die. I just nod and go along.

He does not like the Magyars very much by the way. Is he really Székely? Maybe he just doesn't like people, full stop.

So we go into the market and in our Turkish getup we got by raiding some raiders. And before that he secluded himself in his tent and came out masked like a Turk but I knew it was not a mask at all. I think I'm the only one who knows. We went into the market and he speaks Turkish!! Does he speak any language? Does it come from the shapeshifting? I wanted to show him my blade to see if he can read the Hebrew inscription, but he did <u>not</u> want to look at it and it even made him angry. I did not want to anger him.

He told us to avoid the other Turks in the market (there weren't that many, though they were positioned at choke points) but he went up to them and had a conversation.

Then slowly the rest of the soldiers came in and everyone who could obtain something that looked like Turkish garb. <u>It was as if the Wallachian lord had cast a spell</u> because everyone looked more Turkish than when we were practising in camp. I was confused who were the real Turks. The real Turks were also confused because there weren't supposed to be so many patrols coming in.

And then!!! When the rest of the army arrived at the walls, we attacked the Turks inside the city <u>and cut them down</u>!! Well I personally didn't much cut them down because I know, warfare and all, but doesn't the Gemore say the death of a person is like the death of an entire world, so I'd rather not. I don't know much of the Gemore but I know that one. The lord had <u>no</u> such reservations however!! He fought like a bear and making wild slashes left and right and when his great sword was knocked out of his grip he literally fell upon the Turks and <u>tore them apart with his bare hands!!</u> I have never seen such a sight, you like to say that part from the Torah that nothing is new under the Sun but this was pretty new to me!!

I don't know if he is a monster, he still seems human to me, but that is not human strength. He does have a reputation for evil but <u>he plays up to it</u> for great effect. He had some of the men gather the corpses of the slain Turks and had them impaled on stakes right outside the town, to instil fear in the incoming Turks coming to their comrades' aid, and there was indeed great fear among the Turks so I suppose this worked. People call him the Impaler from his old days as ruler of Wallachia when he supposedly impaled his live enemies, but I did not see that. He is proud of his moniker though and that scares me but he seems no more cruel than the Magyars to be honest, or the Turks. They are all quite cruel. If us Jews had an empire we would probably be cruel too.

This is <u>not</u> a criticism of you!!! G-d forbid.

I am still not sure what Vlad has <u>under his bed</u>. I wish you were a bit less sedentary because you could surely contrive to sit on it. His bed, I mean. But you are sitting in Buda while... Oh you know.

With <u>great respect</u>, Majsi

(I will also try to get more letters for you and send them as I get them and can find your contact. I might not send you more of mine with them because they take much time to compose, and we will soon be on the march again. I ask for your understanding! Again, <u>Majsi</u>.)

* * *

The following letters were enclosed with the above:

July 9, 1476

To the King,

The battles have been proceeding as planned. After our victories in the South, we are turning to the Northeast and making a move on Wallachia. I have devised a few unconventional tactics, and for these I need to requisition an amount of coin from the royal treasury, as detailed in the attached document. The axes are especially important. Please instruct your quartermasters that these be the kind used for cutting down trees first and foremost, not battle-axes to be used upon enemies. I shall explain later; I ask for your trust and understanding in the meanwhile.

Further personal communications will also follow.

Your loyal servant,

Vlad of Wallachia

July 9, 1476

Dear Mátyás,

I apologize for the dry tone of the previous letter; I am sending this one separately because I have reason to suspect spies in our midst. Our gambit with the disguises worked well, and contributed greatly to our military success, but Lord Branković has grown suspicious of me.

I do believe the figure of Vlad will soon outlive his usefulness. For the time being it is highly beneficial for me to be reviled and feared, but battles end while mouths still go on to speak, and eventually someone will no doubt collate all the details and understand my nature. I suspect someone is opening my letters; my errand-boy is dedicated but quite simple, and it might prove easy for a spy to get past him.

I do ask you to allow me a final moment of glory before the planned demise.

How are plans for the wedding proceeding? It is good I learned some Italian from Galeotto and that impertinent brat Janus.

In the meantime I'll spread word of my "wedding"—I will need some help with picking my supposed offspring and my future widow.

Wishing you a good recuperation after your many battles,

Vlad

[*below and in a different hand*]
I am <u>greatly</u> amused!!! But what is that bit about the future widow?!
—Majsi

Letter from Galeotto Marzio to Jakab Mendel the Elder

August 22, 1476

To my dear friend, Jakab Mendel the Elder,

This humble chronicler is always delighted to hear from you. I need to apologize for my delay in responding—we have been on the march to the northeast, and what a difficult march it has been! Periodically the Lord Vlad has the soldiers stop to cut down trees by the roadside and roll them over the road itself, for we have now reached the great Carpathian forests, and he intends to cut off escape routes for the enemy. No doubt also for ordinary peasant passers-by, but as I am fond of saying, the ends justify the means. (One day this aphorism will ensure the continuation of my name, if I dare say so myself.)

Honestly, all were convinced the axes would serve the purpose of making the infamous stakes for impalement, but so far they haven't seen any such use. They have been only used to cut down timber.

Morale is good, if only because all dread Vlad of Wallachia. He makes splendid use of his infamy, as a true leader would. He cultivates an air of cruelty, unlike our friend the King, who tries to appear affable and a friend of the common people. I have assisted both of them with my talents, as I would also be willing to assist you.

It is fascinating that you have taken an interest in the beliefs of the common folk about the netherworld—had I known earlier, I could have regaled you with all the old wives' tales I hear around camp. I have never heard of such a being as this "estrie" that you describe, though many nations do speak of various bloodsucking monsters and revenants. Curiously, what little the Magyars know about such creatures seems to originate entirely with other folk. The Wallachians speak of the "strigoi"—a male creature, unlike your estrie—that could be considered similar, if I have understood this right. Yet you will be hard-pressed to find a Magyar not of Székely origin who has heard of this demonic creature, and presumably the Székely heard it from the Wallachians. My servant Ferenc calls such a monster a "murony," which word must originate in the Wallachian "moroi" meaning a dead person. But your estrie sounds more like the strigoi, which is also a revenant, rising from the grave. You can fight the strigoi with garlic or lovage, whose strong smells drive it away. Some also say marriage can prevent a person from becoming such a monster in death, but I must say most of these folk marry with or without fear of these Devil-creatures—especially in the villages, you cannot find an unmarried adult who is not a widower. And we all know that peasants speculate about people of unusual qualities.

I am still trying to find people in camp who have at least known someone who'd witnessed one of these demons, if they exist beyond the common imagination—which I am skeptical about. We do have some Wallachians among the mercenaries of Mátyás, and some of the better-armed locals have also joined our fight since we started our northward march, but my questions mostly result in confusion. Indeed, it is hard to explain my sudden interest without disclosing yours—the things I do for a good friend!

Pray for me,

Galeotto

P.S.—I do not understand your query about the bedding.

Letter from Jakab Mendel the Elder to Rabbi Izsák the Scribe

With the Aid of the Heavens
The 28th of Elul, the year 5236 since Creation
September 17, 1476

Esteemed Rabbi Izsák,

I wish you to be written and stamped for a good year in the Book of Life, and a blessed High Holy Days season—I know that with your age and your difficulty walking, the complications of this busy time amplify a hundredfold. I do beg you not to try to stand for all the Yom Kippur prayers, like you did three years ago.

I am growing concerned I have not heard from you, but G-d willing my news will soon be in front of your eyes.

My informers in Vlad's army are reporting great victories in battle, and odd events—yet no one has connected these to the legends of the Gentile nations about blood-drinking creatures. No one thinks Vlad's cruelty is out of the ordinary, for the reason that it is not—he is likely no better or worse than other Christian leaders across Europe waging war on the Turks. He has a reputation as a great warrior, they see him in camp and draw courage from his heroic deeds; even if he is mostly out after dusk and before dawn. If on occasion a corpse is found, sucked dry of blood, that can be attributed to any number of malevolent beings that lurk in the Carpathian woods, or even wild animals that still present a danger.

Yet in the letters Majsi has intercepted, some copies of which I am sending, there is an amount of consternation—Vlad seems to be preparing to stage his death, as far as I can tell, and also creating for himself a kind of fictitious family with a widow and heirs. All the footsoldiers would attest that he has had no family with him on the march, but history is not written by the common folk, and Gentile historians will continue to claim what is expedient, as we know all too well. I have no inkling as to what Vlad is planning after he regains his rightful domain, for he seems not to be preparing to govern it again.

In the meanwhile, Mátyás is getting ready to wed Beatrix of Aragon, and I dearly wish Galeotto could still tell me his many courtly tales from the heart of events. The stories reaching me from Italian lands are contradictory and none too positive. I had told the King myself that he ought to marry again, so I should be glad he had finally taken my advice; but I had not expected he would choose such a bride as Beatrix, rumoured to have killed at least one of her previous lovers. The King has been favourably disposed toward Jews, but who knows if that will continue, were Beatrix to sway his heart in the direction of hatred? Or could one say that one creature of the Other Side is drawn to another? I wonder if Beatrix is also an estrie, and these beings are getting ready for a general congress in Magyar lands.

The King has been gloomy, but not hostile to me or our people in the slightest. He has personally asked his majordomo to coordinate with me in great detail about the upcoming festivities, and the Jewish community has been invited to the great marriage parade to present our gifts and blessings.

I am arming all my young men chosen for the wedding march—I

had trustworthy weaponsmiths make them swords carrying the blessings you specified. My son Jakab Mendel the Younger will also join the march as a trumpet-player—please pray for his soul as well as all of ours.

    With peace,

    Jakab Mendel the Elder

The following letters were enclosed with the above:

October 23, 1476

Dear Mátyás,

    I try to restrain myself in these letters. I miss you, and yet.

    Wallachia will fall again without me. I understand what you ask and why, but this is too large a sacrifice. Do you simply <u>need</u> me close, or do you truly <u>want</u> me close? We have an eternity ahead of us, but what kind of eternity will it be?

    Why is it that my death must be staged first? Will you let go of the Crown of Hungary later? We cannot show ourselves in the open forever. People will talk. They already talk—I have exercised the utmost caution, and yet there is word of monsters in camp. That oaf Galeotto seems especially fascinated by these tales. He used to be friendly with me, even after that conflict with Janus; but I feel he is eyeing me with suspicion. The friendliness is gone, and in its place a cautious respect. I cannot say I prefer this. I build up my myth, the legend of the bloodthirsty Vlad, the impaler lord. I have good foundation to build it on, thanks to the tales of terror people have been spreading—as far away as Provence!—while I was held in arrest. The legend makes people fear me, but they draw away from me—all draw away from me, save you. And I can't help finding the merciless <u>convenience</u> in this.

I understand we cannot let go of our lands at the same time—the region would be weakened, ripe for invasion. And I know you want me to rule with you, as much as possible—even if under a different name, a different face. I understand you want me to learn the ways of our kind from you.

I just need to know if you ever considered me an equal.

Yours,

Vlad

October 25, 1476

My dear friend Galeotto,

These are the notes I promised during our last discussion, to help you in your work.

We will need stories and detailed descriptions of my wife—Mátyás has a cousin who assented to this. Her name is Jusztina and she will be at your service once you return from this campaign. (Do stay alive; we need a storyteller, and a merchant of rumours.) Please discuss all the details with her about our family life. I would rather not leave her at the mercy of your galloping imagination.

You also need to invent my children, two at least, three is also good. I leave the details to you. It would be good if you could find at least two capable young men who can lay claim to Wallachia after I'm gone. I would prefer if they retook it by force, to prove their ability to hold onto it.

Any further children can be entirely fictitious.

I would like my family name passed on also in Hungary. You can produce some more distant relatives, but make sure they do not come across my actual relatives in Wallachia, especially my brother Radu. A larger Hungarian town beyond the Danube would be preferable, maybe Pécs or Győr? Though I've never been to Győr.

All this would serve our purposes splendidly. I will convey your regards to the King.

Wishing you good work,

Your grateful friend Vlad

Letter from Majsi son of József to Jakab Mendel the Elder

The 12th of Kislev, <u>the year 5237 since Creation</u> (I did it right this time!)

To the Prefect,

Happy new Year and happy Chanukah in advance! I am sorry I haven't been in touch, but we had such a triumph!! <u>Vlad has reclaimed Wallachia</u>! He chased away that Ottoman-backed pretender and all is well. There was all sorts of jubilant marching and a coronation and all that good stuff! I would love to make it back in time for the new Queen's coronation because to have <u>two</u> events like this one after the other, that would be great! There was also a separate celebration of the alliance with István the Third the Moldavian. I am totally not eating pork! ...But it is tempting.

Vlad has been asking me if I could reach you. No I don't know what he wants or why he wants to talk to you! I'm a bit scared. I think he wants your help. Or my help? My help in getting your help, I think. He said "Fret not, I'm going to write the letter" because I <u>still</u> don't think he realizes I can read and write. But I do think he likes me for some reason.

I will just send the letter once I have it!

I am missing home.

I have been <u>sneakily looking at his bedding</u> and I can report he has a giant sack of something underneath it. It looks like a bag of manure that people spread on their fields for a better harvest, but it does not smell as bad. Though perhaps I am losing my sense of smell in all this military campaigning.

If you are worried, he is not noticing me. I am quite sure of this!

With peace and blessings (I am getting better at this!) <u>Majsi</u>.

Letter from Jakab Mendel the Elder to Majsi son of József

With the aid of the Heavens.
The 24th of Kislev, the year 5237 since Creation
December 10, 1476

My dear Majsi,

I have not received any further letters from you, and I pray every day for your safety. I hope you are doing well, and G-d willing will be among us soon, in time for the royal wedding. The King has asked me and the Jews of Buda to lead the entire wedding march. I am afraid this honour will have a corresponding price.

Have you read Vlad's message before passing it on? I only received your words. Do you know what he was planning on asking me?

Wishing you all the best, with great worry,

Jakab Mendel the Elder.

Letter from Jakab Mendel the Elder to King Mátyás of Hungary

With the aid of the Heavens
The 25th of Kislev, the year 5237 since Creation
December 11, 1476

To the King,

I hereby petition your Royal Personage to allow me to leave my duties in Buda Castle for a fortnight—I have an urgent need to travel in order to pursue some extremely pressing family matters. My secretary has been appraised of the ongoing financial issues and my brief leave should entail no disruption, if the Heavens so desire.

I beseech you to look upon me with favour,

Jakab Mendel the Elder, Prefect of All Jews in the Hungarian Kingdom

Letter from Jakab Mendel the Elder to Rabbi Izsák the Scribe

With the aid of the Heavens
The 26th of Kislev, the year 5237 since Creation
December 12, 1476

Esteemed Rabbi Izsák, my dear friend,

I am wishing you a blessed Chanukah, though by the time this letter reaches you, the festivities will be over. Every time I light a candle, I think of you and the light you continue to bring to the world; a light that is sorely needed.

I hope your health is improving; please find with this letter salts from the Istrian salt ponds and use them for your benefit. Access to the South has been haphazard at best, but I made use of my connections—your wellbeing is of utmost concern.

I have not been able to reach Majsi and I fear the worst. This morning I have finally obtained a travel permit from the Court and I will try to join the returning armies, which are in disarray.

Vlad has allegedly been murdered by Turkish assassins in murky circumstances, but I believe he will return to the Court in hiding and disguise. I need to make certain that amidst all the confusion, my nephew arrives back in Buda Castle safe and sound. If I need to use some of the discretionary funds, so be it. We learned much about the Court already, though this has not been a knowledge that is pleasing to the soul, unlike your own learning.

Beatrix will soon arrive from Italian lands. Once I safely return, together with Majsi if the Heavens will it so, I will make use of your advice and present sacred items among the gifts. I was thinking of a Torah scroll with an ornate cover. If she is likewise an agent of the Other Side, she will draw away from the scroll. I know the King well and he will be cautious enough to keep his distance, but Beatrix might not know as much about us Jews as he does.

If one can believe the paintings, the future Queen has long, flowing hair; though this is likely not a rarity among Italian Gentile women.

I shall do my best to keep you informed. I am growing concerned at not hearing from you.

In peace,

Jakab Mendel the Elder

Letter from Jakab Mendel the Elder to Rabbi Izsák the Scribe

With the aid of the Heavens
The [*illegible*], the year 5237 since Creation
December 20, 1476

Esteemed Rabbi Izsák, my dear friend,

I am writing this with fingers cramped from the cold. We have been on the march, and will soon reach Buda Castle—I might only be able to send this letter from there, but I need to write down all that I had experienced, so that none of it is lost to the vagaries of memory.

I have located Majsi. He, in turn, has lost Vlad—all he had for me was a handful of rich black earth, tied up in a handkerchief. I told the boy that his safety meant more to me than any kind of information he could gather, but he was inconsolable—he still thinks of all that transpired as his personal fault.

He saw the assassination.

Whether it was an assassination is open to interpretation, for it all happened late at night, illuminated only by lightning strikes in the storm raging above. I shall do my best to recount the events as accurately as I can, exactly as I heard them from my young nephew:

Majsi was sitting in the tent, wrapped in a rough blanket and shivering from the cold. Vlad of Wallachia was restless, unable to retire to sleep. Earlier he had let in Majsi so as to preserve him from the cold, and my nephew was wondering if his presence interrupted the bedtime rituals of the lord—rituals he could only speculate about.

The lord ventured outside and circled the tent like a hungry wolf. The lightning cast his silhouette plainly on the wall of the tent, and Majsi was terrified, for it had seemed to him that in this witching hour the lord had begun to change into something inhuman. Yet Majsi had trouble pinning down the details—Vlad retained his human form, by and large, but his limbs lengthened and his stride elongated. He also made a hacking sound as if he had been dying of consumption, when he had in fact been in the prime of his health.

Suddenly he roared—like a wolf, or perhaps even a lion. He lifted his arms against the night sky and his fingers were sharp as talons.

Majsi could see two more figures appear, and there was a consternation, and yelling in a tongue unfamiliar to him, [*the rest of the paragraph is illegible*]

A fight broke out. My nephew crawled to the far side of the tent and hid himself in a pile of garments and assorted pieces of military equipment. It occurred to him that perhaps he should have hidden himself in the bedding, maybe even in the curious sack underneath everything, but he did not do so—and this was truly the work of divine providence, for next the two men broke into the tent and struck the bed with polearms of some sort.

What had they been expecting to find? Whatever they had sought, they could not succeed in their [*illegible*], for Vlad himself returned at this moment, tearing the tent-flap wide open. He proceeded to slaughter the invaders with his bare hands, and as Majsi trembled in his hiding place, he became more and more certain that he was not witnessing something pre-planned, but rather something gone terribly awry.

Vlad wiped blood and gore off his forearms, reached into the beddings to open the sack, and took a deep breath. Then he closed it again, hoisted it on his shoulders, and vanished again into the frosty night outside.

Majsi crawled out and picked up a clump of earth where it had fallen after Vlad lifted the sack. He had expected some kind of treasure, a sack full of golden coins, but if there had been [*illegible*] inside, it had been carefully hidden under a thick layer of earth.

Majsi stole a kerchief and put the clump into it, then sneaked out— he could not spend a moment more amidst all the blood that had been shed, and he was too terrified to follow Vlad.

Since the events of that night, Vlad of Wallachia has not been seen again.

I am convinced Majsi reported what he saw accurately, but I am not certain <u>what</u> it is he witnessed. If this was Vlad's staged assassination, something had gone wrong with it, leaving him to flee. He had meant to exit his own legend of a life, but surely not by such crude means.

Can you advise me on this? I shall do my hardest to comfort Majsi, who has been terribly shaken. I asked a scholar about the clump, a Catholic priest who is knowledgeable about farming, and he thought its consistency and colour was not characteristic of the Pest-Buda area. Wherever it had come from, it must have been transported from far off. Maybe you are aware of such mystical practices?

I am also concerned about Majsi's anguish over losing the lord. He seems to have grown attached to him—even aware of the monster's true nature. He tells me he's only worried he let Vlad out of his sight, as it was his responsibility to keep an eye on the lord, but I feel there is more to it. If you could advise, I would be exceedingly grateful.

All the best,

Jakab Mendel the Elder

Letter from Galeotto Marzio to Jakab Mendel the Elder

December 23, 1476

My dear friend Jakab Mendel,

What got into you? First you join the returning armies—who has heard of such a thing?—and then you cause even more trouble after your return. All throughout the royal dinner, the new Queen was complaining about you and the offence you caused at the beginning of the wedding march. Asking her to *kiss* a scroll! This might be a custom among *your* women, but definitely not ours—neither in Hungarian, nor in Italian lands.

Besides this, there is not much I can report—the rumours took a backseat due to the upheaval after the Queen complained about the seating and most of the guests were ushered out. I was allowed to stay, but the mood was definitely chilly after that. The sky was already dark when the Queen finally agreed to sit at the table. Queen Beatrix did not seem satisfied with the food, she barely nibbled on all those amazing fruits from far-off lands; she only seemed to show some enthusiasm about the game meats, if only to remark that they were overcooked. (I would have begged to disagree, had I not felt it would have been impertinent.) You missed a lot of delicious dishes, though I know you prefer not to show yourself in company where you might be expected to eat Gentile food.

I miss Vlad—he grew on me during the campaign, and I hope the earth will rest lightly upon him. I believe he would get along splendidly with Queen Beatrix, they have similar personalities. Then again, I assume you know the Magyar saying about two bagpipe players in one drinking-hole!

My best regards to your family, too, on this auspicious day. We might not be able to meet for a few weeks at least, as my duties keep me busy. I have Vlad's estate to manage and his affairs to straighten, as I promised to him in his dying hour.

Long live the King and Queen,

Your friend Galeotto (who shall desist from wishing you a merry Christmas).

Letter from Majsi son of József to Jakab Mendel the Elder

The 21st of Teves!!! 5237.

To the Prefect <u>it is very important</u>.

I got this message from the Queen!! Who is probably not the Queen, or the Queen might not be as we know her. It is <u>not signed</u> but it came with her seal.

Do you think you might wish to get an audience with her?

I am a bit afraid but I have my trusty dagger still.

But besides!! I am <u>really</u> all right now and you should not always be so worried.

All the best! <u>Majsi</u>.

*   *   *

The following letter was enclosed with the above:

January 6, 1477

Dear Jusztina,

I am very glad you have assented to our plan, but I am also concerned. You are among a very small handful of people who know my secret, and I don't know you very well. Mátyás trusts you, and so I should also offer my trust, but both my time in Wallachia and my time in this kingdom has made me wary.

Galeotto Marzio suspects but doesn't know. He has been of great help to me in getting my affairs in order and also connecting me to you. He knows much of the plan, but he doesn't understand my true nature—or that of the King, for that matter. This is good, but I am wondering how long it can remain so. Deception can only hold out for so long, and he is cunning.

None of my relatives are aware of this. I have been considering contacting my brother Radu; he might be able to offer help. It could be good to enlist him in our efforts.

Mátyás had a suspicion the Jewish prefect might know, and I tried to reach out to the prefect, but never received a response. I had a Jewish errand-boy on the campaign, and he promised he would deliver my letter to someone who would carry it all the way back to the prefect living in Buda, but maybe it was intercepted en route. I had no reason not to trust the boy, though he might also know; he always seemed to be favourably disposed toward me. At a certain time I thought he might be spying on me, but then I would certainly have heard from the prefect. He was a simple boy and I might have overestimated him. I wonder what he is up to now—I spared him when I got away. My current couriers are slow and unreliable, and I suspect they are also prone to bribes. I hope you will get this letter, at least.

I have a large favour to ask. Do you know of any other people like

Mátyás and I? I have many questions to ask, but the King is busy or otherwise might not be the best person to interrogate on these matters; his mood is rather grim these days, with the news from the South. My absence from Wallachia has also created an absence of power, as we have feared—and I understand this was part of the plan, but I worry still.

If you could help me in this matter, my soul could rest easier.

Letter from Queen Beatrix to Jakab Mendel the Elder

January 10, 1477

To the Prefect of All Hungarian Jewry, Jakab Mendel the Elder,

I have been trying to reach you. I believe you might be my only possible confidante in this wretched land, yet my messages never return with a response. I have lost patience and sought out my former errand-boy to deliver this letter directly into your hands. He looked as if I was about to bite him, and flailed at me with his dagger, so I assume he knows the truth, and so do you.

I await your response after your Sabbath. Please tell him to keep that forsaken dagger sheathed; I have no plans to part with either my hair or my life.

Beatrix, for now.

Letter from Jakab Mendel the Elder to Queen Beatrix

The 27th of Teves, the year 5237 since Creation
January 12, 1477

To Queen Beatrix of Aragon, the rightful Queen of Hungary,

Blessings and felicitations!

I have received your letter with great alarm. I have not received your other recent missives. I will make sure Majsi, who is also one of my younger relatives, will hand-deliver this letter to you.

I would be glad to meet with you; or if you believe that such meetings might not be safe, I can be at your service, reachable by letter.

I promise (without a formal oath, whose sanctity in either case might aggravate you) that I will not make any attempts on your life, nor will I instruct anyone else to act in such manner. In return I ask that you preserve the life of young Majsi and do not act against the interests of Jewry in Hungary, whose interests in any case might align with yours; though this remains to be seen.

I also ask that you do not share our letters with the King if possible, though I do believe this also aligns with your own will.

With respect,

Jakab Mendel the Elder

Letter from Dracula to Jakab Mendel the Elder

January 13, 1477

To Jakab Mendel the Elder,

I will be brazen; I can afford to be brazen. I have so little to lose.

You know. How long have you known? You do not need to say. You Jews are cunning, or is it that Magyars are gullible? You know what the Magyars say about Wallachs, and what they say specifically about me. That's not flattering either, so I will not adopt their attitudes. You are well worthy of respect, though I do not know yet whether you will prove to be an ally or an adversary. You might not know that yourself.

Yet, I think you of all people might understand the price I paid. I regained my freedom and retook the land that was rightfully mine, but in the end neither is my freedom mine, nor my land. All I have is this un-dead existence, where all I can do is pose as the Queen, or sneak out as a Magyar lout or in the shape of a giant rat or the evening fog.

I do make a fitting Queen, if I dare say so myself. My woman-shapes please me just as much as my man-shapes, but they do come with different sets of obligations. I do not yet know what the future might bring. I do not know what would be my own preferences, free of coercion. Mátyás is stronger than me. He has been living like this for much longer, and I can only hope that my own cunning will eventually enable me to overtake him. And to think I had feelings for him, once upon a time! I can only tell you this because you know it already. He had feelings for me too, but his feelings led him astray.

I shall be firm from now on.

I understand you are concerned for your people—I have known for longer than you might have assumed. I have my sources and I am not below hiring a few Magyar lowlifes to reach my aims.

The Turks are certainly coming. I know that you have connections with Jewry in the Ottoman Empire, and your little Majsi certainly helped you with that during the campaign too.

Once I have grown stronger, I will deal with the King as I see fit. I believe he has already made attempts on my life. But I need you to help me plan my escape—either to Turkish lands or to Provence where your friend the mystic rabbi lives. I have noticed he is not eager to return, and lately he has even stopped answering you. It would probably please him to avoid me, but I might need his assistance, regardless of what he thinks of evil forces. I have not ended in this situation of my own volition, and I can already feel my newfound nature starting to influence my mind. His words are with me about the blood and the soul.

I have always lived a warrior's life, and ruled with strength. But strength is one thing, and the needless application of it is another. More and more I struggle to maintain my restraint, more and more I feel overcome with rage even when it is inopportune. I have no idea where this road will eventually lead. I wonder who turned Mátyás; if I were to come face to face with them, could I see in their present my own future. I do not wish to become a mindless animal, and yet where are the other creatures of my kind? I can only assume they have fallen into the straightforward life of the beast—or are they hiding from me?

I only try to drink from the blood of my enemies. But my enemies are many and my friends are few. I have always guided my people with force, unlike you who lead your people with caution, and occasionally subterfuge. I am beginning to see what a great gift it is, to be able to openly yield power. For many years I had not given it a second thought; not even in prison, for I saw my captivity as fleeting.

I turn to your expertise now. As your Jews have flourished under the King, so shall I flourish, if you accept our alliance.

I do not ask for your trust. I could force you—I could tell you how easy it would be to turn the King against the Jews, how easy it would be for me to use his feelings for me against him and against you. It would not be beneath me, truly. But I do believe an earnest alliance based on mutual respect and the shared aims of persistence in face of the King's power could work better.

I am neither Vlad nor Beatrix now; but I shall keep my father's name, that he earned with his knightly deeds. Yet I feel little willingness to write it out in the Magyar way, for as much as my current situation ties me to Hungary, so much has my soul been liberated from it.

Eagerly awaiting your response,

Dracula

*   *   *

Letter from Ya'akov Mendel to Dracula

The 29th of Teves, the year 5237 since Creation.

Dracula,

I appreciate your trust in me. I will preserve the Wallachian spelling of your chosen name; in turn, you are free to address me as Ya'akov. We do not need to yield to the Magyars in everything, even when it is convenient.

It has been a long and difficult road to lead my people, and entirely different from your own. But I do understand the similarities in our situations.

There is one important difference, though, that I must discuss. The King's death (I will not mention any sacred name that I would usually include) would set you free and enable you to act as you see fit. Yet you can surely see that it would make the situation of the Jews much more precarious. I have no guarantee that whoever follows Mátyás on the throne will be friendly toward my people—or, if the Turks take the Kingdom, that they will be any more merciful. I do know many of my people would welcome them, but others are already preparing to flee, digging tunnels just in case. I cannot speak in favour of either option. We need to be prepared, whatever may come.

If you are intent on ruling over Hungary yourself, I would need some guarantee from you of our safety—yet I know that you wish not to be bound in any way, and sacred oaths now no doubt create only revulsion in you. So how could you give me such a promise? Even I cannot make a promise to you, for that I would need to invoke sacred names. I remember your reaction to the Torah scroll.

I am willing to work with you. But I trust that you understand my caution.

With respect,

Ya'akov Mendel

*   *   *

Letter from Dracula to Ya'akov Mendel

January 15, 1477

Dear Ya'akov—if not my friend, then my co-conspirator,

How grim it is that the Magyars accuse Jews of drinking blood, and yet I am the one drinking blood! And you draw away from me even as we plan to work together.

I am not forcing you, am I? Is the situation forcing both of us? I would like to abstain from force—I have had enough of it. Yet I feel the pull of my new, monstrous nature, and it merges well with my old nature, the iron-fisted leader on the Wallachian throne. The only feeling I can fall back on that is distinct from this destructiveness is the desperation of my prison years, when I was shown to ambassadors like a trophy, a secret weapon to be unleashed upon the Turks when the King would see fit. Mátyás is cruel beyond measure—I have always been cruel only with measure.

You benefit from his rule—but for how long?

I need to learn more about the weaknesses of the bloodsucking monster, the one to which I am kin, even knowing that you will be learning about my weaknesses as well.

The King will die—he ought to die—but I might yet roam this earth for millennia more, and even I do not know what shape I might take. I would say, it is better for you to be on my good side, but I do not mean to threaten you. It is simply the truth.

Mátyás has taken even the words of humans from me. All that remains is the pull of the night, the taste of blood. Soon I will need to feast or I shall threaten you too, you who I would like to keep on my good side. You who still need to teach me about your ways.

If there are any rowdy Magyar louts you would not miss, just tell me and I will do you a favour.

Dracula

Letter from Ya'akov Mendel to Dracula

The 5th of Shevat, the year 5237 since Creation

Dracula,

I do not wish to have anyone's blood on my hands; and I would prefer to stay on your good side. Do you think we can come to an agreement? You have plenty of time to depose the King. I understand the wait is hard on you.

If you can make do with animal blood, then as you know, we do not consume blood and bleed out our animals at the slaughter. Some accommodation can certainly be made.

While you are waiting for the right moment, I shall make arrangements to ensure the safety of my community. Would this be agreeable to you?

Let me know,

Ya'akov Mendel

Letter from Majsi son of József to Jakab Mendel the Elder

To the Prefect it is urgent!!

dear Prefect I do not know what is happening! I wanted to speak to you in person but again you were out!

I think V. / B. killed someone at the court and I think it was Galeoto Martzio or how ever it is spelled! Everyone is running around shouting.

No one blames the Queen of course.

Majsi.

*   *   *

Letter from Dracula to Ya'akov Mendel

January 22, 1477

My dear Ya'akov,

Thank you for your kindness. Animal blood does not satisfy for long. I tried this, many months ago, in distress.

I will not be in touch, but I will consider what you have said. I ask you to do the same.

I remain, as always,

Dracula

Letter from Ya'akov Mendel to Rabbi Izsák the Scribe

With the aid of the Heavens
The 29th of Nisan, the year 5237 since Creation

Esteemed Rabbi,

I hope you had a kosher and happy Passover season; here there has been a controversy over butter that kept the entire community occupied. I trust someone else will apprise you better as to the legal niceties.

I have summarized for you all the letters I had received. I haven't heard from Dracula in months—the Queen has assumed her duties, in the meanwhile. In spite of our fears, she hasn't been hostile to Jews; though she has not shown particular friendliness either.

Many in the court complain of her temper. She avoids me and I have been obliging her wishes.

Galeotto Marzio is alive, but gravely wounded in mysterious

conditions; he has fled back to his Italian home for the time being, where he is working on his further chronicles of the King's court. People say he had aroused the ire of Heavens; some even claim he had been hostile to Jews and suffered some kind of divine retribution. How Gentiles can believe this and at the same time loudly claim we killed their Saviour is beyond me. In any case, he never told me anything untoward, Heaven forbid; I did see him make jokes at my nephew's expense once, but that was mere verbal jousting and no one took offence. But I can certainly see how Galeotto in his jocular demeanor can take an anecdote too far, and I am sure that someone still remembers that slight on their person by one of Galeotto's good friends, the learned poet Janus—may he rest in peace.

I will let you know if the Queen takes leave or engages in leisurely travel of some sort—I do believe that one night, someone might pay you a visit. You will not want to be overly friendly, but you do not want to alienate your visitor either. Mist might encircle your house and the eyes of rats and bloodsucking bats might stare at you from the darkness. Out of the mist a figure might step out, a stranger with long flowing hair, tired after the exertions of a lengthy trip. I know you can repel the forces of the Other Side with ease, but for now you might want to hear them out. We also have many enemies, and it might not be wise to needlessly add to their number.

May the Almighty guide the souls of those gone astray from the path, and may He bring us all to safety, speedily, in our days.

Until we meet again, with peace,

Ya'akov

Letter from Majsi son of József to Vlad of Wallachia

Dear <u>Dracula</u> since I believe this is how it pleases you to be addressed I am not good with formalities.

I am sending this letter by courier to the Queenly summer abode because I had to sell my horse and could not come myself. I have to say those people are not as good at the message carrying business. But horses are expensive and I do not have all the money for horse feed.

I have no idea what happened to you!! Even though I read all the Prefect's letters (I do hope you will not tell him or I will be in trouble).

I <u>miss</u> you is that allowed to be said? We fought together though it was you who did most of the fighting. And we marched day and night. Though mostly night.

These days you always seem so grim and distant when I see you from a distance in court and you fight with your Husband. And now you have up and left.

I do not think you are <u>really</u> having a nice summer break.

If there are any messages that need to be carried <u>in utmost privacy</u>, you let me know and I will be your man. If not on a horse, then without. Though needless to say you can always buy me a horse. Most of that tax money goes to military expenses anyway.

I hope the Rabbi will not throw you out though he stopped answering his correspondence. Please do <u>not</u> hurt him if you see him. Also he likes bath salts.

I do not fault you for Galeoto Martzio. He is an ass if you ask me.

With <u>great respect</u> I remain,

<u>Majsi</u> the short one, son of József, and Your former messenger

TWO

NOBLESSE OBLIGE

INTERLUDE

From: Jonathan Holmwood (jwlh1947@amol.com)
To: Dani Văduvă (bornwithteeth@webmail.com)
Date: January 13, 2018
Subject: Re: Mina Harker?

Hi Dani,

Okay, second upload. Most of this is my father's work, done shortly after the Second World War. He'd been looking into suspected vampires in history, and Bathory's notorious killing spree made her an obvious target. He travelled first to the Österreichisches Staatsarchiv in Vienna to find what he could on her trial and conviction, and worked his way backwards from there.

The official records were frustrating. They alluded to a lot, but evidently the court at the time wanted the affair kept quiet—or as quiet as they could. György Thurzó's judgement led my father to more letters and records, and then to a brick wall in Hungary (then occupied by the Red Army). It was only then that he discovered that the Nádasdy family's still active, leading to a brief written correspondence with Count Pál Nádasdy himself, somehow securing access to Ferenc's old letters (my father was a persuasive cuss when he needed to be). But it was Bathory's "day book," dug up from a family library, that was the real find.

Added to Dad's research is... a sort of story, I guess. Apparently one of Count Pál's aunts or great-aunts had written it around 1900 or so, based on the day book and some of the letters, to tie together the parts of the story. Treat it as a species of informed speculation, from that point of view, although Dad was determined it was important—thought maybe the author had access to another, more direct source. Who knows? Take it with a pinch of salt.

More tomorrow.

JH x

NOBLESSE OBLIGE

Adrian Tchaikovsky

With thanks to my test readers Tadhg Ó hAnnracháin, David Stokes, Bru Newhall, Marcin Pągowski and RL Robinson.

"New nobility is but the act of power, but ancient nobility is the act of time."

Francis Bacon, 'On Nobility,' 1625

I.

Excerpt from a letter by Count Jarek Osobyrski, ambassador to the Hungarian Court, to Walenty Dembiński, Chancellor of Poland, 1574

To the right noble and sagacious Lord Walenty Dembiński, Lord Chancellor of the Kingdom of Poland,

My lord, I know of your concerns regarding the further advances of the Turk, such that you wish to be most speedily informed of any developments on that front.

I have been present at Csejte Castle these last seven days as a guest of the Nádasdy family, who have gathered together a number of the more martial of the Hungarian landowners, ostensibly for an early hunt of wolves, but in truth to discuss how best the Turk might be driven from those parts of Hungary under the Crescent.

However, before such weighty matters, I must report that the purpose of our gathering was nearly made moot by the arrival, two days ago, of an ambassador of the Sublime Porte itself, one Azghan Mohammed Bey, who arrived in great style with a riot of their marching music and much pomp. The Turk himself, whilst at pains to stress his apologies for such an unlooked-for arrival, was plainly suspicious of our talk, and it seemed that, other than an outright banishment that might arouse yet more alarm in the enemy, any plans must be laid clandestinely or not at all.

However, this morning the man himself, Azghan Bey, was discovered in the orchard quite dead, and of no natural causes; for his body was set upon a makeshift pike of apple-wood for all to see. At first it seemed that none had seen anything of the execution, or would say anything, but then a witness emerged. This is the young daughter of György Báthory of Ecsed, brought to meet her fiancé, the young son of the Nádasdy. Her story is hard to credit. She claims a 'tall, pale, beautiful man' dressed in a fine robe that sounds, from her words, to be a thing our grandfathers might have affected, came 'from the shadows' as she says and accosted the unfortunate Turk, lifting him in the air by his neck and choking the voice from him before driving him, still living, onto the splintered branch. I would dismiss the tale as the hysteria of a child, save that I had sight of the dead man's throat, where the deep impressions of a single hand were there to be seen.

I had the chance to snatch brief words with the witness herself and asked her if she knew where the mysterious assailant had gone. She seemed half in a daze but claimed he had not departed at all and that she still saw him nearby, or in the corner of her eye. Despite myself, I felt myself shiver on that chill morning.

What strikes me most is the reaction of the locals—these stout men of Hungary. The girl's father said she must be mistaken, and dismissed the story to my face, but many from the East of Hungary seem to have an inkling of what had transpired, and it is a source of both fear and pride to them. Certainly our further talks against the Porte were much emboldened by events. I confess, I have begun to see figures in the shadows myself, after the girl's words.

The girl herself seemed not in the least frightened. Rather, the sight had worked her into a strange passion, and if I had been her fiancé's father I would have been concerned for her fidelity. Her name, for your records, is Erzsébet'or as we would say, Elizabeth' Báthory.

II.

Letter from Doctor Nico Magnus Allavardi, Sárvár Castle, Hungary, to Ferenc Nádasdy, Vienna, 1576

To my most Magnificent Lord and Patron the good Lord Ferenc Nádasdy

My most dear sir, I hope this missive finds you in good spirits and at ease in the court. I regret I cannot ease your heart about matters here, but you were justified in sending my talents to your home. I would travel across the Empire again, and twice as far, to oblige such a wise, benevolent and open-handed patron of the sciences.

The news that reached you regarding your wife's health was not exaggerated, and I came upon your Erzsébet bedridden and very pale, her humours entirely out of balance with a great want of the Sanguine. She is weak and I have found traces of haemorrhaging, with blood found each morning on her pillow. By my arrival she had already endured a decline of several weeks and, had she not by nature a strong constitution, might already have passed beyond the power of medicine to recover her.

Despite this, her manner is euphoric and she seems not to suffer, though she is afflicted by feverish hallucinations, speaking of a tall, pale man that none among her servants have seen, whose visit she seems to be constantly anticipating.

The staff themselves are uncooperative and it would not be going too far to say I detect an undercurrent of hostility directed at your wife, as though she had brought this malady upon herself in some improper manner.

I am, if I may be so bold, a man in command of all that our esteemed Medical University of Vienna can teach regarding physic, and I do not believe any better practises in Vienna even now. However, Man is mortal, and should God call, even the most robust of Adam's line must answer. I have prescribed a diet strong with red meat, minced for ease of consumption, and such exercise as she is capable of, to reinvigorate the ebbing humour; similarly, emetics and tinctures to lessen the hold of the other humours upon her. Had I more time I would be confident in a gradual restoration of balance within her body. However, even since I arrived I have seen your wife decline, and I fear that the techniques I have at my disposal may not have time to be efficacious.

I write this letter to you as something of a confession, therefore. In finding my tried methods too tardy or lacking against this malady, I have taken steps that my peers at the University would frown upon.

In short, there has been a woman come to Sárvár claiming knowledge of your wife's ailment and how to cure it. She is one Dorottya Semtész, and far from being a wild crone, she is a modest woman of middle years, and some small education.

I had grave misgivings about giving her access to the patient, but she was most insistent and your servants here would not bar the door against her. Mme. Semtész has therefore the opportunity of making her own examination and recommendations, and perhaps where education fails some folk charm or prayer may yet bring succour. I only hope I may write with more cheering news. I am afraid it will be soon, one way or the other.

Once again I extend my most heartfelt regrets that I cannot bring you happiness with this missive, and my ongoing thanks for your patronage.

Written this 30th day of October of the year 1576 by your most obedient servant,

NMA

Sárvár Castle, 1576

WHEN DOROTTYA CAME to her bedside, it seemed like a dream to Erzsébet; but her life had become a succession of dreams. The servants glided in and out of her awareness like ghosts. The walls of Sárvár shimmered and danced for her, so that she could almost see through them, into the awful abyss beyond. Even the vain, primping doctor her husband had sent from Vienna seemed like some bladder inflated with life only for the moments he was paraded before her, to have the air let from him when he was out of her sight so he could be more easily stored.

And beyond them all the greater dream, her dread pale visitor. Evening was hours distant, yet the dreadful yearning was already stirring what little blood she had left. She felt a huge slow swell of fear bearing her up, and yet it was a mercurial thing. There was an alchemy to that fear, that could transform it into so many other emotions. She said the prayers of Catholics and Protestants both; she tried to fix the face of Ferenc, her husband, in her mind; she tried to be *good* and yet she knew the fear would decay as the sky darkened, until she was left with nothing but a helpless, weak longing.

And now this woman.

The doctor had come in with her, but now he was absent. Erzsébet had not seen him go. Perhaps he had simply deflated when she was not looking, sagging slowly into a puddle of rubbery skin.

The sharp cough of the woman brought her back to the stagnant, fire-dry air of her chamber. *Dorottya Semtész.* She was dressed in staff livery but it fit her badly, and the role fit her worse. She was plainly a peasant, yet she carried herself with the arch pride of a duchess.

"What do you want?" Erzsébet whispered, because the long, slow hours were drawing towards nightfall and she was to entertain a guest. The thought clutched at her heart with anxiety and anticipation. And yet the peasant woman would not go, and Erzsébet tried to summon the haughty grandeur of Countess Báthory to dismiss her. "What are you looking at?" she rasped.

"A victim," came the stern reply, hard as a governess Erzsébet had once known, who had refused to yield to smiles or tantrums. "Is that all you are, girl? Just one more husk for *Him?*"

"How dare you address me in such a way?" From a peasant! "If I had my strength—"

"But you don't." Dorottya sat on the edge of her bed, staring into Erzsébet's face. *Those gaunt hollows, the darkness about my eyes.* It had been two days since Erzsébet had dared the mirror. "*He's* taking it. Another night, perhaps two, and you'll be lost to the world, though not to him. Is that what you want?"

Yes. But something in Erzsébet rose in defiance, of this woman, of her fate. "*Who?* Who is it?"

Dorottya smiled slightly. "Better. You've seen him, haven't you? He's had the scent of you for a while."

Blood in the orchard at Csejte. Erzsébet managed a faint nod.

"He will have his women." There was an ocean of scorn in Dorottya's voice. "So many. You're nothing special, just the latest he has battened on to. He'll drink the blood of men and children if need be, but it's always the women. One of those tastes he's never let go of, when he's let go of so much else."

"Who?" Erzsébet whispered.

"The Dragon. The pale man with his clothes so fine, his moustaches so long, like a knight from your father's old tapestries. Through barred door and shuttered window with his cold hand upon you, his lips to your throat." The sensuousness of the image died in Dorottya's curt, dismissive delivery. "Did he make promises, or profess his love for you? He does that less and less as he falls away from his proper time. He sheds his skins like the serpent; one day all that will be left will be the hunger. Countess, I know him. I have spoken with those he has leeched off, and some I have seen wither and die; and some I have seen break free of him, at least for a time. But there must be a will, and perhaps you would rather languish in his arms and be his prey."

The thought sent a worm of pleasure through Erzsébet. *To lie in his arms one more time.*

She saw the beginnings of disappointment on Dorottya's face, the woman pushing herself up from the bed. Perhaps it was that look— to be *pitied* by this peasant woman—but she reached out and caught her visitor's wrist.

"I am the Countess Erzsébet Báthory," she hissed. "Through my will and my blood and that of my husband, I sway half the Kingdom of Hungary. I will not be prey."

Dorottya was still and silent for so long that Erzsébet Báthory felt her mind begin to fragment again, losing her sense of the here and now. At last the peasant woman said, "Then perhaps we can do something."

"How?" Erzsébet whispered. "He cares not for doors or guards. How can he be fought?"

"Some say prayer." The contempt dripped from Dorottya's voice.

"Turn the other cheek to the Dragon and you simply give him a new vein to tap. Holiness is for old men and nuns, Countess. We will match him with a strength like his own."

"I have no strength." Even speaking the words seemed too much effort.

"Be guided by me, Countess, and we shall find new strength for you, just as he must replenish his own ebbing power. I have listened to old women tell their lore of his kind, and I have read books that would turn a godly man's hair white. I have gone to the mountains in their season and heard the voices of the Strigoi that issue from their caves and hollows. All these words, all these languages, and but one message, Countess. One path to strength sufficient to defeat the Dragon himself."

"What message?" Erzsébet demanded.

Dorottya Semtész's eyes gleamed. "The blood is the life, Countess. The blood is the life."

Letter from Doctor Nico Magnus Allavardi, Sárvár Castle, Hungary, to Ferenc Nádasdy, Vienna, 1576

To my most Magnificent Lord and Patron the good Lord Ferenc Nádasdy

I am delighted to report that Erzsébet is well on the way to a complete recovery. The remedies of modern physick have, after all, triumphed over the imbalance of humours that afflicted your wife and she is now regaining her strength and speaks no more of this phantasmal figure that was, I believe, the inner shadow of the outer affliction.

In my previous letter (which must be en route even as I pen this) I wrote about a certain local woman who professed some expertise. Whilst her folk remedies may have given some small assistance, my own knowledge and expertise carried the greater burden of the recovery, as you can imagine.

Given the speed with which the patient is rebuilding her strength, I am not convinced that this malady was wholly natural in its nature. Whilst there are no definite signs of a toxin, I cannot rule the possibility out. Suspicion falls upon your staff here at Sárvár. I reported a certain hostility towards Erzsébet amongst the servants. It appears now that, immediately before your wife began her dramatic recovery, two maids disappeared, no-one knows where. Their possessions remain, but they themselves were last seen attending on your wife, and now cannot be found.

I suspect some guilty conscience has prompted them to precipitous flight. Perhaps, seeing her remission, they feared being discovered. What else, after all could be behind such a sudden disappearance?

I will remain at Sárvár for another seven days to ensure no relapse, and then make haste to Vienna.

Written this 3rd day of November of the year 1576 by your most obedient servant,

NMA

III.

Trnava, 1579

HER DARING HAD not lasted long on the road. It was not the coach—the Báthory-Nádasdy fortunes controlled the wealth of half of Hungary, and they were not shy of spending money when they had to. Even Erzsébet's family could not afford to keep every road in Hungary in good condition, though, and so she had jolted and jumped across dirt tracks and potholed paths all the way from Csejte. By halfway she had begun to regard her impulsive decision as unworthy of her dignity. How exciting! How delighted Ferenc would be, that his bold new wife—was four years still new? She had seen so little of him that it seemed so—dared come into the heart of the soldier's world to visit him.

One rattling hour too many, one more stop to mend the wheel, surrounded on all sides by darkness and trees, and she regretted the entire venture, but she was Erzsébet Báthory. She did not back down once her mind was made up. There were too many servants and men-at-arms travelling with her who might prattle of a foolish girl. The thought of it made her ball her fists in fury.

But at last she was in sight of Trnava. The town itself seemed eclipsed by the military camp set up outside it. Ferenc was mustering and recruiting, and Trnava would be fertile ground for him, filled with families who had fled the Turkish capture of Esztergom a generation before.

And she should be proud of her husband, of course, because he was only twenty-three and already named Chief Commander against the Ottoman, a bold knight with the respect of the Emperor and the love of his peers. Yet he had gone from Vienna straight to his military duties, passing through her life like a short-lived ghost. So perhaps this was not such a romantic gesture, after all. Perhaps this was her reminding him that, though the Nádasdy had power and wealth, they were in the shadow of the Báthory pedigree, which underlay Hungary like the very bones of the mountains.

Towards the camp edge, the coach was hailed by sentries. A few sharp words served to give her passage, and she had her servants hunting out Ferenc's livery while the driver manoeuvred the coach along tracks rutted by the ponderous wheels of cannon. All around was the coarse babble of soldiers—their songs, jeers, insults and laughter. Erzsébet shrank back from it, hearing them speculate who might be coming to visit their betters.

And at last one of her people had sight of Ferenc, who was spending the evening with a band of his fellow officers within the town, so that all her winding through this morass of humanity had been utterly in vain. In a vile temper and determined to have her husband regret his choices as much as possible, her servants extricated her from the camp and passed within the walls of Trnava.

Her people asked if they should ride ahead and warn their master of her coming, but no, she would make it a surprise, pleasant or otherwise as she decided. Before long, groping over the cobbles of Trnava by moonlight, she could not imagine how this venture had ever seemed romantic.

At last she had the inn Ferenc was staying at, and she wondered what she might do or say, if she found him with some obliging wench on his knee, or worse.

But she was Erzsébet Báthory. She would not turn aside. That was for the rest of the world to do, when she strode at it.

He was not at play with some harlot. He was not even greatly in his cups. Ferenc's newfound position had brought out in him a love of war and that was the only love he was indulging. Hovering at the doorway, she caught him with a half-dozen men, all older than he, poring over maps and plans of fortifications, discussing the war with the Turk that everyone knew would come sooner or later.

Seeing him there, Erzsébet's anger evaporated. It was not replaced by love, exactly; possessiveness, perhaps, was as close as she ever came, and Ferenc was *hers*. She was seeing a man in his own proper environment, adapted to it as a fish to the river. He was the master of all his companions, and something in her stirred to the confidence and authority he had, that he had never stayed at her side long enough to show her.

Then one of the others was speaking, some portly man discussing the best vantage for an attack against Nové Zámky, the Turk's strongest bastion to the south. Tiring of his drab voice, Erzsébet glanced across the faces of the others.

And stopped, screwing her eyes up. For a moment, had there been…

But that was in the past. She had been too long on the road, too concerned with stoking the fires of anger inside herself. She would find lodgings befitting her station and then greet her husband in the morning…

But there, between Ferenc and the dull fat man, was there not a shadow?

She felt herself tremble to see it, that the air was dark there, as though one more stood in that room than she could account for. She let her gaze slide off it, let it fall into the corner of her eye—as Dorottya taught her—because surely this was no more than fatigue.

For a moment she saw him clearly at her husband's elbow, one slender-fingered hand even resting on Ferenc's shoulder as he leant forwards. She saw his long, pale face, his dark eyes as they darted across the map. In his expression there was an obscene anticipation, seeing on the barren paper the war to come, the blood to be spilled. *For the blood is the life.*

She retreated from the room and put her back to a wall, heart hammering. For a moment she was just a girl in an orchard, violent death crashing into her life. She remembered the terrible measures that Dorottya Semtész had resorted to, to free her from this man's cold power.

But, though so few years had passed, she found a core of stone within her. She was Erzsébet Báthory. She did not turn aside, and just as Ferenc prepared to fight the Turk, so she would fight for Ferenc. It was not love; it was because he was *hers*.

She turned and left the inn and Trnava, back along all the broken roads to Csejte Castle. Even as she travelled, she was sending her servants in all directions with the same mission. *Find me Dorottya Semtész.*

*   *   *

Letter from György Thurzó, Trnava, to Erzsébet Báthory, Czejte Castle, 1579

To the ever beautiful and noble Countess Erzsébet Báthory, on behalf of your husband the courageous and ever vigilant Ferenc Nádasdy

Ferenc being greatly concerned with matters of the camp, it falls to me as his friend to write to you of what has transpired here, as we have won a victory against the Turk outside Nové Zámky. Though it was only a skirmish, it has given great heart to the people who have seen only the depredation of the Ottoman advance in their lifetimes. Ferenc believes that, with proper application of the new guns, we can retake the town in the near future and then set to driving the infidels from the land.

Ferenc, I am sure, would wish to send you all his love and to be by your side as soon as his duties might allow. For my own part, I have a curious matter to broach with you, for I have now three nights together seen Ferenc rise from his bed and heard his voice as though in conference with some informant. I confess this seems much to me like an ill dream, but last night I even fancy I glimpsed his interlocutor: a tall, pale man with burning deep eyes, dressed in antique style, bending low to speak in Ferenc's ear. I even forced myself to rise from my own bed, though my limbs were marvellous heavy, seeking to surprise them—or him, for none beside Ferenc was to be found. When I asked him who he had been inviting as a guest to his home, for such had been the topic of the talk I overheard, he seemed so dazed and uncertain that I thought he too had just woken.

As you are wise, perhaps you can shed some light on these nocturnal incidents. Is this a common habit of your husband when he is at home: to walk and talk while yet asleep?

Your friend, and the conveyor of your husband's love, on this the 29th day of November in Our Lord's Year 1579

G

*   *   *

Csejte Castle, 1580

SHE KNEW ENOUGH to see the import of that letter. Even before she had reclaimed Dorottya to her retinue, her own reading had taught her what it meant to make unwise invitations. Erzsébet had already felt the shadow of the pale man over her when news of Dorottya had arrived.

She had feared the woman might be dead—it's no safe life, after all, to walk between God and the Devil and be despised by both. She had almost been right. Word came of one Dorottya Semtész imprisoned with her apprentice in Horné Saliby and accused of many crimes, some secular and some religious. The latter would have damned her swiftly had the authorities been either wholly Papist or Protestant, but the Church was tearing at itself all through the Holy Roman Empire, and Hungary most of all. Dorottya lived or died on a matter of theological jurisdiction.

The word of a Báthory was iron, though, most especially when that iron was adulterated with gold. Erzsébet sent a letter and a casket to the elders of the town, the former entreating them to show Christian mercy to a poor unfortunate sinner, the latter remunerating them for the time they would spend stroking their moustaches and signing the documents of release. Soon after, Dorottya and her accomplice were on a coach on the rough way to Csejte.

Dorottya had not aged or changed, or so it seemed to Erzsébet. Instead, she had diminished. She was still a peasant woman without any of that class's proper deference, willing to stare her betters in the eye, kneeling only on sufferance. Before, Erzsébet had been weak and Dorottya had the power to bring life or give death its rein. Now Dorottya came to her from the shadow of the noose and Erzsébet sat on a Countess's grand throne and looked down on her.

Erzsébet waved away pleasantry. "When last we met, there was a darkness on this house that you drove away. Now I find you at the mercy of a pack of councilmen and their dogs. Are you fallen so far?" *Are you no use to me?*

"The Dragon has influence in many places," Dorottya said, undaunted. "Many mortal authorities hear his voice in their ear."

"You still fight him, then?"

"And will rid this land of him by and by." Dorottya drew herself to her full height, gathering what tatters of esoteric mystery her imprisonment had left her with. "I thank you, Countess, for your hospitality, but my work goes on."

"And how do you go about such work?" Erzsébet countered, letting a sneer through her regal calm. "My people hear stories of you, Dorottya Semtész. Had they not taken you at Horné it would have been some other town. There is a trail you leave, of suspicion and sudden deaths. I hear tell of poisoned girls, daughters missing, bodies found on hillsides where you have passed. Will you tell me this is all *him?* How far will you travel, to escape those who name your victims?"

Dorottya was very still. "Of all people, Countess, you understand the cost of my work. There is but one currency that can match the Dragon, strength for strength." There was the slightest tremble in her voice. "Countess, *he* has a century and a half to give him strength. I... have had to do such things, but it is for a greater good..."

Erzsébet laughed scornfully, silencing her. "Tell me one thing before I pronounce sentence on you. You said before that *his* prey is women and he loves most the blood of young, innocent maids. What of men, Dorottya? Are they beneath his notice?"

The crafty look that came into the peasant's eyes was far too sharp. "Your husband is gone to fight the Turk, is he not?"

Erzsébet regarded her impassively.

"There are some things *he* retains still, from when he was no more than mortal. Two elements of his nature have survived almost intact: a desire for women and a hatred of the Turk he fought in life. Do you think he is not known, for all his name is not recorded in the rolls of honour? Do you think the Ottoman host will ever go into *his* mountains, or besiege *his* castle? The Kings of Hungary have long known that there is a stretch of their border that need never fear conquest from the south, no matter what else is lost. So, yes, Countess, he may go amongst men engaged in such a venture, and he may touch their minds and steer them, and make them his. And most especially if such work would open the doors to return to you, for he forgets no soul that he has been denied. And so I ask you, Countess, let me continue my work."

"Your murders."

"Will you condemn me, who knows my purpose better than anyone?" Dorottya took two steps towards her. "It is necessary."

"You passed through these lands last year," Erzsébet noted. "I have reports of seven young women dead in your wake. Did you make the most of their blood as you fled their families?"

"Countess..."

"My husband's family bought Csejte for me as a wedding present. All these villages are mine and under my protection."

"Countess, please." Now Dorottya's voice was flat. She stood still, awaiting the fall of the axe.

"Your grand work," Erzsébet went on. "Living from town to town, hiding like a rat, escaping just in time or not at all. *He* will outlive you."

"I do what I can," Dorottya said bitterly. "Who else even has the will to fight the Dragon?"

Erzsébet felt a release, as though some intricate lock, long in the turning, had been released. "I will fight him. And you will be my servant and my teacher, and between us we will break the back of his power."

There was a brief flash of rebellion in the woman's eyes. "My work…"

"Seventeen villages around Csejte," Erzsébet pronounced. "More around Sárvár and Németkeresztúr. *Mine*, Dorottya. The beams and bricks of them, the bodies and souls. And the blood; of course, the blood. Is it not time that your *work* found a proper patroness?"

Dorottya just stared at her, like a woman who thought she was seeing a lantern when in fact it was the sun.

IV.

From the Day Book of Erzsébet Báthory

9th February 1582, Sárvár

Word from Dorottya at Németkeresztúr. Under my writ she has recruited three for service and had them confined within the castle. She reports limited gain from light beating and remonstrance, but reluctant to proceed to bloodletting without my being present. Instructed her to progress to pins and I will travel to join her as soon as I am able.

Judit has been clumsy at service here and, when reprimanded, had a definite defiance in her eye. Had her held upon the battlements unclad until third hour past midnight then brought to me. In her weakened state, merely touching her chilled flesh resulted in a minor gain of strength, which made me suspect she had been brought close to death. Applied pins beneath fingernails as per the usual procedure to draw blood. She was all apology and contrition now, not realising her repentance was no longer sought, nor even an object lesson for others. Her screaming and invoking of saints and pleas wore at my nerves. Judit has always been shrill. Informed her she could take the pins out herself if she wished to suffer the consequences. Watching her try to remove the pins with chilled fingers was amusing, as she often struck against the metal without dislodging it, causing yet more pain. After, I had her fingers struck off. The result exceeded previous cases by a considerable factor. A curious thing: the hope given her definitely affected the drawing process—at first inhibiting the gaining of strength from her, later, when that hope was dashed, greatly enhancing it. Must write to Dorottya suggesting further experiment.

Ilona is gone to Pozsony to procure more staff, but no word from her yet.

Németkeresztúr, 1583

WHEN SHE WAS very young, Erzsébet had watched her father execute a gypsy. The man was accused of selling his child to the Turk, but in truth he was simply a gypsy who had been caught with a few coins on him, and who would miss such a man? She remembered the thrill she had felt, at the death. The man had been so vital before, so full of cries and begging, and then he had been dead, and where had all that life gone?

Later, before her marriage, she had demanded perfection of the women who waited on her, and the servants below them. She had them beaten if they failed her. She had beaten them herself more than once. In the bonds of pain, she had felt something pass from them to her. And after all, she was their mistress, their ruler. Everything of theirs was hers, and if so, surely that included blood and life and soul.

When the pale man had killed the Turkish ambassador, she had felt the moment when the life passed, the strength fleeing at the point of death to vanish into the shadow of the Dragon's cloak. The blood was the life, yes, but so were all the stages on the road to it. Simply opening a throat like a worker in an abattoir would waste all that power and vital essence. They needed to gather it, husband and harvest it so that Erzsébet could steep herself in that strength. *He* had been drawing on the strength of others for centuries. *He* had shown that the dominion of a feudal overlord was a thing not limited by mortal constraints or mundane power. And if they were to overcome him, they must follow him on that path. Dorottya had the knowledge, but she had never been able to properly refine her methods. Only now, her head bowed to Erzsébet, did she have the opportunity.

And they could not do it alone, just the two of them, and Erzsébet could trust none of her family retainers in the work. Oh, the servants could bring girls in and the guards could lock them up, but that was not the *true* work, after all.

Ilona Jó was Dorottya's apprentice, a peasant who had suffered some depredation of *his*—Erzsébet didn't care about the details, so long as Ilona was dedicated to the cause and did not seek power on her own account. By now, Dorottya had already passed the tipping point, so that the peasant deferred to the noblewoman, as it should be. When they were together drawing strength from the blood and the bruises and the screams, it was Erzsébet first to the table, and Dorottya grudgingly content with her leavings.

A year ago they had recruited Fickó from a prison; a stunted little creature, half-mad, he had lived with the wolves out in the forest and bloodied his teeth on their kills. Unlettered and wild, still he had ended up on the same scent as they, drawing the strength of others into himself for all he could not use it. Dorottya hoped his grisly feasting would unlock some vital secret, for they still fell short of what *he* could accomplish. They could not drink the pure well of life with the blood, nor devour it with the flesh. They could merely tap the cask imperfectly, with rods and switches, pins and knives. When *he* came at last, they would not be able to contest sovereignty with him; he would make Erzsébet bow the knee once more. And she was done with humbling herself before anyone else's dream.

*   *   *

V.

Letter from Zsófia Perényi to Count Árpád Perényi, 1586

To my honourable and noble husband, your wife sends greetings,

  I regret that I have cut short my visit to our cousin Erzsébet. I made announcement of news from you that requires my attendance at your side with all haste, and am sending this missive ahead of me so that you will know what must be said if questioned, for I fear the lady of this house has means of hearing rumour from afar and sifting it for any grain of truth that might offer insult to the name of Báthory.

  I know you desired to make a closer alliance with Ferenc Nádasdy. This alliance is not to be effected by way of becoming a confidante of Erzsébet. I no longer wish to share walls with her, kin though she may be.

  Ferenc himself was not present. I understand he had barely seen the birth of his first daughter before he returned to his military duties, which caused Erzsébet some irritation. Nonetheless, she dotes on the child, Anna, with a mother's proper love, but that is the one fond thing I will write in connection with her.

  Matters started uneventfully enough. I had heard that she was a harsh mistress to her servants, but you and I have both had cause to discipline our staff in our time. In the first few days of my guesting I was incited to see a girl whipped, and though Erzsébet took distinct joy in the act, a proper order must be maintained in every household. Later, while I and several others were at talk, Erzsébet suggested we watch her servants perform a traditional dance of Sárvár Castle, which we readily consented to. She called in a girl who could not have been older than thirteen, and had papers placed between the child's toes by a brutish, unshaven dwarf she keeps close to her. These were then lit on fire, forcing the screeching creature to cavort about the room in a display not devoid of humour. Seeing my amusement, Erzsébet leant close and suggested that she would have more choice entertainment later on that night, fit only for those of a certain temperament. At the time, seeking to woo her to us, I feigned enthusiasm and agreed.

That night I was sent for, and advised to have my people dress me for the coldest weather, since the snow was falling thick. I was led beyond the castle walls by certain low-born women whom Erzsébet appears to give an untoward authority, and there our cousin was with the same servant girl, quite naked in the drifts. 'First fire, now ice,' she said, and her people proceeded to pour icy water upon the wretch as she pleaded and cried out to God. This continued long enough for the chill to work its way through my furs, but by the midnight bell the girl had expired. In truth it was not the glee that Erzsébet took in the death that so unsettled me, as comments I overheard by her peasant women that, with a cold death, 'the blood would keep for longer.' I cannot put any interpretation on these words that does not affright me severely.

Worse was to come when we returned within the walls to find that, without precedent, little Anna had become sick. Some malady had touched her so that she seemed very weak and pale, and although I well know what realms of illness the youngest are subject to, Erzsébet appeared to fear some specific complaint that drove her into a frenzy of fear and rage. I caught the older of her peasant women eyeing me with disturbing manner and she commented to her associate about the pedigree of the Perényi line and the purity of our blood. The predatory way she spoke convinced me to make my excuses immediately the next morning, before Erzsébet had arisen. I will not count myself safe until I have met with you again.

Written on this xii January Anno Domini 1586 by your loyal and penitent

Zsófia

*   *   *

Csejte, 1586

THE WOMAN WAS the least appealing example of Hungary peasant stock Erzsébet had ever set eyes on. *She makes even Dorottya look like a fine lady.* "Did you hear the story of the Lithuanian Jew who made a man from clay?" she asked idly, circling the creature. "I imagine the thing must have looked much like this. Why do you bring me here to see it?"

The lumpen woman's heavy-jawed head swung to stare at Erzsébet, and for a moment she felt a frisson of fear that those huge heavy arms would reach for her, brutal as an ape's. Instead she just looked down with coal black eyes from a height that would have put Ferenc in her shadow.

Dorottya was in the corner of the room, reckoning something on the stones of a rosary. "They call her Katarína Benická," she explained. "I found her chained in the cellar of a church. She's a murderess, by law, but in such circumstances that they were still debating it when I found her."

"What is it to us?"

"Katarína, tell the great lady what you did," Dorottya prompted.

The burly peasant woman turned that flinty stare on her, then shrugged hugely.

"It was only I was hungry," she said thickly.

Erzsébet felt her patience slipping. "Dorottya—"

The witch held up a hand. "She was a taverner's wife. Her hunger took itself out on their guests, and her husband, when he found out. She wasn't subtle about it. When they came to take her, a neighbour put a pitchfork through her gut. A militiaman put a crossbow bolt through her, and the local butcher, a cleaver between neck and shoulder. All of it she lived through. They say God touched her, to make her well enough to stand trial, but I have studied her and I have seen her at her trencher. She is a clear channel for the vital essence, and no wonder she hungers for it."

"This... *thing?*" Erzsébet demanded. Again that dull black stare turned its disinterest on her, and Dorottya was nodding fiercely.

"We need more subjects, Countess. We don't have much time before *he* finds us here. We need subjects, and we need to study how Katarína is able to master the *vitae* as we have never been able to."

"Is she one of *his?*" Erzsébet wondered.

"She is a freak," Dorottya said, almost proudly. "Some taint of her heredity. There were darker things than *he* in Transylvania in the old days, and some had mortal offspring whose blood is with us yet. But most of all she is a gift to us, and we must seize it while we still have time."

THEY HAD FLED Sárvár immediately when Anna was found shivering and weak in her crib. It had been a warning, but one intended only to sharpen Erzsébet's fear. *He* had turned his attention back to her at last. *He*, who had been roosting like a crow at all the battlefields Ferenc had contested with the Turk, had finally grown tired of bloodshed by the sword, and recalled unfinished business.

They had gone to Csejte, even though it was practically under *his* shadow. For Erzsébet, the castle there was still her stronghold. Anna had wailed all the way, until she had thought she might even strangle the infant herself, but the child had lived. Ferenc and Erzsébet's first child, and she had lived.

But *he* would find them, and Erzsébet knew that they were weak. They were uncovering lore from first principles that *he* had been steeped in two centuries gone. *He* had been an alchemist, a scholar, a student at the Devil's own lectern, if the stories were to be believed. And the world had turned, since then. The Age of Reason had driven the shadows back until all Dorottya could glean were scraps and old wives' tales, just as the Protestants were driving away the cobwebs of old Rome.

Ilona and Fickó moved through the villages in the castle's shadow, announcing that the Countess had returned and the castle was alive again, and lucky young girls could find money and preferment in service at Csejte. Enough families were desperate or greedy, had too many daughters without dowries, that memories grew dull and the girls were volunteered. Some would indeed be maids and cleaners until other uses arose for them, or until they crossed Erzsébet's temper. Others went straight to the cells for Dorottya and Ilona to experiment with.

And Katarína was an education. Dorottya often speculated on what twisted rusalka or leshy lurked in her heritage. She did the work of three men, and when Ilona and Fickó teased her or beat her, she took it like a stone. Her one passion was her hunger, and she could fill her belly with bread and turnip mash over and over without taking the edge off it. Only flesh filled the void in her; flesh, and human flesh most of all. And of that flesh she made strength, becoming yet more ogrish, heedless of the knocks and scratches of the world.

"Only under the night sky," Dorottya concluded. "But that has always been a time for witches, even as it is *his* time. The sun destroys shadows, makes things clear and plain. Katarína was taken at night, at the peak of her strength. And I have found how she unlocks the doors to the vital essence, draws life from the blood." She brandished pages of tangled diagrams and equations at Erzsébet, who waved them away.

"Dorottya, my Anna was weak in her crib when I went to her this morning. She did not cry, but stared at me with eyes not her own; with *his* eyes. We have no more time. Does all your paper-scratching amount to your being ready?"

Dorottya was about to make some plea—more time, more practice, more study—but she plainly saw the thunder in Erzsébet's face, the violence in her crooked fingers. There was no safe answer but, "Yes."

SHE WAS WAITING for the Dragon when he came, standing between the window and Anna's crib. Erzsébet had retained one maid and the babe's wet nurse, both kept trembling in the room's shadowy edges, but besides them, she had her true helpers, her fellow dabblers in blood. Dorottya stood at the crib's head, Ilona at its foot, while little Fickó and hulking Katarína were on hand to either side to ensure the servants didn't run. Erzsébet couldn't recall the name of the maid, or even the nurse. It wasn't important to her.

Moonlight lay out a path across the chamber floor, turning the rugs and stone into a miniature landscape, as though Erzsébet flew high above some unknown land of forest and wastes. It was along that path *he* came, entering the room like a coil of darkness that writhed and fought until it had unfolded into *him*. The maids began screaming and even Fickó let out a bark of shock, but Erzsébet was ready.

She had seen him in the orchard on her first visit to this castle, but the memory was smeared by fright and youth. He had come to her after her wedding, seeking to make her his own, but she had been feverish and under his sway. When he had been amongst Ferenc's officers, he had been but a shadow, a whispering knot of hatred and bloodlust spurring them on. Only now could she look at him properly.

He was tall, perhaps the tallest man she had ever seen, and very fine-featured. His skin was pale as an albino's, save for his cheeks and lips, which shone with a rose of ersatz life. A stab of glee shot through her, to know that he had not simply strode in to feed, but that he had gone elsewhere to build his strength before trying her.

He had a long moustache but no beard, and his eyes were dark and powerful, deep wells of arrogance and power. If she had met with that face under other circumstances, she would have admired its cruel lines, the strength of purpose that burned from it, because those were the virtues of nobility. Except she knew his purpose now, and it was no more than the grave worm's or the clutching ivy: to go on, to exist, day after day.

But she would greet him as befitted his station. "My lord, many years has my husband held out an invitation to you. I am only surprised you have left your visit so long."

The sanguine line of his lips curved, and she saw the sharp white points behind them. "Countess Báthory." His voice was deep, hard like stone, hollow as a cenotaph. He looked her over, as though she was staff for the hiring, some trembling village girl lured by the promise of service. "But you have changed," he murmured. "What is this that has laid its hand so heavy upon you? What has creased your fine skin and coarsened your hair? Can it be *time?*" His words stole upon her, and suddenly she realised he was standing right before her, close enough to touch. "Is it five-and-twenty now?" He bent close so the words were for her alone. "Six-and-twenty? Seven? How the years pass, Countess. And yet, had your Strega slave not thrown such a muddle of blood in my path before, you might have been six-and-ten forever."

For a moment she faltered, feeling the claws of age on her as though she withered there and then. She let his words master her. She was no longer the girl she had been, and soon there would be an old woman looking back at her from the glass, and *he* would be young, young forever. And so might she be, if she would just submit…

"I am Erzsébet Báthory," she hissed, barely more than a whisper, but so full of venom! "What I desire, I take." And she met his eyes. The act of will was almost more than she could bear, to stare into the dark void within him, but she forced herself to it. She had not bowed her head or subsumed her name to her husband, and nor would she to *this*. "And what you desire, you shall not have. My child is beyond your reach."

He was a step further from her, though she had not seen him take it. His eyes blazed, lips curling back from ivory fangs. "Your *child?*" he spat. "A scrap of flesh for my dogs. But *you* I shall have. You shall kneel to me and do my will, and you will love me for it. What are you, that you *dare* defy the Dragon?"

Erzsébet was aware of the whimpers of the maid and nurse, the squalling of Anna, the reek of Fickó soiling himself. The air in the room seemed to bend around her and she felt *his* will like a vice, like a hawk's talons clutching at her skull, like a hand at her throat.

"You speak of age and time," she managed, through clenched teeth. "You have paid a price, to hide from them. A hollow man, I see before me, who must forever fill himself with the life of others. What is left of the man you were, the great scholar, the great soldier? What do you study now? What wars do you win, except through the feats of others?" And again she made herself meet that furious, all-consuming gaze. "When I follow your path, *old man*, I shall do better. It shall be Erzsébet Báthory who lives forever, and not merely her shell."

She had gone too far. She saw the moment when his temper snapped, and then he had her by the neck, her feet off the ground, her world shrinking to his rage-twisted mask. Her thought in that moment was not of death but of lost opportunity. Here was her mirror, who knew himself master of all, who brooked no insubordination. *If only we could have shared the world.* But they were neither of them capable of admitting an equal, of bending the knee.

Distantly, she heard Dorottya shout for the others to do their work. Fickó already had his knife out, swarming up the maid like a monkey to plunge the blade into her throat. Katarína was more direct, taking the old nurse in her huge hands and twisting, the explosive retort of snapping bones shocking through the chamber.

That would have been the moment for betrayal, but Erzsébet had bound Dorottya to her with chains of threat and promise and sheer power of personality, and the witch and her apprentice gave unselfishly of all the strength they had harvested. Erzsébet reached out and took hold of *his* hand, prying at his claw fingers until her throat was free and watching him stagger back from her, his eyes wide with a fear he must not have known since his last mortal breath.

Ilona had caught the blood of the maid in a cup, and now she came to Erzsébet's elbow, proffering the spattered vessel. The taste was salt and iron in her mouth, but most of all it was *life*, the life of others made to serve her own; for what else was nobility for? She felt it flood through her, lending her a strength that would not last—they were still practising their new skills, after all—but would serve for now. When she advanced, *he* fell back to the window, diminished to a shadow in the moonlight.

"My blood is poison to you, Count," she told him. "Go prey on the witless and the ignorant in the shadow of your home, but know that I banish you from this place. One day I will come for you, and you will bend the knee to *me*, or I will destroy you."

His lips writhed and his eyes burned, but he was a mad dog chained. He could not raise a hand against her, nor even curse her. A moment later he was gone, bursting out into the night and speeding invisibly away, darkness against darkness, and she was free.

All our work, all the blood, has come to this, she thought, *and I do not need to trouble myself any more.* But her eyes slipped from the night outside to the emptied vessel in her hand. It was lined, that hand, save where the blood had touched it. *Time,* said the Dragon and, though he had fled, Time remained behind to stalk her, which would never touch *him*. It was not enough. She had won only a reprieve and not a victory.

"Dorottya," she said hoarsely. "You must hire more servants. There is more work ahead of us."

* * *

VI.

From the Day Book of Erzsébet Báthory

19th December 1591

Word from Pozsony that Anna has been asking to see her new sister. I have instructed them to tell her it is not possible. She must not be here until Orsolya has been properly 'baptized' as Anna herself was. No daughter of mine shall be the shadow or possession of another.

Dorottya and Ilona have returned with new recruits, although they have had to go further afield. Another four for the cells. Three are to be chilled and drained. This morning I noted the skin of my hands is losing its firmness again. Have instructed Dorottya to prepare a new bath, but each application suffers diminishing returns. Time, he said. How was he able to sever himself from Time when I am not? No matter how long I bathe, how much I drink, I am only borrowing the vital essence, denied true title to it. I must preserve my youth until I can perfect myself and follow him into that other country, and wrest lordship of it from his cold hands.

Ferenc is present, and so we must be circumspect. He stays two nights at Csejte before going before Rudolph to discuss the war. I have instructed him to gain access to the Emperor's library, as by all accounts Rudolph has collected texts which may throw light on our studies, and which may give me an advantage over the Dragon should he ever return to trouble me. Ferenc can barely write his name, the oaf, and I fear any requests I make will be lost in the hollow of his skull. Save when he comes to my bed and thrusts upon me, he is nothing to me, but then I could not abide an attentive husband who might notice things.

*   *   *

13th February 1592

Dorottya believes she has improved her incantations, so we shall attempt a major bath with warm, rather than cold-preserved.

Materiel: 7
Hungarian, age 14, fair
Hungarian, age 15, fair
Jewess, age 15, dark
Slovak, age 15, fair
Hungarian, age 17, dark, blemish on left cheek
Serb, age 17, fair
Hungarian, age 21, fair.

Results: greatly improved success, all agree that I look some years younger, 25 perhaps, or even 20. Change persists after rising.

15th February 1592

My face in the mirror shows the burden of years. The blood washes off me. The materiel was imperfect or insufficient. Have sent Ilona and Fickó to recruit more subjects. I feel him out there. Time is a river that bears me off while he just waits on the shore.

Letter from the staff of Ferenc Nádasdy, Prague, to György Thurzó, Trnava, 1593

György, from your fellow soldier Ferenc

Never have I had greater joy than today. The Emperor has at last given me leave to reclaim our abused Hungary from beneath the Crescent.

I will meet you at the muster outside Trnava and we shall embrace, and then we shall fall upon the Turk like tigers. Rather the armies of the Porte than to be home any longer than I must, and be with Her.

Your comrade

Ferenc

Dictated this 29th day of July in this year 1593

Letter from György Thurzó, Esztergom, to Prince Matthias of Habsburg, Governor of Austria, Vienna, 1595

My right worthy and worshipful Prince, I recommend myself, your humble servant, into your good graces.

Messengers will already have outstripped my words to tell you that we have taken the town, but that General Von Mansfeld's wounds were mortal and he has followed after the many men he led into the breach, leaving the army under my command and that of Ferenc Nádasdy.

Your Highness, as you know, I have on occasion conducted investigations for your Imperial brother Rudolph to further his interest in matters unusual and arcane, and so consider myself something of a familiar of the mysterious. The matters I write of have a touch of darkness about them, but I must make plain I do not send this message as an attack upon our friend. Instead, pure concern moves me to broach the subject with one who knew him at Vienna, and who was there to see his pride when His Imperial Majesty your brother conferred upon him his current prestigious command.

There never was a more courageous soldier than Ferenc. I say without fear of contradiction that of all who secured Esztergom for us, none played a greater role than he. These last few years, however, I have felt as though a different man sometimes watches me from his eyes. Since even before the war began, a strange distance has attached itself to him. He has joined less and less in the merriment of camp life. Small matters have brought a temper out in him so that his hand is often raised towards his subordinates. At other times he has shown a curious fear of things that should be of no account to a bold warrior: rats and other vermin, darkness, the sudden rise of mist. Most of all he seldom speaks of his wife, but when he does there is a tremble in his voice and he will not meet my eyes, as though terrified by her. His visits home are brief, no more time than it takes to warm the marital bed and then be gone, and I sometimes think the joy he takes in battle compensates him for what he cannot derive from his home.

What troubles me greatly is a habit that has been sporadic with him for some years, but is now almost nightly. When all are abed, as I have seen and his servants have confirmed to me, he often rises and walks out under the stars, though I cannot say whether he still sleeps or no. There he speaks to himself in such a way that he seems to hold conversation with some other not present. I have stolen close and listened to Ferenc's words, and the impression is of a man being goaded and instructed to terrible things. I hear him speak of the Turk in terms that go beyond even those of a soldier faced with a vile enemy, and there are curses for his wife, couched in dreadful terms.

When he is properly awake in the morning, he has no apparent recall that any such perambulations occurred, but I have watched him with Turkish prisoners whom he has ordered hung, scourged, drowned, and he has muttered the echo of some words I heard overnight. Before the gates of Esztergom, he had one such impaled upon a stake, placed slow upon it so that the man was a long time dying. He said it was to break the spirit of the defenders, and it may have done so, but it shook me and many Christians who witnessed the act, not least because we many of us recall the practice from our histories, and that it was abandoned because of the reputation of that Wallachian who put it to greatest use.

I fear for our friend, Your Highness. If you have any advice for me, I would gladly welcome your wisdom.

I am your man and ever will be, by the grace of God, which ever have you in his keeping.

Your servant and soldier ever, on this the 28th day of August in Our Lord's Year 1595

G

VII.

Sárvár, 1596

FERENC HAD NOT cared, after the births of the girls. He had not much wanted to see them, and his visits had been perfunctory. Erzsébet, after the shadow that had been cast over Anna, had sent each girlchild away as swiftly as possible. She had set aside money for them, made arrangements for their nursing and their education, but she had not wanted them near her. And they had thrived, out of her shadow. No mysterious ailments; no pallid, bloodless faces. *I have saved them from* him, she told herself, and did not consider whether it was her influence they were better rid of.

Anna, Orsolya, Katalin, three scions of the Báthory-Nádasdy line, born to the most powerful and wealthy family in Hungary, to whom even the Habsburgs came cap in hand when their coffers were bare. When grown, they would be the most eligible women in Christendom, ripe for sealing alliances or marrying monarchs. Ferenc barely acknowledged their existence, and as for Erzsébet, she sought a different posterity. Let her name live on in however many generations it might, she planned for a future that she would be there to see.

But the birth of András changed all of that. András, first male heir of the line. She expected to resent him, the moment she purged his tiny form from her body, gritting her teeth and forcing it into the cruel world. When Dorottya declared the babe a boy, she should have sought to have the little shred of flesh destroyed. After all, a boy would inherit, and that made him an enemy for the future, a rival for power over all she had.

But she held him in her arms and felt a connection none of the girls had sparked in her. *András*. She sounded his name in her head, and who knew what future the boy might have. What might she teach him, in the long, long years of her life? He would be bright and cold like ice, she knew. He would be clever and cruel and follow the long path she set out for him, her eternal viceroy in a world dominated by the name of Báthory.

And Ferenc came back from the wars the moment he heard he had a son. He stood and beamed down at András, who stared back at this huge stranger with measureless courage, and Erzsébet thought, *We are almost like a family*.

Her happiness lasted two days.

She had been at her studies, marking entries in her day book as one of the new girls trembled, red, on her table. She had some idea about Tartar women—perhaps the fierce warrior spirit of those people might offer improved results—and had procured a few for experimentation. At first she thought the screaming was her own work, or some echo in her mind of all the screams that had gone before. Then she recognised the voice: no nameless peasant fit only to be used up for the advancement of Erzsébet's life and work, but one who had become most dear to her: Dorottya.

Dorottya was old now—fifty years at least, though she had always been strong-framed. When Erzsébet found her at the foot of the nursery stairs, at first she assumed the woman had stumbled. Ilona was already crouching by her teacher's side, too distressed to be of help, and Erzsébet came within a breath of just storming back to her studies, cursing the clumsiness of menials. Then came Katarína's bellow from up in the nursery, and she realized that something far worse was at hand.

She took the stairs three at a time, feeling that monster Time dragging at her even as she did so. *Slower, weaker, duller.* There was blood on the nursery floor.

Katarína, the behemoth, stood before András's crib. A slash of crimson crossed her face, another her outstretched hand. In one corner of the room, Fickó lay insensible, half his face a purple bruise.

As Erzsébet entered, Ferenc was lashing at Katarína again with his curved cavalryman's sword. It was an artless stroke, no soldier's work, and it gashed her upraised arm. The huge woman plainly wanted to get in close, where she could break Ferenc in half like a stick, but fear of the sword kept her where Ferenc could whittle her down.

For a moment Erzsébet tried to make the scene one of her husband defending their child from a servant gone mad, but András was at Katarína's back. She was spending her blood to keep her mistress's son from his murderous father.

Erzsébet shouted her husband's name. She had learned certain ways of speaking, as part of her studies, ways that *he* might use, to twist the minds of the weak. Ferenc's mind was weak. He was a barely literate thug good only at killing and siring children, the only virtues noblemen valued. She yelled at him as she would castigate a dog.

When he turned, she saw it gouged into his expression. Another hand was there, another voice in his mind. The hatred writ large there was not Ferenc's hatred, however hot that might burn, but another's. *His.*

The sword came up, and she ignored it, fixing Ferenc with her eyes, pinning him as she sometimes pinned the girls to her table, when they just wouldn't stay still to be studied. She sent out her will to smother him, to fight over the ravaged terrain of his consciousness. For a moment he was slipping through her grasp, and the bloodied silver of the sword blade approached her, but he was *hers*. He was part of her dominion, and she *did not share*. She lunged forwards, gripping his face, gouging him with her nails, speaking his name again and beating in the doors of his mind with her own. There was a moment of infinite fragility and then the sword was ringing on the floor. Ferenc collapsed like an abandoned marionette, his eyes those of an animal, weeping and trembling.

That was how Erzsébet learned that *he* had no more forgotten her than she had forgotten him.

From the Day Book of Erzsébet Báthory

17th April 1600

The protections are holding. He has been close to Sárvár once more, but András is untouched. I am glad I sent Pál away immediately after his birth. I cannot spare the strength to defend more than one, and András is my firstborn, my heir. Dorottya says there are diminishing returns to the warding blood, just as when I bathe. She says we cannot keep him out forever unless we refine our techniques. I know his temper and I had hoped he would be moved to a rash confrontation that we could take advantage of. It has been four years! But he has all the time in the world.

Materiel for the wards today: 4
Székely, age uncertain circa 16, dark
Székely, age claimed 19, dark
Hungarian, age 12, fair
Jewess, age 23, fair

All our material goes towards protection and I can no longer look in the glass without despair. He is taking my life from me and I must find a way to turn the fight upon him. Materiel is grown hard to come by and the latest batch was of inferior quality. We can no longer rely on peasants offering themselves up for service. Have dispatched Ilona with Katarína and Fickó and some ruffians to go between the villages and seize on any who may be taken. The time for subtlety is past.

Letter from György Thurzó, Esztergom, to Prince Matthias of Habsburg, Governor of Austria, Prague, 1602

Written this 11th day of October 1602

My right worthy and worshipful Prince, I recommend myself, your humble servant, to your good wisdom and patience.

As oft before I do not write on the matter of our victories against the Turk, which you will be more fully informed of by better messengers than I. Once more I write to beg your guidance regarding our friend.

Since the birth of his son and his return from Sárvár, Ferenc has been a man further changed from the stout comrade-in-arms of our youth. He will abide no mention of his family, and when a visiting officer happened to commend himself to Erzsébet Báthory, the very name sent Ferenc into a kind of a fit, so that he was swiftly removed from the view of subordinates to preserve morale. His sickness is now very advanced, and there are times when he is not able to stand or recognise his friends, though thus far the advent of battle has banished any and all symptoms.

I do not believe Ferenc suffers from any infirmity of body. He is like a man at war with himself: a war of factions, ambuscades and treachery. Outside of battle he is beset by timorous moods, weeping, tearing at his hair and shaking. Once the fray is joined he becomes a different man, but still not the man I know. His commands now are such that the most hardened soldiers dread receiving them. After the action against the Turk near Braşov, he had one hundred and thirty-four prisoners impaled alive, as he said, to send a dire warning to those enemy yet under arms, yet he had the army halt for half a day while he sat and watched them die and would brook no interruption. Amongst the men, and as I hear amongst the enemy also, he is called 'The Black Captain' for his moods and the punishments he exacts.

For the matter of his wife and the apparent terror she holds for him, I wonder if Your Highness has heard the name of István Magyari, whom we came upon preaching the Protestant faith amongst the followers of the army. He was brought before me after his sermons raised calumny against Ferenc and the Báthory-Nádasdy family. I had intended to run him off with just enough civility to show respect for his place, given that many of the soldiers and officers are of his doctrine, but instead proceeded to a most alarming conversation with the man concerning Erzsébet. He has made wild claims regarding the fate of many scores of young women around those places that Erzsébet has made her own—Sárvár, Csejte and the like—and claims to have taken the testimony of many whose daughters have gone to serve at the castle and never been seen again, or who have had men in Báthory livery come and take their girls by force. What becomes of those taken is uncertain, but Magyari claimed tortures of such cruelty that the Turk himself would pale. Were such accusations made in isolation, I should have had the man whipped or hanged for shaming so noble a name, but I will confess to hearing rumour of similar abomination and I have the shadow of my friend Ferenc to add substance to these thoughts. Magyari claimed that he had written to you, as one always concerned with the health and wellbeing of Hungary and its people, and perhaps you have already read his deposition. I released him, though I cautioned him to stay away from the army lest harm befall him.

Your Highness, I do not know what to make of these things, but I commend them to your greater wisdom. You have previously offered me Ferenc's command, and say once again I that it would be an unjust reward for one who has served the interests of Hungary and the Empire as determinedly as he. And yet I fear for the man he was, and I fear more the man he has become.

Your servant and soldier ever on this the 11th day of October in Our Lord's Year 1602

G

Csejte, 1603

SHE COULD HEAR Ferenc's hoarse, ragged voice from anywhere in this wing of the castle. Most of the time he was roaring out old soldiers' songs, the words so slurred they sounded like another language composed entirely of anger and despair. He left off only to bellow at the servants for more pálinka. The castle would be dry of the brandy long before dawn, and what he would do then was anybody's guess. He had turned up two days ago, already drunk and in a foul temper, demanding to see his son, looking at Erzsébet as though suspecting she had murdered the boy. Faced with little András, he had broken down weeping and the boy had fled the unshaven, ogrish stranger, screaming hysterically until Ilona had comforted him.

Since then, Ferenc had begun to drink his way through the cellar, seeking freedom from some guilt plainly not soluble in alcohol, and Erzsébet had tried to get on with her preparations.

Fickó had brought news the day before of a girl found bloodless and cold in the woods outside one of the local villages. She had been left where it was easy to find her, and Erzsébet had recognised the message for what it was: a polite indication to the local nobility of a visitor to their domain. She had been preparing for the confrontation ever since the day Ferenc had attacked András, seven years before. She should despair, that the fight was never-ending—

that *he* grew no weaker, even as the years clawed away at her—but she was a Báthory. She applied herself with grim determination and, for a while, it had seemed as though she had succeeded. But they were building on sand. Whether it was a protective ward or their attempts to hold back the ravages of time, their results were always short-lived. The wrinkles returned to the skin. The face in the glass was just as haggard in the morning. All *he* needed to do was wait.

And now they were short of materiel. Mothers around Sárvár were hiding their children or sending them to distant relatives. Erzsébet had ridden through villages filled only with glowering old women and white-bearded ancients, no fit subjects for her work. So she had come to Csejte hoping that memories would have faded and the promise of service would draw new girls in, but the same stories were whispered here. She had to rely on travellers ambushed on the roads, on girls kidnapped from further afield. She had even made clandestine overtures to the Turk in the hope that they would have Christian captives to sell at their slave markets; yet here she was, in direst need, and the cells below the castle were empty.

After the drained girl was found, she knew, if she were not to be hounded out of her last sanctum, that she must turn and face the huntsman. Unwilling to flee, and knowing that to be caught on the road would be fatal, she had chosen the fight. Even now Dorottya, Katarína and Fickó were out with some thugs, taking by force what would not be offered willingly. Once they were back, Erzsébet would wield the knife herself, painting the whole castle with blood if she needed, to overpower the Dragon and banish him yet again.

She heard them return as evening was drawing in, and stormed down to castigate them for dragging their feet. There would barely be time to effect their preparations, and *he* would even now be stirring in whatever hole he had dug for himself, surrounded by the soil that fed his strength.

When she found them, still kicking the mud off their boots, she realized the late hour was the least of their worries.

Dorottya's grim look confessed to their failure from the start as she hobbled to stand before her mistress. Katarína was bruised, one eye swollen where a stone had struck her, and Fickó was nursing an injured arm. Erzsébet felt the urge to just beat them all herself, to scream at them for their failure. *Don't you know what you might have cost me?* But she needed to know what had happened. Never had her people returned empty-handed.

"There was a priest," Dorottya spat, leaning on her cane as she lowered herself to sit. "Magyari, his name was. He had them all riled up against you, my lady. He was preaching that you were the Devil's willing servant, and that you would be cast down like Jezebel."

"And why have you not brought him here for punishment? Or just his head?" Erzsébet demanded.

"Countess"—Dorottya's voice was an exhausted whisper—"he had the people of three villages together, with fire and staves and axes. Many of your men are dead. We only escaped because Katarina slung me over her shoulder and Fickó can run like a dog. He *knows*, my lady. This preacher has heard the stories, and seen what you have done."

"What I have *done?*" Erzsébet demanded. "I am the Countess Erzsébet Báthory. These are my lands. They are my people. They are *mine*. If their blood will make me strong, or young, or merely happy, then that is their *place* in the world! They cannot tell me *no!*" Her eyes widened, the rant dying almost before it had begun. "But for this to happen now, when *he* is close... He has set this preacher in motion. He has spread word against me."

"The preacher said..." Dorottya visibly considered the wisdom of her words before soldiering on. "He said he had written to the Emperor to denounce you."

Erzsébet laughed scorn at that. "And will Emperor Rudolph come from Prague to sit in judgment on me? Will his nephew, that spendthrift

Matthias, take the part of these ignorant peasants against one of his own? I shall have this Magyari flayed alive. I shall make an exception and bathe in a man's blood this once, and see if his precious sanctity rubs off on me. I shall " And the words dried up, because she heard Ferenc's voice, still roaring drunk but singing no longer. He was hailing someone out of the window, just two rooms away.

"Come in, come in, fine fellow!" they heard him shout. "The house is yours, my honoured guest! Come in!"

"*No!*" Erzsébet shrieked, but the words were lost in the boom of the castle door being thrown open. She stared at her followers with manic eyes. "Fetch the cook, fetch the stable boy, the last of the maids, all of them! Open their damned throats and drain them to the last drop. *He* is here, and we have not the strength, we have not the strength to keep him out!"

A chill wind seemed to gust through the castle, as of the passage of some great, cold thing through the halls, heading upwards, ever upwards.

"The nursery," Dorottya cursed, and they heard Ilona cry out in terror.

By the time Erzsébet had struggled up the stairs, it was too late. *He* had not even given her the courtesy of staying to gloat at her expression. Ilona lay senseless in a corner, and in the little bed lay her son, her seven-year-old boy, eyes open but never more to see. Frost lay on his skin, dusting his eyelashes and hair with white, just like the girls Erzsébet had left out for the winter. His blood was all still in him. That was the ultimate insult; the blood of her son had not been a vintage that *he* had deigned to sample.

Erzsébet stared down at the slight, frozen body for precisely three heartbeats, as Katarína and Fickó caught up with her.

"Bring them," she instructed, no feeling in her voice at all. "The stable boy, the maids, all of them. Bring them and make them ready."

"But it's too late?" Fickó asked hesitantly, looking past her at the still form.

Erzsébet slapped the hunched dwarf hard enough to knock him off his feet. "It's not too late!" she screamed at him. "Bring them *now!* Bring them and empty them! And bring ice from the cold rooms, all the ice we have!"

Letter from György Thurzó, Sárvár, to Prince Matthias of Habsburg, Governor of Austria, Prague, 1604

My right worthy and worshipful Prince, I write under the most dolorous circumstances and recommend us all to the Lord's mercy.

I shall be sure that no messenger out-speeds my own, for it is my solemn duty to report the death of the Black Captain, Ferenc Nádasdy.

I have kept you appraised of the malady that has long touched my friend and your loyal commander, and since his return from his home and the death of his son, it has reached new heights. In times of peace simply walking, standing, sleeping has been beyond him. With battle and bloodshed at hand, his actions were such that the dread he was held in, by the Turk and the Transylvanian rebels both, only grew with every skirmish. All things must pass, however. In this last clash, his conduct was above and beyond the call of valour as he plunged his destrier in amongst the enemy, ahead of the vanguard of our forces, ready to rout them alone.

At the peak of his charge he gave out a great cry, heard across the field, and toppled from the saddle. When his body was recovered to Sárvár, there was no wound or mark on him that might have been dealt by the enemy, not even a scar upon his armour. Instead, and I almost fear to recount it, his body was strangely wasted inside his mail, as though all the strength that had sustained him over these last hard years had been abruptly withdrawn.

I will mourn my friend, but I feel that I lost him some years hence, and the expiry of his mortal shell was only the post-script. I pray that the Lord has mercy on him for the services he has done for Christendom, and forgives those actions that, in themselves, were less than Christian.

Perhaps Ferenc had premonition of his fate, for the night before, he called notaries before us both, with documents to the effect that, should anything befall him, the care and keeping of his surviving children were to be mine, and these documents I enclose herewith. He was emphatic that his wife should have no control over them and, in those last moments before he retired, he seemed a man in utter mortal dread for his soul.

Your Highness, I have served you well both in the war and outside it, and you will recall the many services I have done for you and your brother the Emperor in pursuing the truth of matters obscure and unnatural, when my sword was not being bloodied against the Turk. In the name of this service, I ask a boon. I have many times given Ferenc audience on the matter of his wife, and have spoken with the priest Magyari, who made such alarming accusations. I beg you now, grant me your writ to follow these rumours and dispel them if I may, or else to bring to light what lies hidden, for I am more and more convinced that when so many tongues wag of such deeds, there may be a very dire cause.

Your servant and soldier ever on this the 5th day of January in Our Lord's Year 1604

G

VIII.

Prague, 1605

ERZSÉBET HAD COME this far on a path of gold, favours, threats and one actual murder—a court official of minor family who had felt that neither a full purse nor the gratitude of the Báthory family was sufficient to let him bend his duty. Well, for all that his was a weightier corpse than any number of mere peasants, Erzsébet had buried it deep, and priggish gadflies of the court were a pest that swarmed in any season.

She had risked a great deal. She had travelled to the heart of Empire almost without retinue, desperate to move fast. Now, crossing the threshold of Emperor Rudolph II's most private library, she had only Ilona with her. Dorottya was too crippled to leave Csejte these days, and neither lumpen Katarína nor odious little Fickó could read a word.

There was a curious quality to the air within the library, as though all that convoluted lore had folded it like a piece of paper, giving the high-ceilinged, shelf-lined room a sense of vast unseen realms packed away at every turn. Opening the shutter of her lamp, Erzsébet cast its beam about ranks of books, each of them a select volume of occult knowledge hunted down by Rudolph in his mad desire to *know*. Erzsébet had met the man on state occasions, when his attention was plainly anywhere but on the business before him. He closeted himself with alchemists and sorcerers and artists while his brother Matthias slowly extended his hand towards the reins of state. Wise heads claimed Matthias would be Emperor sooner rather than later, as Rudolph's eccentricities tried and taxed every part of the Empire, and perhaps that would be to Erzsébet's advantage. Matthias owed fortunes to the Báthory line, a veritable king's ransom; when he *was* king, she would have him by the throat with a cord of gold. By then, though, this library would likely be beyond her reach or scattered across Europe. She needed the mystical Rudolph, not the debtor Matthias.

Ilona had a list of works reputed to be in the Emperor's private collection, and they had some small space of time in which to search. They lit the half-melted candles they found there and set to untangling Rudolph's idiosyncratic shelving.

They had been at it for perhaps twenty minutes, efficient and silent as seasoned thieves, with one volume already located and set aside. Then Erzsébet heard a long, drawn-out breath, and realised they were not alone.

She and Ilona turned in concert. In a shadow alcove, surrounded by stacks of bookmarked tomes, sat a long-faced man with a tangled beard, wearing a nightgown, once bright Chinese silk of incalculable worth, that was now faded and worn. For a long while, Erzsébet stared, before finally sketching a jerky, reluctant curtsey to their host, Rudolph II, King of Bohemia, Hungary and Croatia, and Holy Roman Emperor.

His gaze showed only a tentative acknowledgement of reality, but then he sniffed ostentatiously as though Erzsébet or Ilona had brought something in on their shoe, and said, "I know who sent you."

Perhaps she should have bluffed, then—pretended to be some menial and shirked responsibility for what she was about—but that was not in her nature. "Nobody sent me," she told him icily. "I am Erzsébet Báthory, and I go where I will."

His next words chilled her. "I can smell *him* on you. You've come at *his* command." His voice was ragged with misery, and the way he pronounced '*he*' matched her exactly, when she spoke of the Dragon.

She crossed to him immediately, heedless of place and propriety. "Your Majesty, I know of him. *He* is my enemy, as surely as he is yours. You are the greatest scholar of hidden lore in the world. Surely you have found a way to overcome his power—or to duplicate it, to fight off death..." Under his melancholy scrutiny her words tailed off, for if this old, sad man could have achieved any such thing, would she be meeting him in such circumstances?

"He always wins," whispered Rudolph, leaning close to her. "He promised he would teach me, if I made war against the Turk he hates so much; against another of his kind—a 'brother,' as he puts it—who he believes orders them as *he* directs me. But now the war has exhausted my Empire and all I know is how much I do not know. And he goes on, my child. He always goes on." One frail hand took in the ranked spines of the library, or perhaps all the books there ever were. "Read any of them, read them all, there's nothing in them that will let you go where he has gone. Shadows, all of it. Cobweb and shadows."

"No, Your Majesty, no," Erzsébet hissed, but he stared through her, not consenting to her existence, as though she was one more shadow that a movement of the candles might dispel.

Letter from György Thurzó, Németkeresztúr, to Prince Matthias of Habsburg, Governor of Austria, Prague, 1606

My Most High Prince, I write this day from the Báthory holdings at Németkeresztúr.

Glad I am to do my duty by you, my Prince; less glad in the particulars, for my investigation has for some time now been work that would daunt the strongest of men.

The impasse that I had been at with certain of the Nádasdy has at last been circumvented. The application of money and your recent peace treaties have conspired to permit me access to the apartments and chambers used by him and his wife when they were present here, as I was able to in Pozsony. As there, I have uncovered cells and chambers not to be encountered by a casual visitor. As the Countess is absent, these were untenanted, but I found plenty of circumstantial evidence to back up the claims of the people hereabouts. I would guess that, at their height, the secret prisons here could have held a score of souls altogether, and there are also alchemical paraphernalia and certain tomes which your brother Rudolph would doubtless twitch to lay his hands upon, for their subject matter was nothing less than pure witchcraft and the darkest magic.

I have accumulated a considerable body of evidence from here and Pozsony and, as I understand the Countess is to return to Csejte in the New Year, I shall attempt a similar discovery at Sárvár while she is away from it. My informants tell me that the rumours of her practices have not lessened at all with her husband's death, and indeed her activity suggests some single-minded project consuming her notice so that I may gather my evidence undetected.

I will provide my fullest report when all is ready, and I know you will have faith in my diligence from my similar services to you in the past. You will recall, perhaps, the werewolf of Rusovce or the supposed witches of Eichbüchl, and how the tale had grown so much in the telling, though in truth there was hardly a mad dog in the one nor a single malevolent crone in the other. This is not such a case, and what I have uncovered already overshadows the worst that any tattling tongue has spoken, for each of those complainants saw only a small part of a work that has been conducted across the Empire wherever the Báthory coat of arms has been displayed.

I shall write again once I have conducted my inquisition at Sárvár.

I am your man and ever will be, by the grace of God, which ever have you in his keeping.

Written this 2nd of December in the Year of Our Lord 1606 by your servant

G

Letter from King Matthias of Hungary, Pozsony, to György Thurzó, Sárvár, 1608

To my loyal György,

Your congratulations on my coronation are duly welcomed, though I would as lief be without the clutter of ceremony that so impedes the ability to accomplish any good act. Likewise your condolences on my brother's infirmity and retreat from many aspects of governance. I write to you with good news, that wheels are set in motion to confer upon you the mantle of the Palatine of Hungary. I anticipate my own eyes will be more turned towards Prague and Vienna as my brother's support amongst the families wanes.

Your further report from Sárvár I commend in its meticulous detail. You must find excuse to bring your investigation to Csejte, even though the Tigress seems ensconced in her lair there. You have herewith my writ to take whatever steps you must to dispel this great shadow from our land.

Given at the court of Pozsony on the twenty-seventh day of the month of September, in the year of our Lord one thousand six hundred and eight, by Matthias, second of that name, King of Hungary and Croatia and Archduke of Austria.

IX.

Csejte, 1609

"I BEG YOU, Countess, do not attempt this." Dorottya Semtész's voice was weak. *She* was weak, an old, old woman all crumpled up by time, eaten away by pain. Erzsébet brushed past her as if she were no more than cobwebs and shadows, ascending to the high tower room with a sweep of her gown while the witch had to conquer each step one after another, her dire predictions fading to echoes.

Up in the high room—once a nursery, but there were no more children here, not any more—everything was being brought to readiness. There was a great stone bath there—Katarína and five strong men had hauled it up with block and tackle. There were eleven girls taken from the villages by Fickó and those same men, all whimpering and naked and shackled, awaiting the knife. Their weeping would have stirred a passion in Erzsébet once, but now she was all desperate purpose. Time enough for pleasure later, when her task was done.

Time, her enemy. *He* had been right about that. Time that sunk its claws into her—almost fifty years, now, and if the glass showed her younger than she was, still it did not show her *young*. Time, that had loomed like a monster over her every day since *he* had taken András from her.

She would not allow *him* his victory. She was Erzsébet Báthory, even here, even desperate. She ceded the field to nobody, not even the Dragon.

Those five strong men, they were in attendance in spirit if not in body. Ilona had drugged their food and Fickó had cut their throats and then strong Katarína had hauled the jars of their blood up here. It was not maiden-blood, which Erzsébet had relied on all these years for her power, but blood was blood. It would be made to serve her as it served *him*.

And beside the bath, into which Ilona was even now pouring that blood, was the casket. What had the peasants thought, to see her shrinking entourage move from castle to castle with a little coffin in tow? What would they think, discovering she always chose the high mountain passes and travelled in winter, or if they had touched the casket's gilded sides and found it icy cold and slick with meltwater?

As if I should care what peasants think.

They had crossed themselves, those ignorant serfs, but she took their superstitious fear as her due, just as she took their daughters.

She had wrung Rudolph's library for what scraps of truth it contained, sifted the work of Dee, Flamel and Michael Scotus for hints and whispers of what she intended. It all came back to *him* and his ilk, those who stepped aside and let time rush past them, those who used the blood of others to cheat death forever. *For the blood is the life.* And just in time, for that mundane-minded Matthias was King of Hungary now, soon to be Emperor, most likely, and poor Rudolph practically a prisoner, his precious books scattered who knew where.

She could hear Dorottya's weak voice rising from the stairwell. Of course the old witch would come to cry doom over everything Erzsébet was trying to achieve, but it was too late for that. Tonight she would finally conquer the great work. Tonight she would defy the laws of nature and time. And not selfishly, not for vanity; she would wield her mother's love like a knife.

"Place him within," she whispered, and Katarína cracked open the casket. Within, half afloat in the ice-melt, was András. She wanted to think, *He looks so peaceful*, but that would be a lie. He was purplish in parts, greenish-yellow in others, whilst the backs of his limbs were puckered, fishbelly-pale. His gut had bloated out and his eyes were dreadful sunken hollows.

And yet is this a six-year dead corpse? It is not. All her art and lore, and all the ice in the Kingdom of Hungary, had gone to frustrating the claws of time. András looked as though he had been dead mere weeks, perhaps. *It is not too late. I have worked so hard.*

Katarína shrank back from the dead flesh at first, she who feasted on the slain after they had been drained for Erzsébet's pleasure. In the end Erzsébet had to beat her, whipping her with a switch until the huge lump of a woman took the little body in her hands and decanted it into the bath. *It's the only language she understands.*

The blood of her thugs would not be enough, of course. They had been coarse creatures, *men*, they would add little power; and yet even that little was worth ending their lives for. Now she needed sweeter stuff, and Fickó was already scuttling forwards with his ever-ready knife. The first of the girls was hauled up and bent over the bath, her screams setting the rest of them off. Katarina had to slap and cuff them until they stopped. *I will not have them ruin my triumph.*

She took the knife and opened the first throat herself. *Drink deep, András. Come back to me. Live.* For a moment she thought something more than the wind battered at the shutters. She thought another voice was raised high above the death-shout of the peasant girl. *Is* he *here? He's come to stop me this last time?* But she had drawn red wards at the windows and the doors, and though he might tear through them in time, it would be time enough.

"Countess," wheezed Dorottya from the doorway, "you must not. It is too much. You cannot open these gates. You don't know what will come through."

"András will come through," Erzsébet snapped. "Hold your tongue, old woman, if you want to keep it. Bring the next." And another weeping serf was dragged over to give her all for her Countess. They were peasants, it was what they were *for*. It wasn't as though they had finer feelings.

She heard the castle echo to shouting and imagined *him* beating at the wards, fighting to thwart her will. *But this time I will hold you off. I will undo your work, you monster.* And she reached for the next girl as Ilona manhandled her over. But Ilona was slowing, staring down into the bloody corpse within the vat.

"Mistress," she breathed, half-horror and half-wonder.

Erzsébet looked down at what she had wrought and saw András's shrivelled eyelids, so long closed, twitch and shiver.

In her mind she pictured Time and Death, two cadaverous pale figures just like *him*. She pictured them howling in outrage at what she had done. She pictured them in her cells, impotent against her. She would not bow to mortal authority, nor to the might of the Dragon. Why should she bow to the limits of the universe? She would break Time on the wheel and have Death torn apart by horses. She would live forever, be young forever, and all it would take was all the blood in the world.

Then András smiled and opened his eyes, and she met his dead gaze and screamed. Because she knew it. She knew what sat behind her son's face like a toad. She had shed the blood and spoken the incantations, but it was *he* who leered at her from behind her son's discoloured, half-decayed face.

She shrieked with rage and drove the blade down, hacking and hacking at flesh so soft and sagging that it came apart like overcooked meat, until the blood of the bath was swimming with pieces and corruption and nothing like a human form remained.

It was then that they thundered into the room, knocking Dorottya aside. She turned on them, spitting curses, ready to look *him* in the eye and strike him down, but it was not the Dragon. It was mere soldiers, uncouth peasants with swords and fists knocking down her servants, beating Katarína with clubs, striking Fickó so hard blood came from his ears. And behind them, a lean man with a thin face and a sharp dagger of a beard, some face she thought she knew from long ago. She commanded him to leave her castle. What did he think he was doing?

His expression—all that disgust and pity and loathing—made her drop the knife and put her hands to her face, for surely she was hideous, all of a sudden. Surely only truly ugly things could gather such a look as that.

Letter from György Thurzó, Bytča, to King Matthias of Hungary, Pozsony, 1610

Your Royal Majesty, I commend myself to your continuing wisdom.

I have brought the Countess Báthory here to Bytča, away from her holdings and people; less for fear of some attempt to free her from captivity and more that no vengeful relative should seek personal justice before proceedings are complete.

Whilst evidence to convict all the prisoners has hardly been lacking, I have been concerned that justice may be seen to be done for all those injured by the Countess's reign of terror, and she herself has proved uncommunicative. For some time it seemed as though I would always be leaving loose threads behind me, even once the sentence had been handed down, but I finally found the lever that allowed me to separate one of her followers from the rest and obtain her cooperation. She is an ogrish creature, simple-minded and of appalling appetites, but I judged her low intellect as less culpable than the rest. She has been imprisoned amongst nuns of a severe regime, away from the others, and her hunger for human flesh has been transferred to a hunger more numinous, in particular the taking of the host, which she perceives as devouring something more precious and powerful than simple meat, which I suppose it is.

This servant, one Katarína Benická, has provided me with the locations of the Countess's 'day books' in Csejte, and just today my swiftest messenger has returned from there with the texts in his possession. They make nightmarish reading, but I have been diligent, as I know your faith in me. I have read through the Countess's deranged writings and can at least make a tally of her victims since she began this foul trade. I believe that her bloodlust has consumed at the very least 650 souls. I will freely confess that I have lived a life of strife and war, and yet nothing has so unsettled me as reading the Countess's matter-of-fact accounts of torments and murders. The books I enclose for your perusal should you wish, though I recommend you burn them unread.

Of the matter of punishment, I know you have recommended death, and for the uncooperative servants, naturally, no other course can be followed. However, the execution of one of her blood and high family may stir untoward passions in a land so recently riven by war and civil division. It would not do for the lowly to believe that they can pass judgment upon the mighty, and perhaps it would be better for the Countess to fade from memory rather than to become too striking an example.

I submit myself to your judgment and will, on this the 14th day of June 1610

G

From the Judgment of György Thurzó, 1611

...for their part in such crimes, the witches known as Dorottya Semtész and Ilona Jó to have their fingers, which committed such wicked deeds, plucked from their hands with heated tongs, and thereafter to be hanged by the neck until dead. The villain János Újváry, also known as Fickó, likewise to be hanged until dead. For that servant woman Katarína Benická, whom the court has found to have been dominated and led by those other wicked examples, she is to be imprisoned for the rest of her life in the hope that she may atone and assuage the stain upon her soul.

For the "Tigress of Csejte," the Countess Erzsébet Báthory, so that she may long consider the bitter wrongs she has performed, she is to be immured alive within that castle she has most been associated with, seeing no visitors save for those instructed to watch over her, and there she shall remain until death comes for her.

X.

Csejte, 1611

THE WORLD WAS a room and the room had no doors and no windows. It was like a dream she'd once had, but in the end the dream had bent to her will and she had knocked down the walls with a thought and walked free. Here, in the heart of what had been her domain, nothing would obey her command. She had a bare slit left where the door had once been, and that sufficed for all transactions with the outside world.

Her contact with others was limited to one set of footsteps and the gruff voice of her jailer, twice every day. Had anyone asked her a few years before what value she placed on human company, she would have laughed them to scorn.

Today was different. Today there was a second set of footsteps. A jolt of excitement shot through her—*They will let me out!*—and just as swiftly it was replaced with one of fear. *What if it's* him? He couldn't have forgotten about her, she knew. The whole world must still buzz with the fear of her. And she would *make* them fear, if she ever got outside these walls. Of course *he* must still think of his rival, his equal.

But then the footsteps paused, by the slot they used to feed her. She heard the jailer's muted voice receding; one must yet remain.

She summoned her courage and dared herself to look out into those deep-set burning eyes.

It was not him. She saw a blandly handsome man in fine clothes, his hair cut very short and his beard and moustaches trimmed to points. Not Thurzó the inquisitor, not one of Ferenc's fighting comrades. His eyes were narrow and suspicious, and she knew him at last from those. Erzsébet Báthory stared through the gap in her world at Matthias II, King of Hungary.

"I am to have no visitors," she said flatly. Human contact suddenly seemed overrated.

Matthias smiled blandly. "When the Emperor wishes to see such a spectacle, who shall tell him no?"

"Rudolph is gone, then?" She remembered the miserable mumbler in his library and felt nothing.

"Almost. He pushes to resume the war with the Turk, and the Empire will not stand for it. So costly! I've a stack of letters begging me to take my brother off the throne for good."

She scowled at him. "I know someone who will not like your peace with the Turk."

He regarded her for a long time, and then shrugged. "My brother has evil counsellors. They are none of mine."

Then he stepped back as she was abruptly at the slot, hands crooked about its edge, staring out at him. "Then let me out, Your Majesty. I can teach you how to fight *him*. I can make you strong. I can make you live forever!"

His contemptuous laughter hurt her as keenly as András's death. "I see captivity hasn't cured you. Do you know, you even had poor György believing there was something behind your killings, beyond mere madness? But I told him, this is an age of reason. I am still rooting out the last of Rudolph's pet mystics, all those who took gold and turned it to dross in defiance of their claims. I am not here to let you out, Erzsébet. I am just here to see a prodigy and rejoice that my reign has started with the righting of a great wrong."

Erzsébet tried to lunge at him through the slot, but her arm would not go past the elbow, and he had already put a prudent distance between them. "And have you never beat a servant?" she demanded. "Or perhaps you take joy from watching others wield the lash. But you are like me; had you known what I knew, you would do what I have done!" And she waited for the inevitable denials, the sanctimony.

But Matthias was, after all, a man of reason. He only smiled slightly and shrugged. "Bohemia is crawling with Protestants decrying the excesses of church and state, and philosophers preaching the equality of the common man. And probably there's truth in it. What do any of us do, we kings and lords? We all live off the blood of those below us, do we not? But there's metaphor, and there's literal truth. You took your little games too far, and we have to show the peasants that there's order in the world." He shrugged again, already turning to walk away. "And in the end, Erzsébet, I just owed you far too much money, and the Crown is not obliged to repay a murderess, and can do what it likes with her lands. So after all poor Rudolph's striving, perhaps I am the better alchemist, for I have made gold from blood."

Csejte, 1614

IF SHE STOOD at just the right angle, she could see through the corner of the slot, down the corridor and to a place where the light of the sunset fell. The sun itself was denied her, but each evening she would stand *just so* and watch the last red rays of the world face to an unrelieved grey.

When the jailer had come to take her plate and pail, this evening, she had told him she was cold, that her hands were numb with it, and he had told her to sleep. Sleep was no balm, to her. Only nightmares could creep in through that slot. Nor did they absent themselves when she woke. The vacant halls of Csejte echoed with voices conjured from her memories. She heard Ferenc's bellow, Dorottya's whispered imprecations. She heard András crying, far off.

When *he* came, at last, she was not sure if he was real or just a figment of her torment. The sun was long down, by then, but she woke to a darkness more profound than she had ever known, buried deep in midnight with not even an echo of the moon reaching her. And yet his paleness seemed to shine from it, the pallor that told of what he was and the road he had taken, the man who stood unharmed on the far side of death and time.

"Countess Báthory," she heard him say softly. "What is this cage, that you allow to hold you?"

She stood, drawing to herself the little dignity they had left her. "Has the Dragon come to gloat?"

She heard his cold laugh. "Are you not free, yet, O Countess? Shall I show you the way?"

And despite herself, something broke in her. She remembered him in the orchard so many years before. She remembered when he had come to her after her wedding, his lips on the flawless white of her neck. She had fought him so long, but she had been fighting to *be* him, not to destroy him.

She asked, in a child's voice, "Are you here to take me, at last?"

His laughter hurt her as much as Matthias' had, years before: the laughter of a man who had done with her and can walk away. "You might have been mine, Countess, for a moment, or for a lifetime. But I will not take you as you are now. If you will follow me, you must do it yourself."

Anger brought her back to herself. "You took from me the means to follow you. My servants, my books..."

"It was not servants or books that delivered me from Time, Countess," he told her. "Nor, alone, the gift of blood my own master bestowed on me. It was *will*. What, beyond my will, keeps me in the world? What staves off time and gives me command of the things of night? It is nothing but will, the refusal to be bound by the fetters that might cage a lesser creature." And he was close in the darkness. She wondered what he saw, staring at her haggard face. "Where is your will, Countess? Has it grown brittle in this place? Follow me, if you dare."

And he was gone, or else he had never been there, and she lay back down and felt the unseasonal cold leach into her.

Excerpt from a Letter from Father Tamás Kovács, Hrachovište, to Péter Pázmány, Primate of Hungary, 1621

...As I know you have an interest in the curious, and as my heart has been obscurely troubled by a matter, I write to share a most unusual deathbed confession in case you may shed light upon it.

Whilst the identity of the deceased shall of course go undisclosed, it will not offend if I reveal that he was amongst the staff at Csejte Castle guarding a most particular prisoner, and indeed was on duty one night six years ago when that prisoner, whose name I am sure you can guess, went to her final rest to the relief of all Hungary.

He was plainly troubled by some thought of it, and strove mightily to give his confession, so much so that, in light of she whom he had warded, I was prepared for an act of great darkness. However, when the matter came it out, the act and the guilt could not readily be correlated. He told me that she had called out to him and pledged to tell him where certain treasures were buried if he swore to perform a service for her. There would come messengers after her death, she said, who would order him to inflict curiously specific mutilations upon her corpse, viz., beheading, impalement and the like. Her request was simply that he say he had performed these acts, but yet not defile the body and instead let it go into the ground unmarked.

That very night, so he told, she died, and such an order did indeed come from no less a man than the Palatine of Hungary. Moved either by Christian propriety or by love of the treasure, he complied with the prisoner's last wishes, gave the lie to the Palatine and instead had the body released whole for burial in the family crypt.

I told him he had done a noble and worthy thing in not permitting the body to be thus desecrated, and yet am left with an unaccountable worry. Word from Ecsed, where lies the crypt, is that none can say where the body lies, or even if it was conveyed there at all...

THREE

A STAKE TOO FAR

INTERLUDE

From: Jonathan Holmwood (jwlh1947@amol.com)
To: Dani Văduvă (bornwithteeth@webmail.com)
Date: January 14, 2018
Subject: Re: Mina Harker?

Hi Dani,

Hope you got my emails last night. On with round three!

This one was my work, back in the 'sixties. Romania and Hungary were still largely out of reach behind the Iron Curtain, but Yugoslavia was a bit more negotiable, with the right resources. I'd come across references to the vampire hunts in eighteenth-century Croatia, and figured it had to be a promising lead.

Of course, I didn't speak a word of Croatian, and my German only got me so far; but I found the inestimable Ana Horvat through university friends back in Cambridge, and funded her to unearth, translate and organise the material that follows.

It wasn't quite what I was expecting. I find it almost comforting—it shows a humanity I daresay my great-grandparents would struggle to recognise in their enemy.

It's getting late, so the last section may have to wait until tomorrow.

Jon

A STAKE TOO FAR

Milena Benini

Dear Mr. Holmwood,

Enclosed please find the transcripts and translations of all the documents I could find following your instructions. A part of them were indeed in Vienna, as you supposed, but the trail also led me to the National Archives in Zagreb, and then to the archives of the city of Varaždin. Following the clues I found in this initial corpus, I managed to track down the descendants of Mrs. Magdalena Hranić, who kindly allowed me to rummage through their attic. There, I discovered a small box of documents that obviously belonged to Mrs. Hranić, so I included them in the collection.

I am also enclosing excerpts from the diary of Marcel Bordchamp, acquired through the kind services of my colleague, Prof. Antoine Bordchamp, who was intrigued by the possible familial connection and unearthed the diary at the Alsace Regional Archives, in an improperly catalogued bequest from a private donor. I have only included portions that seemed pertinent to your inquiry; if you should wish to obtain a complete translation of the diary, please let me know.

I have tried to put the documents in chronological order, although, since many were undated, a lot of the ordering had to be based on external clues and/or pure guesswork. This is probably why the events that underlie the documents appear so fantastic. I hope you will be able to reorder them so that it all makes more sense.

Also find enclosed the receipts for all expenses incurred in the research process, and the final bill for my services as research historian and translator (as separate items). It has been a pleasure working for you.

Yours sincerely,
Ana Horvat

Excerpt from Marcel Bordchamp's diary

MY NEW EMPLOYER is... odd. I have no better word to describe the man. But I am willing to forgive him. What other man would take an obviously sick man such as myself into his service? Admittedly, he claims he only did it to spite my former employer, M. de Veuxtort, who sent me packing the moment I confessed I was suffering from consumption. The Count doesn't seem to mind my sickness, and is only interested in two things: my efficiency, which is, he says, good enough for his purposes, and my loyalty to him, which he claims must be absolute. He has some very strange turns of phrase like that, and an idiosyncratic sense of humour. Maybe that's because he's a foreigner—his ancestral lands lie far to the east. He has arrived with a small staff comprised of people I could swear were Slavs (correction—Ilan says he is Muntenian, which I have noted), but they all dress in the French fashion and speak perfect if uneducated French. There is probably a story there, but I do not know what it is, and have no intention of prying. They all accept me in their midst and are kind enough, but I have no illusion that they would not turn against me the moment I failed our master. All of them meet the requirement of absolute loyalty, of that I have no doubt.

People say that is too much to ask, but I don't care. He has promised to provide my mother, should she outlive me, with a small pension. For that, I would die in his service. When I told him that, he laughed, and said, "I am counting on that, Bordchamp."

Strange man.

Addendum No. 34-46 to the dispositions of the Medicinal Office

To the attention of Simon Aigner, Esq., Medicinal Office Assistant.

Following the instructions from Her Majesty's chambers, and with the approval of the Directorium in Publicis et Cameralibus

We issue the following decision:

To be added into the budget:

the sum of 6 times 360 Taler, as annual salary for 6 field physicians, or a total of ....2,160 Taler;

the sum of 6 times 16 Taler, as coverage for expenses of the field work (travel expenses, accommodation &c.) for said physicians, or a total of ....96 Taler;

This being a total of ....2,256 Taler.

To be held in reserve:

the sum of 120 Taler, as reward for successful findings of cases of vampirism, to be disbursed in amounts of 20 Taler per head of the vampire found & documented; should this amount be exceeded by any given physician or physicians in the field, Her Majesty shall be informed immediately, as she has pledged to reward any possible further findings from her personal coffers.

This being a total of ....120 Taler.

In Vienna, on the 3rd day of January, 1746.

[*signed, left, with seal*]
Gerard van Swieten,
Personal Physician to Her Majesty,
Maria Theresa, Holy Roman Empress

[*signed, right, with seal*]
Count Friedrich Wilhelm von Haugwitz,
Head of Directorium

The following note was attached to the document:

Pick the least promising fellows, Simon. This is a wild-goose chase, but we must humour Her Majesty.
   Gerard

Excerpt from Marcel Bordchamp's diary

HE IS FURIOUS, and I am seriously afraid. I have never seen him like that: normally, he is always calm, as if nothing touches him as it does the rest of us mortals. But this morning, he received a letter that threw him into a veritable explosion of rage.

I had left him reading his private correspondence and enjoying his morning meal. Although in many ways an unconventional and open-minded employer, the Count never eats with me, or even in my company; I am served my meals in the small salon, unless I choose to have them with the staff in the kitchen. It's just another one of his little oddities, and I have grown used to it by now. I had gone to deal with the business mail when I was disturbed by loud crashing. For a moment, I thought the house was falling down around us!

I ran into the dining room, whence the noise had come. What a sight! The great dining table was overturned. It is a twelve-seater made of solid oak; if asked, I would have reserved at least four workers to move it. And yet, it was lying on its side, four chairs broken beneath it, as if someone had swept it aside in anger. His chair lay on its back, and the Count himself stood among the broken dishes, a small vase of flowers miraculously preserved at his feet.

He heard me open the door and whirled around like a wild beast. His eyes were completely red: not red as if from crying, either, but a deep, crimson red that seemed almost to glow eerily in the soft light that penetrated the thick curtains. (He likes to keep the curtains closed at all times. Prevents unwanted visitors, he claims.)

For a moment, he just stood there, watching me. After the clatter, the silence was downright ominous. Then he muttered something— I'm guessing a curse—in his native tongue and rushed past me out of the room. I was about to follow him when a strong hand gripped my elbow, making me jump. It was Ilan, one of the Muntenian servants.

"You are a very lucky man, Monsieur Bordchamp," he said. "Do not test your luck."

I understood his meaning immediately, and bent and started collecting the broken dishes from the floor. Strangely enough, I did not see any traces of food. Perhaps he had just finished eating when whatever it was made him jump up in anger. Just out of curiosity, I tried righting the table on my own. I couldn't even move it. I am a sick man, it is true; yet, later, it took six of the Count's servants to set the massive table straight.

As we were straightening up the room, I found a piece of paper on the floor: a letter, crumpled and thrown away. At first, I put it in my pocket without thinking, fully intending to give it back to the Count when he had calmed down some. But he stayed away all day and most of the night—he gets up after twelve anyway, so most of his "day" passes in darkness—and, in the end, curiosity got the better of me. I took the still-wet paper out and looked at it. I wanted to see what could send my normally poised employer into such a rage. The letter must have landed in the wine the Count had been breakfasting on, and what little I could read explained even less. Yet I kept the letter, and will have to try and think of a way to breach the subject with him.

Ah. He has finally returned, and is calling for me. I shall finish this entry later.

The following loose page was inserted after the page:

Vlad,

I know you have no reason to help me. But if you don't, I will surely die—I am barely holding up as it is. We have betrayed each other many times, Vlad. You can betray me one last time and be done with me forever. I will not even hold it against you when next we meet in eternal flames, yet— [*remainder illegible: the majority of the page is preserved, but has been soaked in wine, or perhaps blood*]

[*recto empty*]

The next entry is undated, but may be a continuation:

IT CANNOT BE. It simply cannot.

* * *

Bill of sale, from Magdalena Hranić's effects

Sekula & Krayach, Household Goods
Kaputzinerplatz 6,
Warasdin

Bill of sale

Date: 17th of February, 1746.

Item: candlestick, silvered, well-preserved, 1 pc:	3 Gr.
Item: set of silverware, 1 spoon missing, 27 pcs:	15 Gr.
Item: travelling writing set, in leather case, 1 pc:	7 Gr.
Item: pipes, Meerschaum, carved, reasonably preserved, 2 pcs:	4 Gr.
Item: cuirass, used, but well-preserved, 1 pc:	6 Gr.
Item: dessert plates, set, well-preserved, 12 pcs:	8 Gr.
Total:	46 Gr.

Paid to:

Magdalena Dorotea Hranić (widow), née Jurić.

[*signed, left, illegible*]

[*signed, right*]
Magdalena Hranić

* * *

Letter from Bartol Povšić to Marcel Bordchamp

Topliss, 18th of February, 1746

Dear Mr. Bordchamp,

It is our pleasure to inform you that, as per your request, we have reserved a suite at our establishment for the use of your employer for an indefinite period, starting with the 2nd day of March this year. We hope that the Count will find our waters, that first found their use in Roman times, beneficial to his health.

Of course, we shall also do our utmost best to provide the Count with any comfort he might require. I must confess that the request for additional ground floor accommodation with a private garden is somewhat unusual. If you believe this could suit your employer, we do have at our disposal a fine little house somewhat apart from the rest of the bathing complex. We could equip the house with our finest furniture, and provide all the gardening tools your employer might need in the pursuit of his hobby. If this should not be satisfactory, please, advise us as to any modifications to this arrangement you would like us to undertake.

With the expressions of our sincerest regards,
Bartol Povšić,
Hauptdirektor,
Warasdin Topliss Baths

[*in bottom left area of the paper, in a different, wider hand*]
It will suit. Confirm.
V.D.

[*below, in a third, small and neat hand*]
Notified by return post. B.

*   *   *

Letter from Anneliese Lehner to Erhard Ferdinand Pradl

Vienna, 19th of February

Dearest Didrl,

Please, <u>please</u> tell me that Papa was joking when he said you were going away! You <u>know</u> I couldn't bear to live in one of those horrible provinces! If we are to marry, we can only ever live in Vienna or, in the worst of all horrible cases, in Graz—in short, somewhere where there is music, and salons, and where, every now and then, you can smuggle me into your working rooms so I can see your experiments and assist you when no one is looking! (I understand that in Graz, they are very keen on cutting up dead people, which I should probably think is rather horrible, but I must confess it would be interesting to see the inside of a person for once. Can we arrange that? And do not say a <u>word</u> to my brother, of course. He would die of shock.)

In any case, if that's what makes you happy, yes, I shall settle in Graz and love it, even though it will mean being far from Mama and my friends and the court. But a province! Where they still burn witches! That cannot be! Reassure me promptly, please!

Yours (if you stay in <u>civilisation</u>)

Anneliese

Letter from Erhard Ferdinand Pradl to Anneliese Lehner

Vienna, 19th of February

My dear, dear girl,

Lay your fears to rest. Your father was not joking, but, at the same time, I am not planning on moving into any of the provinces you find so distasteful, believe me. I have, however, accepted the position of field physician, as part of a small, informal group that Herr van Sweiten has put together to investigate some rather disturbing reports we have received recently. I shall not bother you with details, sweet Liesel, but I want you to know that one of the main reasons I have accepted this position is exactly so that I could provide you with the life in the capital in the style that you deserve. The salary I have been promised is very good, and there is the possibility of additional monies.

At the same time, I hear life in the provinces is significantly cheaper, so I am hoping to save up a good portion of what I earn, and use the lot as payment for a house in Vienna. In that way, you would not have to live under the same roof as Mater, which I know would make you happy. It is not, trust me, that I think you do not like my family, but I am aware that your youth and exuberance suffer when you have to subdue them as you are obliged to do before my parents.

Furthermore, if you will excuse my boldness, I hope to start a family with you as soon as we are wed, and Mater would certainly not take kindly to the bustle and clamour of little children in the house. As things stand, to be honest, we could barely afford to keep a decent household in Graz, and we would be obliged to rent. In this way, we might not have to move at all. And I don't even have to tell you that, as a doctor having worked more or less directly under van Sweiten, I shall also have significantly better prospects of building a career.

It will only be for a year, dear Liesel, which means that I shall return six months before our wedding date as it is now set. I expect it to be a long, dreary year, so far away from you, but I could not pass up the possibility to make our future life so much better. Please, tell me that you will wait for me, and write to me every day while I toil among the savages.

I kiss both your sweet hands,
Erhard Ferdinand Pradl

*   *   *

Excerpt from Marcel Bordchamp's diary

MY DUTIES ARE getting stranger every day. They aren't necessarily any more difficult, and to be completely honest I am having quite an interesting time—more interesting than I had ever hoped to have within my secretarial duties. But sometimes, I get stumped by what is expected of me. The other day, I was required to locate some obscure place in one of the Austrian provinces. It seems that we will be travelling there. And taking along a coffin! The Count insisted on getting one here in France; apparently, he has had some bad experiences with poor workmanship in less developed areas.

After the Revelation (some day I might cease to feel the need to capitalise that word, but it still seems too momentous to me now), my relationship with the Count has changed. Not much, but in several significant ways. I am not even sure if it is for the better: now that he no longer needs to keep the mask on for me, I sometimes see glimpses of the creature that can overturn a twelve-seater in a fit of rage. His attitude towards the rest of the world, which has always seemed filled with dry humour and a trace of disdain, now comes to me without the veneer of politeness he previously maintained. And yet, when something goes well, I see him smile, and his satisfaction, when I earn it, is given just as freely. It seems strange. Ilan tells me it is normal: in his first life, the Count had been a warrior, and at the battlefield, nobility is judged by deeds, not blood. It is not that he doesn't believe in his superiority, of course—he has every reason to. But he appreciates mere humans who help him navigate the profoundly changed world of new centuries. Sometimes it makes me feel like a favourite dog, or a performing monkey. I would be lying, however, if I didn't admit it is flattering to be considered worthy—not only by a nobleman, but an immortal one, at that.

I am learning Muntenian, the Count's mother tongue, in which all of his servants communicate. It is not as difficult as I had expected; there are many similarities with Latin and French. Of course, there is also the purely selfish aspect of it. I have been thinking on it for several days now, but I am still not brave enough to bring my proposal to the Count. I should probably wait until we are done with whatever it is we're going to do in that Godforsaken place.

The following note, in the wider hand, was pressed between the pages of the diary:

Bordchamp,

Have you found a decent coffin yet? We are leaving in two days. I do **not** intend to deal with local craftsmen. And you know that there can be no delay. Do not make me regret that I have spared your life. That can always be remedied.

V.D.

Letter from Father Andreas Toth to Magdalena Hranić

Varaždinske Toplice, 24th of February 1746

Dear Mrs. Hranich,

Thank you for your contribution. You are, I am sure, aware that it is not nearly all that is required. Being the understanding person that I am, I shall not make a big deal out of it. I do, however, feel obliged to remind you that it is my duty as shepherd of our small flock to protect it from all untoward influences, even if that might force me to appeal to higher authorities. As Heinrich Kramer teaches us, evildoers do exist in our world, and must be eradicated. If you wish to convince me of the sincerity of your agreement with these sentiments, dear Mrs. Hranich, I have no doubt that you will find a way to do so—let us say, perhaps, by the end of next week?

Yours in Christ,

Father Andreas Toth

Letter from Erhard Ferdinand Pradl to Anneliese Lehner

Warasdin, 2nd of March

Dear Liesel,

I have arrived, finally, to my destination, and my first act was, of course, to sit down and write to you. Literally: as I write this, I am sitting in my landlady's salon, waiting for the final preparation of my rooms to be finished. As you can imagine, I have as yet nothing of interest to say about the town or about my work, but I thought you might find a little note about the journey itself of interest.

I will not bore you with detailed descriptions of my travels, even though some of the scenery was lovely, and I do believe we should one day visit this part of the Empire, merely to enjoy the nature, which is often quite virginally untouched.

But when we do that, we shall travel slowly. Lovely views are no compensation for spending a week cramped in a carriage! I would never subject your delicate constitution to hours upon hours of sitting still and having to suffer whatever company happens to appear at one station or another. From Tattendorf, I shared the coach with the most boring couple, who insisted on telling me stories about their grandchildren—at one point, I seriously considered taking a horse at the next post station and continuing my journey in the saddle, regardless of the difficulties.

Luckily, I did not do so, for we ran into a savage storm soon afterwards, and the horrible weather followed us for two days. Now, not only was I forced to listen to stories of precocious children, I had to do it while suffering bitter cold and pervasive moisture that neither the coach nor the blankets with which our drivers supplied us seemed able to keep out.

And then, around Lockenhaus, we had a bit of excitement. At the post station, we encountered two gentlemen who had been travelling in a private coach, but their horses had apparently slipped in the storm, so the coach overturned and their axle broke. Faced with the choice of waiting for the repairs or continuing on the public coach, the two gentlemen decided to join us. At first, I was less than enthusiastic—it was cramped enough with just the three of us in the coach, and now only one seat would be left unoccupied—but I soon changed my opinion, for the two gentlemen made the rest of my journey a lot more interesting.

One of them presented himself as Count Dragonneau (Comte Dragonneau, I suppose, since he pronounces the name à la française, although his accent doesn't ring quite French to me, so it may be affectation), travelling to Topliss to take the waters there, for apparently they are quite famous. Time permitting, I shall visit the baths myself, to see what they have to offer. Herr Doktor van Swieten claims that Roman medicine can teach us a lot, and might appreciate my account of the baths. That would perhaps make it easier to catch his eye.

But, to get back to my story: the Count is exceedingly interesting in appearance. He is tall, but also rather large of shoulder, and walks with the easy self-confidence of people who have command in their blood; he may only be playing at being French, but that he is an aristocrat born and bred, I do not doubt. He has a pale face, cut by a long nose and topped with deep-set eyes that seem to look right through you. I know, I sound fanciful, don't I? Believe me, dear girl, the Count's presence has that kind of effect. Even the boring couple kept their mouths shut after the Count gave them one of his profound gazes.

To make things even more interesting, he is not at all aloof: as our journey dragged on, I exchanged views with him on many a subject, and he listened to me with profound concentration and offered intelligent commentary, not merely pretending to attend to me for politeness' sake. Of himself, he spoke very little, but his conversation left me with a most favourable impression of both his mind and his manners. A true example of nobility, if I ever saw one!

His secretary, a certain M. Bordchamp, is a different story altogether. His accent genuinely sounds like he might be of French or similar origin, but his German is poor, and his Latin overly complex and near-unintelligible. He also coughs a lot, always careful to put a kerchief before his face, and seems to be rather poorly. Yet he never complained once, and seemed grimly determined to see this journey through. In the normal course of things, I would have expected to have more in common with him, as he is merely a burgher like myself and, I suspect, closer to me in age than his master, who might be anything between 30 and 50. But the fellow barely spoke to me at all, and eyed me constantly with a frown, as if I were a potential threat. There is no doubt that he is fiercely loyal to his employer, and perhaps that is the reason the Count keeps him by his side.

In any case, once the two newcomers joined our company, the journey seemed to go quicker—helped, I suppose, by the weather clearing; we arrived at Warasdin in glorious sunshine. I invited the Count to join me in a short stroll around the town's main square while the coach changed horses, but he declined, claiming tiredness and a great sensitivity of the eyes. Only then did I remember that he was on his way to what is, after all, a medical establishment. Can you imagine, Liesel, dear? Me, a doctor, forgetting that I was travelling with an invalid! I was so visibly embarrassed that even the ever-scowling M. Bordchamp felt pity for me, apparently, for he offered to walk a while with me.

This was the first time that the Count showed his more capricious side: he immediately cut the plan short, speaking in a language I did not recognise. Whatever it was, it did not please M. Bordchamp, I can tell you. He turned to his master and seemed about to argue, but one sharp gesture stopped him. We said our goodbyes then, and I promised the Count I would come and visit him in Topliss as soon as my work here allowed it. And I intend to keep that promise, my sweet girl: I have a strong suspicion no one I could meet in this poor corner of the Empire will be half as interesting as the good Count.

And now they are calling me, which means, I hope, that I can finally get out of my travelling clothes and take a few hours' rest on a bed with clean sheets. I shall write again this evening, when I have something to report.

I hope you are doing fine in my absence, and are not too unbearably bored. Please, also, extend my regards to your parents.

Kissing both your sweet hands,

Erhard Ferdinand Pradl

Letter from Magdalena Hranić's effects

My dear Matko,

My dear, dear Matko. I miss you so much, I don't know how to put it in words. That is why I'm writing this: if I went to visit you and started speaking to your grave, people would think me crazy and put me away. They're half waiting for an excuse to do so anyway. And, I must confess, it is disheartening to try and talk to cold stone. Yes, I did try it. Don't worry: I did it at night, and wore a thick shawl over my head so no-one could recognise me. But it was just stone, Matko. You were not there.

Where you are, I know not, but in this way, writing to you, I can at least pretend that you are merely travelling, away from home for a few days, and will be back soon enough to laugh away all my sighs. Kiss away my frowns. Wipe away the tension from my body. Oh, Matko. When I think about the way you would hold me when we haven't seen each other for a day or two, I can only *(next few lines illegible, as the handwriting becomes too shaky and irregular. Legible portion continues below)*

There is, I must confess, another reason why I'm writing. I am deeply, deeply troubled. I fear... saints in Heaven and all the godlets of every brook and hill, it's scaring me to even write this! But Matko, my love, I fear that I can sense another one of <u>them</u>.

Letter from Marcel Bordchamp's records

Very esteemed Count Dragonneau,

On behalf of our establishment, I wish to express our most heartfelt welcome. We hope you enjoy your stay.

Attached to this note are the keys to the small house you have requested be put at your disposal. It is situated a few dozen paces south from the Palace, at the very edge of the grounds. Despite your secretary's claims, I have instructed our Majordomo to set aside appropriate servants for the upkeep of the house. Should you wish to avail yourself of their services, you have but to ask.

Also, as per your request, I am leaving you the most detailed map of the area I could find. I have taken the liberty of marking (in red pencil) a few of the paths that would provide you with the most charming views and the greatest calm. I hope this is satisfactory.

Should you require anything else, please do not hesitate to tell me.

I have been warned of your nocturnal habits by your secretary, but I assure you, I shall personally forego my rest every night to provide you with all the comforts you can desire.

　With our sincerest regards,

　Hauptdirektor Bartol Povšić

Report to the Gentlemen's Bird Appreciation & Observation Association, Topliss

Report on observations, pertaining to the night of 2nd to 3rd of March, 1746.

All times recorded according to the clock on the church tower.

Left the house at: about 5.30 p.m.

Arrived at Park at: about 6.00 p.m.

Observation time: about 4 and a half hours

Birds observed:

Common nightingale

Nightjar

Scops Owl

Remarks:

After around 2 hours of being in the Park, I noticed, again, a very big flying creature, gliding with surprising speed just over the treetops. I am convinced it is a Siberian Fish Owl. First of all, the only other nocturnal bird that could, even theoretically, grow so large would be the Eagle Owl. Moreover, it was flying near the Public Baths—it is only logical to assume it was looking for fish.

I know that you will no more believe me now than you did before. But while I might have made a mistake—or even dozed off, as Lojzi suggested—once, this is the second time in as many months that I have seen the creature, and I am sure I did not dream it.

In the end, if you refuse to believe me, I shall be forced to kill the bird just so I could prove to you all it is not a figment of my imagination. However, I would like to conclude the matter amicably, and leave the magnificent beast to roam our night-skies freely. To that end, I intend to keep vigil in the Park every night until I repeat the sighting, and any member of the Association is welcome to join me.

Antun Sustar,

merchant of this parish

Letter from Magdalena Hranić's effects, unaddressed

My dear friend,

I know you are not satisfied with the latest from the widow Hranić; neither am I. But we must be patient. I have it on good authority (Mrs. Tišljar, who makes it her business to know everybody's business in the town, bless her bored soul) that a number of expensive things are gone from her parlour. It is reasonable to suppose she is selling things, probably in Varaždin. Let her, I say! She might have enough left for one more payment or two, but eventually, she will run out of possessions, and then she will have no option but to sell the house.

Trust me, please. Malleus Maleficarum is a powerful weapon and, although I doubt that was the intent of its authors, it is also very useful in the settlement of certain, shall we say, less spiritual issues. Just have patience. God's hand cannot be rushed.

I hear that Vienna is now as afraid of vampires as it is of witches. Have you considered looking into that option? There even seems to be a reward of some sort. I dare not ask too many questions myself, for obvious reasons. You, however, can show as much curiosity as you want. See what you can find out—apparently, there's a doctor in Varaždin right now tasked with looking into the matter. I am sure he could be persuaded to visit the baths. That might be all it takes, you know? Subtlety, my friend. In all matters, subtlety.

I shall see you on Sunday.

Excerpt from Marcel Bordchamp's diary

HE CAN FLY. Never in a thousand years would I have believed it had I not seen it with my own eyes. He just stands straight, spreads his hands, and—flies. I look at the words I've written, and they seem absurd; yet they are true. Last night, he asked me to accompany him from the Palace, where our regular rooms are, to the small house we rented extra. Ilan and two other Muntenians were there, having finally driven the coffin over from France. He conferred with them for a few moments, and then took off. For a moment, I thought I was dreaming, or that my sickness had made me imagine things. Silhouetted against the night sky, he seemed more like a huge bat or a bird. Then I blinked, and in the next instant he was gone, just a suggestion of motion somewhere among the stars.

"You'll get used to it," said Ilan. I don't feel like I ever will—but I would, I suppose. I am like a child here, lost in a world that, only a month ago, I wouldn't have believed possible at all. Ever since my childhood, I believed that we were living in an exceedingly lucky time, the Age of Reason, when men are finally starting to discover the truths underlying the great clockwork of a world in which Our Lord has seen fit to put us. But now it all seems to be falling apart. I do not know how I feel about this—any of this. Sometimes it seems as if I had fallen into a swift, cold river, and the only thing I can do is swim along, or else I shall perish. Maybe, once I reach the shore, I will have time to think things through. But not now, not yet.

SO, TRYING TO keep my head above water... I am still in the dark as to what we are really doing here. I asked Ilan, but he is, or pretends to be, just as ignorant of our master's intentions as I am. I do know that the coffin is partially filled with dirt the Count keeps in the cellar of our house in Paris—he needs to sleep on the soil of his homeland every now and then, to keep his strength up. It is not simple, being what he is. I am still hesitant to write down the word.

He returned a few hours later, clearly frustrated and unhappy. He complained about the brook that runs nearby: apparently, those of his ilk can have trouble crossing water if the wind blows in the direction opposite the water's flow. So we waited a little, until the wind calmed sufficiently, and then he flew off again. Whatever it was he was trying to do, he failed again, and returned just before dawn. Ilan tried to make him get some rest in the coffin, but he declined.

"It is not for me," he said. If that is the case, who *is* it for? How many of them are there?

Document from Magdalena Hranić's effects

TO PROTECT YOUR house from vampires, ghouls, incubi and other pests:

Take a little bit of your Moon's blood, and put it in a box made of white birch alone, with no nails or metals of any kind.

On the first Thursday of the month, take the blood, still in the box, and put it in a bowl. Make sure that the bowl is not of metal, but it should not be wood, either. Around the box, put three leaves each of the following:

—laurel (can be dry)

[*in the right margin, in faded pencil, visibly different hand*]
Laurel substitute—usually thyme. Quantity?

—sage (fresh)
—granny's finger (fresh or dry) [*literal translation of the name; I have been unable to identify the plant*]
—dandelion (make sure each leaf comes from a different flower, and leave the flowers themselves be. This will make the ward last longer.)
Also, on top of the leaves, put three cloves of garlic, at equal distances (this is not important for the leaves). Cover the whole with leaves of grass or dry hay.

Taking care not to lose a single leaf from the bowl, take it to a place nearest your house from which you can hear but not see water. If this is impossible, take a pitcher of water (anything will do) and put it behind the easternmost corner of your house, then move northwards until you no longer see it. You should still feel the presence of water. (If you do not, you have no business doing this in the first place, and the spell will fail.) Dig a shallow hole in the ground using your hands or a wooden stick, then place the bowl into the hole and set it on fire that you brought from your own hearth. Let it burn to ashes, then cover the remains with earth, taking care to leave no speck of ash about. This should keep your house safe for the next three months.

Alternatively, build a moat: water will stop most pests, except for incubi. You might not want to stop them, and it is easy enough to chase them away in the morning. (Wild carrot and rosemary)

[*below, in the same hand as the margin note, but in ink*]
Wild carrot is sufficient. Use pennyroyal in a pinch.

* * *

Letter from Erhard Ferdinand Pradl to Anneliese Lehner

Warasdin, 4th of March

Dearest Liesel,

Well, I have rested now, and finally had the chance to look around town, and inspect my new office. The town itself is very pretty, I must say. Of course, it cannot compare with Vienna, but the houses are quite charming, and with the spring coming, the gardens look just lovely. I cannot specify the flowers, but there are very many of them, in all hues imaginable. I suspect even you would like it here. I am not saying that as a roundabout way of suggesting a move to the provinces, never fear! But should your parents be so inclined, you might perhaps come visit me in the summer. I miss you, my dear girl. Truly I do. I hope you miss me, too. ~~You will not forget me while I am far from you, will you, dearest?~~

As for my office, it is not grand, but it is noticeably larger than the small room I had to share with Franz and your brother at the Medicals. It is situated right next to the Franciscan Monastery, of all places. This is for convenience; the Franciscans have a pharmacy, so any equipment I might need is available. At least that is what the man who took me there said. Frankly, I am not sure what kind of equipment I might need at all, because it seems the services they expect from me here have little to do with medicinal research, much less with doctoring. At least that is the impression I got from the man whose request brought me here.

The man introduced himself as Gašpar Katych, predialis. This is some sort of tiny local nobility, I am told—a knight, perhaps? The man owns a nice piece of land lying between Warasdin and Topliss, and commoners in the area seem to expect such landowners to take upon them the defence of their lands. That, obviously, includes unnatural dangers as well as natural ones. Hence the locals all turned to Katych with their complaints, and Katych in turn worked what connections he has to get me here.

Now, my sweet, I do not want to bore you with stories of my work, but you always said you found my regular work-stories interesting, and I believe you will find this story even more so. Therefore, I am recounting here the events that led to my coming here, as they have been related to me.

About two months ago, Katych received first reports of dead beasts in the area: one of the peasants from the nearby village lost a ewe, another a whole cow. In neither case were the animals dragged away: rather, their bodies were found, mutilated and drained of blood. (I have to stop here and tell you how incredibly happy I am to know that I can write of such things to you, and you will not faint! Immediately I finish this letter, I shall cross over to the monastery chapel, drop to my knees and thank our Maker for the gift of you.)

To go back to my story: since it was then still winter, it seemed possible that a hungry wolf or even a bear had wandered close to the settlements and killed the beasts, but lacked the strength to drag them away. Katych gathered a hunting party, and they searched and searched for the renegade animal, but found nothing. They even bivouacked in the forest, but to no avail. The following morning, they concluded that, whatever it was, it had probably died of hunger or some illness before they'd even started the hunt.

Imagine their surprise when they arrived back to the village in the morning, only to discover yet another dead cow. How the creature could have avoided them, they could not imagine—the forest is not that big, and they had kept vigil throughout the night. This time they set up guards on the side of the village closest to the woods. The knight and his men, armed with muskets and swords—even the peasants with their tools—stood and kept watch throughout the night.

Now, the following portion of the story made even me uneasy, just listening to it. I am hesitant to talk to you about it, and shall skip the most gruesome parts. Do not read this all alone, or at night! I know that, for a woman, you have strong nerves, but for once, do heed me, please.

The knight and his men settled to wait out the night. The knight himself took up position just outside the forest. To his right was a small brook, to his left a wide footpath from the village to the road. He calculated, rightly, that whatever was coming out of the forest would keep away from these, and take the shortest way to the village. He found a small patch of raspberries to hide him from sight, and crouched behind it.

The weather was favourable for the hunters: the sky was clear as it sometimes gets in bitter cold, and the moon, half-full, shone brightly. Katych had brought a thick fur coat to keep warm, and wrapped his hands in woollen mittens to be able to fire quickly. He had oiled and loaded his musket—a fine Spanish specimen, he tells me, though I know very little of such things—and loosened his sabre in its scabbard for good measure. Time passed, and the only sounds he heard were a few owl calls, and the tinkling of ice-covered twigs when a night breeze shook them.

Then, as night grew deeper and thicker, Katych heard another sound. Very soft, and slow: the squeaking of snow under someone's feet. At first he thought their vigil was paying off. He checked his musket once more, and looked intently at the forest; but the squeaking stopped. For a heartbeat or two, silence was complete. Convinced he had imagined it, the knight was just about to put down his musket, when the steps continued.

As they moved closer, Katych struggled to make out something, anything that would tell him what kind of creature was walking over snow. He stared at the dark mass of the forest in vain: no yellow eyes flickered, no brown fur flashed in the moonlight. The woods were shrouded in darkness. And still the snow crunched, slowly, rhythmically. Although he could see nothing, there was no mistaking the cadence of the steps. One foot, then another, moving with care, betrayed only by the frozen snow.

Katych concluded he was dealing with a bear. Although bears do not like walking on two feet, they are capable of it, he says, and are very intelligent. It is not by accident that Gypsies often steal bear-cubs and raise them as family, teaching them to dance and even steal. It was easy to imagine a bear was raiding the village, knowing to approach it on two legs to make less noise and leave a slighter trail. The sound continued, and Katych raised his musket, aiming at about the height where the chest of a bear standing on its hind legs would be. He could still not see—and was loath to waste such a good chance—so he waited.

The steps stopped again. As Katych stood aiming at the woods, he noticed a few wisps of fog rising from the ground. This was strange: the night was far too cold for fog. Yet it continued to rise, as if exhaled by the earth itself, and Katych could see snow rising and whirling in it. He looked around, trying to find an explanation, when, all of a sudden, the fog coalesced into a thick, dense cloud.

The cloud started towards the knight. It wasn't moving very quickly, but Katych could still hear the crunching of steps inside it; he gave an involuntary cry.

Just then, the cloud flew towards him.

For a moment, Katych was too confused to react. That was all the thing needed: it hit the knight at full force—he says it was like being hit by a bear—and attacked. The knight felt claws grabbing at him, and only then remembered he was holding a musket. He pushed it into the roiling cloud and fired.

The shot turned the night into a pandemonium. In the village, dogs started howling. On the edge of the forest, scores of birds flew up from the branches, alarmed by the report. There were shouts from other village guards, and the clatter of running feet. And above it all, like a saw passing through all their heads, a deafening, piercing cry that could have no natural cause. The horrible screeching made Katych let go of the musket and cover his ears. The claws grabbing at him let go, and he fell to the ground, calling for help.

He felt a horrible sensation, as if ants were crawling all over his body. He tried to get up, but was pushed down again by a strong gust of wind. On his knees, he looked up, and saw an enormous silhouette, like that of a huge bird or bat, rise to the skies. It flew uncertainly, erratically: first it started towards the forest, then seemed to change its mind and turned away from it. Men were arriving from the village now, shouting and aiming their muskets in the air. The creature turned again, this time towards the brook. As it crossed the water, it let out another horrible cry, then rose higher and disappeared in the night.

The men helped Katych to his feet, and took him to the closest house to check his wounds. The thick fur coat saved his life, it seems: in the light, they saw it was reduced to rags, torn by the creature's immensely powerful claws, while the knight himself escaped with only a few deep scratches. He showed them to me, and I confirmed his judgement. If it had happened in the summer, he would have been grievously wounded.

In the morning, they found the snow around the village covered in blood, and followed the trail. Unfortunately, the thing seems to be endowed with intelligence. Judging by the traces, it flew over the brook until it had stopped bleeding, so it was impossible to find.

Katych fell down with fever that same day, and nearly died. Once he'd recovered, however, he decided it was time to look further afield for help, and joined his report to the others being collated by the Court. And that, Liesel, is what I am here to do. Not to study the vampires, nor to see whether they are real. By all appearances, I am here to kill one.

I only wish I had any idea how to do that. My first instinct is to consult a library. Some time ago, I acquired that interesting pamphlet by Johann Christoph Harenberg, Sensible and Christian

Thoughts on Vampires or Blood-Sucking Dead, but, alas! I never took the time to read it in detail, nor am I familiar with Allatius's work, which would probably be even more pertinent here. The libraries here in Warasdin have neither work, and it is doubtful that I shall find them in Agram, either. I am therefore addressing a plea to you, my dearest. Would you visit my parents, and ask them to send me my copy of Harenberg as soon as possible? Also, if you could locate a copy of De Graecorum hodie quorundam opinationibus, I would be most grateful.

In the meantime, I shall return to the Franciscan library—one of the kind priests there told me he might have a volume that would offer at least some enlightenment on the subject—and also visit Topliss. It is work, too, in a way: the events Katych described took place in a village just outside the town. Also, it struck me as a good idea to try and consult the Count Dragonneau. He is well-travelled, and very knowledgeable. We did not discuss any similar topic during our journey, but for some reason, I have a feeling his opinion could be instructive in this matter.

I do miss you, my sweet. I hope your parents are well, and look forward to your answer. It doesn't have to be long, just a line or two to let me know you have not forgotten me completely.

Wishing I could kiss your sweet hands,

Erhard Ferdinand Pradl

Expenses report from Marcel Bordchamp's effects

Expenses incurred, 2nd to 6th of March:

[*encircled in black ink*]
Three workers, for the digging in the garden—9 Gr. (3 Gr. each)
Two workers, for the transport of the coffin—8 Gr. (4 Gr. each)

[*in the margin in black ink, in a different, wider hand*]
Why the difference?

Transport of workers to and from Topliss—3 Gr.

[*in the margin in black ink, in the wider hand*]
Per ticket price?

[*below have check marks next to them, also in black ink*]
One fully grown pig, live—1/2 T.
Food for said pig (temporary; the man said it can eat any kind
of scraps)—1 Gr.
One metal vat—2 Gr.
9 milk vases—18 Kr.

Total: 53 Gr, 7 Kr.

[*at the bottom, black ink and wide hand*]
Bloodhound!
  V.D.

Letter from Magdalena Hranić's effects

I am afraid, my darling. I am very afraid.

I have performed the spell for the protection of the house. I had
no laurels, so I used three sprigs of thyme. It should have been three
leaves, but they looked so tiny, and laurel leaves are big. I do not
know if it will work, or how well. I can only hope. Our house needs
protection. I need protection.

The one who took your life is still alive, somewhere. I can feel
him. I hear his movements over the water. It is odd, for a pest, to

keep so close to the water. But I know it's there. Hiding. Waiting. Given enough time, it will recover. I know I should go out and look for it, but I dare not. Not yet, I keep telling myself. Once I have bled, it will be harder for it to sense me. I will be stronger, directly afterwards. It is wiser to wait. I keep telling myself. But I am afraid that is all it is—fairy stories I use to hide my cowardice from myself.

What kind of a witch is it that fears a wounded vampire, you would ask, wouldn't you, Matko? You would say something funny to make me feel brave. To help me forget that awful night, help me think with my brain again, not my bowels. But you are not here, my love, and my fear is strong. I do not fear death, of course. But un-dead life? That scares me beyond words. Also, unless my craven senses are deceiving me, there are two of them now. I have to investigate this, I know I do. It is the duty of the witch to protect her lands from all pests. Should I fail in that, too, I shall truly lose any right to call myself a witch.

I remember telling Mother Bara, when I first decided to marry you, that marriage and witchcraft need not be opposites. I remember promising her I would never, ever shirk any of my duties, never turn away one in need, never fail a sister. And I kept my word, didn't I? I was a good witch, and a good wife to you, wasn't I? It's only now, when I am suddenly without you, that I sit in the house wrapped in a blanket like a true widow. Only now that I am afraid to move. This has to change. I would be betraying everyone if I let my fear get the better of me. Soon, I shall go out and look for the creature, and finish it. Then I shall see what I can do about the other one.

Oh, and if that wasn't hard enough: that horrible man came by again yesterday. He is still trying to make me sell the house, threatening to denounce me as a witch to the diocese. I paid him off, selling a few trinkets I don't need any more. But if he keeps it up, I will have to do something about him, as well. He has this idea that our house would be the ideal place for an inn. He thinks the fashion of the baths will spread, and burghers will start visiting the place as well as nobility. What folly! As if us ordinary people had the time and money to run about just for the pleasure of it. In any case, he is dead set on that plan, and helped by you-know-who, of course. I am tempted to turn both of them into frogs, just to try it out. I wonder, once the transformation is complete, where does the rest of the bulk go? Or do they simply become really big frogs?

I am rambling, my love. It's time to turn in. I need to get as much rest as I can, for I have a difficult battle ahead of me. Wish me luck, dearest Matko, and watch over me, wherever you are.

With all my love,

Magda

Letter from Magladena Hranić's effects, unaddressed

My dear friend,

I hear from Mrs. Tišljar that our widow has recently taken to leaving the house at night. If we could persuade the magistrate to come with us one evening, we could catch her in the act. Would you be willing to endorse such a course of action? Frankly, I am losing patience. I tried reasoning with her again yesterday, but she remains as stubborn as ever.

If she is found to be a witch, her house will become property of the township, and it will be easier to buy it, although the price will be higher. But I need your support in this; the magistrate is lazy and will not budge on my word alone. What do you say? Do we dare the gamble? Let me know as soon as possible.

B

* * *

Record from the Monastery Library of St. John the Baptist, Varaždin

On the 7th day of March of the year of Our Lord 1746, taken out of the Library of the Monastery of St. John the Baptist, and set out in the reading room for the perusal of the visitor, one Erhard Ferdinand Pradl:

> Johannes Weickhard Valvasor: The Glory of the Duchy of Crain, tome 3.

Said visitor was also provided with a fresh candle, a set of writing implements and a sheet of paper.

In gratitude for said services, the visitor left a donation in the amount of 6 Gr.

Letter from Erhard Ferdinand Pradl to Count Dragonneau

Warasdin, 7th of March

Most esteemed Count Dragonneau,

I hope I am not intruding upon what is, after all, your time of convalescence. I have come across a rather interesting problem, and would dearly like to consult a man of intelligence and learning such as yourself. I am therefore writing to announce that I should like to use your kind invitation to visit you in Topliss, and intend to take the liberty of calling on you tomorrow. If this should not be convenient, please, let me know; as a doctor myself, I understand the needs of those suffering from an illness take precedence over the whims of us blessed with robust health.

With my greatest respect,
Erhard Ferdinand Pradl

[*at the bottom, wide hand, black ink*]
The sooner we see him, the sooner we'll be rid of him. Accept.
 V.D.

Excerpt from the diary of M. Bordchamp

THE GOOD DOCTOR visited us today. He is still as pompous as he was when we first met him in the coach. I really do not like the mores of the Austrians. On the other hand, I should probably be happy that he is so silly: he is here to find vampires, and I would not like it if he were better at it. I suspect he would like the consequences even less, although I have yet to see my master do anything truly reprehensible. Maybe he still hides things from me.

The doctor asked a few general questions regarding the Count's health and the spa, then turned the conversation to the subject of his work. He told us very little about the story that had brought him here—I think he was uncertain as to how much he could trust his source—but he had also done some research which, in his view, showed that this part of the world had long suffered from vampire infestations. That was the exact word he used. I couldn't help but glance at the Count at that moment, but he merely lifted an eyebrow, as if he was trying to decide between scepticism and amusement. When the doctor claimed he could prove it, he was cordially invited to do so.

Thus, with much excitement, he told us a story about the first vampire recorded in these parts. The man allegedly died, but kept returning to pester his neighbours, even demanding marital congress from his wife. In the end, the people from his village gathered and killed him, led by their parish priest. The Count listened to the story carefully—the doctor was all excited about it, since he'd found it in a book by a man so respected as a scientist, he was even made a member of the British Royal Geographical Society—but at length merely shook his head.

"The man may have been very good when it came to describing rocks, but I'm afraid, my friend, that he wasn't equally gifted when it comes to common sense."

"What do you mean?" asked the Austrian doctor.

"Let us look at the evidence you have presented," said the Count. "This alleged vampire knocked on the doors of his neighbours in the middle of the night, and usually someone died soon after. Is this correct?"

"Yes."

"For sixteen years? How strange would it be if no one died in a village for sixteen years?"

"Well, yes—" started the doctor, but the Count didn't let him continue.

"And if you were raised on such a story, as children of the village undoubtedly were, would *you* resist the temptation to knock on doors now and then?"

"I should hope—"

"Let us be honest, Herr Doktor. Perhaps you were indeed the paragon of virtue at the age of twelve, but I know that *I* certainly wasn't. And in a village, where youth has little imagination and even less scope for it? Come on. The knocking was either the natural sound of old wood, or else tasteless youthful mischief." The Count smiled and settled more comfortably in his chair. He'd received the doctor sitting at his desk, with me by his side prepared to finish the conversation should he feel so inclined, but now he seemed to be enjoying himself. "Now, for the second point: when they opened the grave, they saw a body that seemed to be laughing at them. Correct?"

"Yes." The Austrian dragged the syllable out, expecting what was coming.

"You are a doctor yourself. You must have seen dead bodies in the course of your education. At least a skeleton."

"I did, but—"

"You know, then, that we all end up laughing in death, do you not?"

The poor man was by now quite disheartened. "Of course." He sighed. "But wouldn't they also have noticed that it was a rotting body they saw?"

"In the middle of the cemetery, when they have already come prepared to deal with a monster?" The Count shook his head slightly. "Do you know so little of people?"

"I thought we were living in the Age of Enlightenment."

"*We* are," said the Count. "But those peasants in the middle of nowhere, almost a hundred years ago?"

The Austrian had no response to this, but the Count was not yet finished. "And as for the monster looking for his wife's affection... obviously, someone saw a man sneaking out of her house. What better protection than to claim she was being pestered by her dead husband? The woman was clearly having an affair."

"But she was widowed... if she wanted, she was free to marry again."

"You truly are young, my friend. What reason do you have to think her lover was also free?" Seeing the doctor's shocked face, the Count added, "Widows are women with too much time on their hands. Dangerous creatures."

The doctor left soon after this—a little shaken, I think, but still determined to conduct a thorough investigation. When he left, I expressed my admiration for the way in which the Count had torn down the 'vampire' story.

"Oh, the story is true," said the Count casually. "I've even met the gentleman once—if I can call him that. He was a coarse, uncouth soul with no idea of discretion."

"But how did he become a vampire?" I asked.

"He had been turned by... another vampire." Unexpectedly, a tiny frown appeared on his usually clear brow. "An irresponsible creature, who turned a peasant to cover his own tracks."

"Cover his tracks?" I couldn't wrap my head around the idea of something that would make a vampire flee. "What was he running from?"

The answer was simple.

"Me."

Inserted after the page is the following note:

I, Marcel Bordchamp, do hereby attest that on the 8th day of March 1746, I have, on behalf of my employer, Count Dragonneau, taken possession of the dog, Garo, a trained bloodhound, from Josip Raukar, villager of the Topliss parish, who raised said dog and trained it in hunting. I promise to return the dog, unharmed and unspoiled, within the next three days. Should I fail to do so, I agree to pay the price of 46 Kr., separate from the monies already paid.

[*signed, left*]
Marcel Bordchamp

[*signed, right*]
Josip Raukar

[*initialled, bottom left*]
V.D.

* * *

Continued diary entry on the next page:

After that, I waited for a while, hoping for an explanation, but the Count offered none. Instead, he reminded me that I needed to finalize the arrangements for tomorrow night. As I was leaving, he muttered, "The sooner we end this, the better. It's been dragging on for far too long."

This time, I didn't even wait to see if he would tell me anything. I am learning. I can only hope it will be worth it.

Letter from Father Andreas Toth to Magdalena Hranić

Varaždinske Toplice, 8th of March 1746

Dear Mrs. Hranich,

We seem to have a misunderstanding on our hands. I do not want to be a bother, but I really do feel that the situation, as it is now, cannot be allowed to continue. I am therefore appealing to your better nature, as well as to your common sense, and proposing that we meet to discuss possible solutions. Would it perhaps be agreeable to you to meet at one of your usual outings and try to reach an agreement?

Oh: I hear that the Crimson Lobelia (the Cardinal's flower, I believe you would call it) sometimes flowers very early in the year, particularly around the area of the little bend in our brook. Perhaps tomorrow's full moon will coax a few buds? You are, I understand, very knowledgeable on all subjects relating to local flora and I am, alas, but an ignorant priest, if very willing to listen and learn.

Yours in Christ,

Father Andreas Toth

* * *

Letter from Bartol Povšić and Father Andreas Toth to Gašpar Katych

Topliss, 8th of March 1746

To: Gašpar Katych, Esq., Magistrate's Representative for this parish

We the undersigned wish to turn Your attention to the problem of witchcraft in our parish. We have been informed by sources who, from fear of retribution, wish to remain anonymous, that a widow of your parish, a certain Magdalena Hranić (born Jurić), does engage in acts that go against God and Church. Said Magdalena Hranić collects strange herbs from the woods, and has been known to use them to produce unnatural potions, which she then sells or even gives away to women and young girls in the parish. Some of her victims claim the potions ease women's pains, which is in itself of dubious moral value, since any such pains a woman suffers must indeed be part of her atonement for the Original Sin; but it has also been claimed that said widow Hranić can produce potions that will make it harder for a woman to become with child, or get rid of one while carrying it.

Furthermore, one witness, when confronted, admitted she had purchased from said widow Hranić a potion that would, if ingested in wine and during the Moon's waning, make a young man's blood boil with desire for the one who provided him with it. In addition to this, we have had reports saying that widow Hranić often leaves her house at night. Whither she goes, we know not, but an honest woman would not use the cover of darkness for her business, so it can reasonably be surmised that she is attending a witches' coven or consorting with the Serpent. In view of all this, we also cannot help but wonder whether the death of said widow's husband, Matko Hranić, although seemingly by accident, when he drowned in the brook, could not have been brought about in some magical manner.

In view of this, we appeal to You in the hope that You will condescend to take prompt action and investigate the case. We propose that You join us tomorrow night in secretly following said widow, to see whether the allegations of her leaving the house at an unseemly hour are correct, after which You will certainly have a sound basis for Your decision.

With the expressions of our most humble respect,

Bartol Povšić, burgher of this parish,

Father Andreas Toth, pastor of this parish

Letter from Erhard Ferdinand Pradl to Anneliese Lehner

Topliss, 9th of March

Dearest Liesel,

I am now completely convinced that something strange is going on here, but let me start from the beginning. As I told you in my previous letter, I went to consult Count Dragonneau regarding the possible vampiric situation in these parts. I told him the story of the first sighting in the wider region, which I had found in a much-respected book on the Crain, yet he dismissed it as part invention, part misinterpretation of facts. Now, I am aware that some, perhaps even many people doubt the existence of vampires, but the author of this book, Johannes Weickhard Valvasor, was a member of several renowned institutions of philosophia naturalis, and remains widely respected. It only goes to show one cannot judge anyone on short acquaintance: the Count is perhaps well-read, and is certainly well-bred, but in some ways, he is definitely behind the times.

After the Count, I spoke to Katych again. He has received a very strange letter indeed, from the local priest and some burgher. These two men claim that one of the local women is a witch. There have been quite a few cases of witchcraft documented in this area, so it would not be particularly strange, but it does seem too much of a coincidence that a witch should be spotted so soon after the events Katych had previously related. It seems only natural to suppose there is a connection between the two. Because of this, I have arranged to accompany Katych on the fact-finding mission that the letter proposed. So, my sweet, to-night, I shall participate in what might be a real, actual witch-hunt!

I shall confess to you (and only to you—you are not to mention this to anyone!) that I feel a certain amount of trepidation at the prospect. I have read some accounts of witch-trials, and the deeds described therein are indeed gruesome. Add to that the hair-rising story that Katych himself had told me, and you shall understand why my heart is uneasy. But at the same time—for such are the vagaries of the human heart—I am excited. I came here, to be completely honest with you, fully expecting that I should do nothing more strenuous or interesting than supervise the unearthing of a grave or two. As things now stand, before I return to Vienna, I shall have amassed experience with all manner of supernatural creatures, and—I am only starting to dream of the possibility now—perhaps even claim one of the rewards offered for confirmed cases of vampirism.

Having read Valvasor's account of the conflict with the vampire, I armed myself with the largest cross I have in my possession. Perhaps you remember it: it is the one my Mother bought on her pilgrimage to Mariazell, that has been blessed by the Archabbot himself, directly before the sacred image that is said to work miracles. Katych is also going armed, with both sabre and musket. I hope that the parish priest will remember to bring holy water, as it seems that it has some effect on vampires, and it is supposed to burn witch-skin. Thus equipped, we shall wait for nightfall, and watch the alleged witch's house. Should she leave it—it seems she is given to night-time excursions—we shall follow her, and see what she does. Katych had shot his monster; perhaps she is nursing it back to health? I am almost afraid to hope for such luck. Imagine finding a vampire weakened enough to be captured and studied at leisure! Wouldn't that be something to bring to Vienna?

Of course, maybe this whole story will turn out to be nothing, just a lonely woman walking in the night or meeting with a completely mortal lover, for I am aware that some cases of witchcraft have been proven to spring from sheer jealousy. Thus, my dearest Liesel, wish me luck tonight, and remember me in your prayers.

Hoping I will live to kiss your sweet hands again, I remain, as ever, yours

Erhard Ferdinand Pradl,
vampire- and witch-hunter

Report to the Gentlemen's Bird Appreciation & Observation Association, Topliss

Joint report on observations pertaining to the night of 9th to 10th of March, 1746, as made by Antun Sustar and Stjepan Novak, both members of the Association of good standing.

All times recorded according to the clock on the church tower.

Left respective houses at: about 5.30 p.m., met at road.
Arrived at Park at: about 6.00 p.m.

Observation time: about 3 hours (effectively, followed by unexpected events)

Birds observed:
Common nightingale
Scops Owl

Remarks:

After some 3 hours of careful observations, we were about to call it a night. I (Antun Sustar) tried to convince my companion to stay a bit longer, hoping that my Siberian Fish Owl would return. As we had been keeping vigil nightly for seven days now with no unusual sightings, Štef was not willing, and we argued a little, after which he agreed to stay a bit longer, but no more than a quarter of an hour. This interval being close to passing, Štef said he would wait no longer and got up to go, and just at that moment, my Owl flew out of the woods. It sped over our heads, then turned in the air and started back towards the woods, only to disappear completely from our sights. We looked at each other, and without superfluous words started running in the direction in which the huge bird had flown.

Once in the woods, we lost our way and wandered for a while in the darkness, when we heard some sort of commotion over on the side towards the brook. We started towards it, but made little progress before a veritable pandemonium broke out, as if each and every bird in the woods had woken up at the same moment and taken flight in panic. Nightingales and common sparrows criss-crossed the sky, whizzing under the wings of magpies and tawny owls. Impossible, yes, but we saw it!

We clung to each other, filled with fear, as the frantic flapping of wings surrounded us and distraught birds cried all around us. Just as inexplicably as it had begun, in a moment or two, the pandemonium settled. In the sudden calm we heard the single cry of an osprey, and then the woods fell silent again.

After that, we decided it was very late indeed, time to go home and get to bed. We did so immediately, crossing through the woods to make our journey shorter.

We are now both convinced that an unexpectedly large bird does indeed live or has at least made its temporary home in our woods, and see no further need for nightly watches. Lojzi can say whatever he wants, we know the truth.

    Antun Sustar,
    merchant of this parish
    Stjepan Novak,
    boot maker of this parish

Letter from Magdalena Hranić's effects

My love,

    Of all the stories I never expected to tell you, of all the things I never expected to write, what happened tonight is definitely the strangest.

    You know, as I write these letters, I always have the same image of you in my head: I see you reading by moonlight, sitting in that attic room you had while you were apprenticed to Master Žiga, chewing on an empty pipe and laughing at the silly things that pass through my mind. This is how I want to remember you, always—young, and handsome, and happy. And this is why I will stop writing to you after this letter. I have a feeling, irrational as it may be, that, if I continue, you will grow old with me, and fade away, and I do not want you to. Not if we can't do it together. I will go on, because I have to. But you can stay forever the dashing apprentice printer who first captivated my heart. That manner of eternal youth, no matter how painful for me, is infinitely better than the other kind. I would not take that from you, so I shall leave you here.

    Yet, I owe you the end of the story that we have started together. It would be unfair to make you wait until I am dead too. I am trying, right now, not to imagine you standing behind St. Peter's back, hopping from foot to foot in that impatient way of yours as I approach the Pearly Gates. And you would, I know you would, so instead, here is the rest of the story.

I told you, didn't I, that Bartol Povšić is trying to force me to sell our house? He has the support of Father Toth, whom Povšić has convinced they would both become rich. Unlike Povšić, though, Father Toth is cunning. His threats are always couched in language ambiguous enough to be explained away should I try to turn the tables on him, yet clear enough that I cannot mistake his meaning. In his latest missive, he invited me to discuss the situation, and added some apparently unrelated sentences that made it clear he wanted to meet with me at night, at the small bend of the brook where I sometimes go to gather plants. You know the place I mean.

My first instinct was to ignore the invitation. There was nothing any one of us could say that would change the situation: these two want me to sell them the house, preferably at a low price; I do not intend to do so. That should be the end of story, although of course it isn't.

Thinking about it, it occurred to me that the place was close to where we'd fought with that vampire who killed you. I know that this is horribly bad of me, and a very non-witchy thing to do, but please, please, try to understand. I am now alone. Mother Bara is dead. You are dead. Yes, some of the women in the villages support me—but only when their husbands and fathers cannot hear them. If Povšić or Toth were to carry out their threat, there would be no one who would speak for me. I could, perhaps, just pick up and leave, but where would I go? This world is not welcoming to a woman alone. Here, at least, I have my house, and the sound of water that puts me to sleep every night, and the fields and woods I've grown up with. Here I have the memory of you, and can re-live it in every blade of grass where we once walked together. This is my home.

So I decided I would try and solve two problems at once. You are already guessing, I think, as to the how. I knew the vampire we'd fought was still around here, somewhere. We had used enough silver and garlic and rosemary to kill all but the sturdiest of the creatures, but even so, I would have sensed the relief in the atmosphere had the monster breathed his last.

I also knew, no matter how strong, it would be at half its powers at best.

Povšić and Toth, on the other hand, no matter how pious a face the former makes at Mass, or how ostentatiously the latter carries his Malleus, do not really believe in witches, or any other supernatural creature. They would come expecting to meet merely a stubborn but helpless human woman. All I needed to do was get them to walk into the swamp a little way: vampire senses would do the rest. And while the monster is feeding—it would be half-crazed with hunger, by now, and would lose what little self-control it has—I would have enough time to take careful aim and hit it full in the chest with the stake, then proceed to decapitate it properly.

My two tormentors would die, and I must say, my heart was not easy with that decision. If I believed any kind of persuasion, logic or reasoning could reach them, I would have adopted that course instead. I didn't. Maybe this is not something you wanted to know about me; I'm sorry if I disappoint you. Ruthlessness is a trait that any good witch must possess, at least in some measure, you know. It helps make the hard decisions. Witches' lives are full of them. I hope you'd understand—no, I know you would. Or if you wouldn't, don't tell me. After you've gone and got killed like that, the least you can give me are a few comforting lies. You would <u>not</u> care.

There, that's settled, and I can go on with the story. Now, my plan was far from perfect, as well I knew, so I made careful preparations. I went to the bend early, and planted stakes in the reeds, where they would be invisible unless you knew what you were looking for. I then returned home, and carefully prepared a whole bag of vampire-hurting stones. I took the Silbergroschen that we prepared the last time—I didn't want to touch them even when Toth demanded money—and wrapped every single one of them carefully in herbs, then soaked them in holy water. I also took a bag of ordinary stones, in case I had to defend myself from human attackers. Lastly, I checked my sling, made sure it was undamaged and ready for use, and tucked it in my pocket.

I felt like a knight preparing for a fight. If I still had the armour that wandering soldier had paid with when I treated his boil, I believe I would have donned it at that moment. Not for protection, you understand, but to gird myself; I was ready to do battle with all my enemies, be they human or not. In the end, I settled for my black widow's scarf, wrapping my hair and tying it back as if I were going to do the washing. Thus equipped, I stepped into the night.

This is what I mean when I say "home." I should have been frightened. I <u>had</u> been frightened, at least a little bit, while I was doing all those things that had to be done before I could be on my way. Then I closed the door behind me, and my fears vanished. It was dark outside—it's still early enough in the year, so the night comes swiftly, and the Moon had not yet risen. Heavy black clouds rolled over the skies, bringing with them the threat of a storm. And I was about to face two men who wanted nothing more than to see me broken, and at least one true monster with good reason to hate me specifically, more than he hates the rest of humankind. And possibly another, if what I had sensed was correct. Yet, as I walked through the darkness, my fears dissolved. This was <u>my</u> night, <u>my</u> darkness. I knew its every sound. The air was cool, but to me it felt as comfortable as our marriage bed. I felt as if nothing and no one could defeat me.

That feeling carried me all the way to the brook, and allowed me to touch the crimson heads of the flowers there with calm, unshaking fingers. I stopped and looked at the skies. It was still relatively early. Toth's convoluted writing couldn't convey an exact time, but his mention of the full Moon made me suppose he would wait at least until it was clearly visible. It suited me fine. I could hear the nightlife stirring in the woods behind me. In the distance, I could even hear some of the bumblers from the "Bird Appreciation Association" imagining themselves silent enough not to frighten away their quarry. I found a rock far enough from the water to serve as an acceptable chair, and settled to wait.

I kept all my senses open to any trace of a monster. All the self-assurance in the world will not save you, and vampires are murderous foes, as you well know. I heard and sensed nothing other than the general unease that signified the beast was not yet dead. And then, somewhere in the woods, I heard—sniffing.

At night, there is usually a lot of sniffing going on: it is, after all, a matter of life and death for most forest-dwellers. Small noses, close to the ground, search for safe passages; larger ones, higher up, look for food. But this was different. Louder, and more excited than anything else. This nose did not sniff out of life and death. It sniffed... deliberately. Professionally. And fairly quickly, moving through the woods towards me.

A few heartbeats later, I could also hear steps: human steps, trotting with the same easy pace as the sniffer. I closed my eyes, trying to discern how many there were. I was sure about one, two; maybe three. The "maybe" worried me: humans do not have that lightness of gait.

But vampires do. Even when they're wounded and still recovering.

As I concentrated on what was coming through the woods, I forgot to look around me. It was only when a thin hand grabbed me from the darkness that I realised it was a mistake.

The monster's fingers closed over my forearm like a manacle. I screamed, pushing my free hand into my pocket. No time to take out the sling, but holy water and herbs and silver would burn it a little and—wrong pocket! Those were the ordinary stones. I grabbed them all, and threw them at the monster all the same.

The creature was no longer quite sane, and that was my salvation. As the sling-stones dropped, it let go of me and grabbed them with filthy hands. I heard sounds coming from its lips as it collected them, one by one. I did not recognise the language, but the motions and my poor Latin suggested a meaning. "Unu, doi, trei, patru..."

He was counting.

I didn't know what kind of a miracle it was, but I wasn't going to waste it. Slipping from the creature's suddenly slack grip, I stepped backed and grabbed another handful of stones; just ordinary pebbles from the banks of the brook. But they worked, too. I threw them at the creature. As soon as he heard the rattling, he let go of the stones he'd already counted, and started anew.

I moved toward the banks of the brook. If I could reach one of the stakes I'd planted there, I thought, I could kill the monster. I no longer cared about my plan. I just wanted to stay alive.

Steps rattled behind me. I turned and saw a group coming from the woods. At their head, a large black hound was running with its nose almost touching the ground. Three shadows came after the master-sniffer. One was short but stocky—I learned later that his name was Ilan. He kept up with the hound in long easy steps. The other one, Bordchamp, was thin, and ran as if his legs were about to buckle under him. Behind them, a third shadow was almost impossible to discern in the darkness. As soon as I saw it, I knew. The other vampire.

The hound raised its head and let out a satisfied bark. The two men following it slowed down, the thin one breathing so heavily I thought he must be very old, or very sick. The tall shadow didn't even slow down; it passed over the men and the dog, or maybe through them. Or just too quickly for the eye to follow, I don't know. All I do know is, in the next instant, the two vampires were facing each other.

The wounded one had been kneeling, frantically collecting the stones to his chest. Now he let them trickle from his fingers, and looked up. His lips formed a new word, not a number—at least, not one that I recognised.

"Vlad."

The other one kept silent for a moment. Then he answered. "Radu."

As if this was a magic word, the wounded vampire jumped up and slammed into the other with full force. Both fell. The hound barked. The two vampires rolled on the ground, pebbles faintly clicking under them. The short stocky man grabbed the dog and jumped backwards.

"Master!" screamed Bordchamp.

I didn't even know vampires could have servants. Not the kind of observation to have under the circumstances, but in my defence, my head was full of confused thoughts and unanswered questions. First and foremost among them, however, was how to get out of there alive.

The two vampires separated, and the tall one, Vlad, lifted a hand. The wounded one stopped. There followed a flurry of words in that language: Muntenian? So frustrating! It sounded as if I should be able to understand it—almost Latin, but not quite—yet I couldn't, or not enough to make head or tails of it. The two men with the hound apparently could, following the exchange with tense faces. At last, the wounded vampire, Radu, stood up. He was not sure on his feet. As he swayed, Vlad offered a hand, but Radu pushed it aside. He looked towards us.

That, my dearest, was when I became truly afraid. When he'd first attacked me, I had no time to think; and things went from strange to stranger with such speed I could barely keep up. But now I was standing still, and staring at me was the vampire we had jointly wounded, the vampire who had killed you. And who, without a shadow of doubt, wanted to kill me.

I reached into my pocket for the witched stones. From the corner of my eye, I saw the two men step away from me, understanding that the vampire was selecting me for his victim. I took my sling in a slow movement. My hands didn't even shake, you know. I could feel myself tremble inside, but on the outside, I was as calm as the night.

The Moon had risen in the meantime, and fought its way through the clouds for long enough to light the scene. I could see that the damage you and I had done had almost healed, but another wound, fresher, spread over Radu's chest. Black spots of dried blood covered the tattered front of his shirt. His face was distorted with hunger, animal instincts taking over again. That is what happens with vampires: it is not easy to keep the inner beast in check, even in a single lifetime. Through an eternity, it becomes nearly impossible.

The other vampire was still in full control, though. He spoke in a soft, almost sad voice. "Radu, nu." That, I understood: *No.*

Radu shook his head and took a step towards me. I put a stone into the sling. Lifted it. Took aim.

"Lord our saviour, deliver us from evil!"

The shout in German made us all look towards the woods. The wounded vampire let out a long hiss, like a giant cat, and leaped towards the source of the cry.

It was Father Toth, of course, leading his would-be business partner and two other men whose faces I couldn't discern in the dark. The wounded vampire jumped at the priest, who took out a large silver cross from his robes and started banging the vampire over the head with it. It would have been ridiculous if it weren't so deadly. Povšić turned to run, but tripped over something and fell, pushing the third man along. The last one—I recognised predialis Katych—raised a musket.

This prompted Vlad to react. He rushed at the newcomers. Bordchamp also took a step.

"Stay here!" commanded Ilan, pushing the by-now frantic hound into Bordchamp's hands. He then took out a flintlock pistol and raised it towards the group.

Vlad grabbed at Radu, and their hands locked on each other's throats. The priest dropped to the ground, and the unknown man freed himself from the panicking Povšić, reached into his shirt and took out a smaller cross on a chain. Radu screamed; even Vlad let out a furious hiss. He pushed the man aside. Father Toth scrambled to his feet, his cross forgotten, reached into his robes and came out with a small flask. He unstoppered it and started sprinkling it over the two fighting vampires. They both roared, whether in pain or in anger I could not tell. Clouds coalesced about them, and the air became a whirlwind of darkness, human and non-human screams mixing with the cries of the newly-disturbed birds to create a cacophony beyond understanding.

A shot tore through the chaos. For a moment, it seemed as if everything had turned to stone. Then a lone osprey call echoed somewhere far up in the sky, and as if the piercing cry had freed us from some spell, we all started talking and moving at once.

In patches of moonlight, I could see Father Toth lying on his back, his throat and chest torn, his mouth gaping. Povšić was curled on the ground, his left hand cradling his right, moaning. A dark stain spread over his coat. Next to him, on his knees, the unknown man was taking off his coat and folding it neatly; it would have seemed absurd had I not recognised the calm competence of a physician with a patient. My suspicion was confirmed when he asked, without turning his gaze away from Povšić, "Could someone provide me with a knife?" He lifted his hand, fully expecting the world to meet his demand somehow. Only surgeons have that kind of calm in a crisis.

And witches, of course. I stepped forward and took out the knife I always carry strapped to my thigh. The man accepted it with a short nod—politer than some surgeons I've known, let alone some witches—and started cutting away Povšić's coat.

I later learned he was indeed a medical doctor, from Vienna. Quite a change from the operating rooms he was used to!

"I'll need light, too..." he was muttering, but I couldn't help him there, so I turned to see what had happened with the others. Katych leaned on his musket, a dazed expression on his face. Ilan also seemed confused. They were looking at each other, as if wondering which of them had fired the shot that wounded Povšić. From my position, I saw another pistol, partially hidden by Povšić's body, and remembered how Mother Bara always used to shake her head at the mention of firearms. "Never use a weapon that can turn around and bite you," she used to say. It seemed that Povšić had tried to fire a shot and the flintlock exploded in his hand. But that could all be figured out later.

Bordchamp was still holding the black dog in his arms, both shaking wildly. The man had his eyes closed; the hound hid his in the crook of the man's arm. Shock, I thought distantly. They would need warmth and peace to recover. I could provide them with both back at the house. But first...

But first, the vampires. The wounded one lay on the ground. In an echo of the two men not ten paces from them, the other knelt by his side. It was obvious that Radu was at the end of his strength: even for a vampire, his skin looked sickly, and his body was twitching spasmodically. The other vampire lifted his hand, curled in a claw, the way vampires do when they're about to strike. The clouds parted again, lighting his face. A glittering trail of tears streaked his cheeks. He swallowed. Closed his eyes. Then tore at his own neck.

I let out a small cry of surprise. Vlad leaned closer, lifting Radu's head and directing his lips to the flow of blood. After only a few sips, he grew visibly stronger. He swallowed and blinked, much as Vlad had done before. Lifted a hand to Vlad's neck, as if to stop the flow.

"Nu..." he muttered through swollen lips. The rest I couldn't understand. I turned to Bordchamp.

"What is he saying?"

He wasn't very good at the language yet, but my frustration at least penetrated the fog of shock. He frowned, concentrating.

"'Don't try to save me,'" he said.

Vlad grabbed at the hand at his throat.

"'I have to try,'" Bordchamp translated. "'Despite everything, I have to try.' And the other one says, 'It's no use. We're too far gone our separate ways.'"

Radu tried to smile, and added another sentence.

"'But I do appreciate the effort.'"

His hand, until then pressed against Vlad's throat, now slid up to cup his brother's face. He started to say something more but was cut short by a low, rumbling shout in German.

"In God's will and His eternal glory!"

Father Toth, whom we had all assumed dead, tottered towards the two vampires, brandishing his heavy silver cross like a dagger, longer side out.

Before anyone had had time to react, Radu pushed Vlad aside and spread his hands, grabbing at Toth's sleeve. The priest threw himself at the vampire with the last of his strength, striking a blow in the middle of Radu's chest.

A shriek cleft the night. It was a sound I cannot describe, and can only hope will never hear again. The sound of a vampire dying.

And this, my love, is where I shall stop my story. There is almost nothing left to tell, anyway. The story of two brothers who fought over love and faith and power through centuries, yet somehow still loved each other, is not really mine to tell. Suffice it to say that, after the sound dissolved in the night, Vlad remained prostrate, his shoulders shaking. No one dared approach him. Ilan merely stepped between us and crossed his arms, his back turned to his master. After a while, Bordchamp joined him, still carrying the dog, and the three of them stood silent guard.

I went over to see what could be done for Povšić. He will never regain the full use of his hand, but will have some movement— that little Austrian is a decent physician, and I provided him with poultices to prevent inflammation and rot. He will live because of me—in his hometown, not here. That was the deal we struck and, after everything that's happened, it wasn't difficult to talk him into leaving Varaždinske Toplice forever.

Predialis Katych agreed that the events of last night would best be kept secret. He wrote a short report, merely confirming Dr. Pradl's claim that we had all witnessed an instance of vampirism, but that the problem was resolved in a permanent fashion. He also agreed that a witch, provided she is discreet and benevolent, isn't a matter to take up with the Court. Vienna cannot understand the way we do things here. It helped that his wife and both daughters are clients of mine, and that he now knows where the ointment with which he treats his own rheumatism comes from.

He also wrote to the Diocese, asking for another priest. We debated on whether to paint Father Toth's death as heroic, or dismiss it as accidental. In the end, we agreed that heroism would be closer to the mark. Yes, he was a hypocritical, lying, greedy scoundrel; but he has three sisters and a younger brother back in Szeged, and they have done nothing wrong. Let them have a pleasant memory, at least, and what small pension they can get from the Church.

All of this was arranged at our house, where we had retreated after the eventful night. Yes, including the vampire, Vlad Dracul, Prince of Wallachia. He is more than three hundred years old, he says. I don't know if it's true, and I don't care. He apologised for his brother's behaviour, and insisted on paying for my services and the physician's. Before they left, he took me aside and asked if there was a cure known to witches for consumption. His man, Bordchamp, suffers from it, and His Highness suspects he thinks becoming a vampire could be a solution.

"That is not a fate I would willingly impose on anyone as kind-hearted as he," said His Highness in a quiet tone. He looked through the window. In the back yard, Bordchamp was sitting, wrapped in a blanket, still holding the frightened black dog in his arms. The two seemed to take comfort from each other.

"Why do you care?" I asked.

"I beg your pardon?"

"Why do you care? If you are more than three hundred years old, how can the life of a mere human being mean anything to you?"

At that, he smiled and nodded towards the man and dog in the yard. "Did you ever have a pet, Mrs. Hranić? In my country, witches are famous for it."

So I gave him the list of herbs for Bordchamp. They will not cure him—there is no cure for consumption that I know of—but they will diminish the symptoms; if he sticks with his medicine and takes care of himself, he will have a long, fruitful life. I have told His Highness as much, and he told me to add another Taler to my bill.

"That is too much."

"I'll pay it in Silbergroschen," he said. "That way, when next you need it, you will have ammunition." He smiled again, and of a sudden, I understood full well where myths of vampiric charm came from.

I was glad that he was leaving, my love. Not because I couldn't live with being grateful to a vampire—life is strange, and one has to take help where one can find it. But because I knew that, should he stay, I would become just as loyal to him as the others in his entourage. Not a bad fate for some, perhaps, but not one I would have wanted for myself.

So, now you know everything, my love. Your sacrifice was not in vain: despite his lucid moments, Radu was too far gone to ever regain control of himself. He was indeed a danger, a pest that had to be dealt with. But Vlad... Vlad is different. And far away. If he does lose control at some point, he will be someone else's problem.

You can't save everyone, as Mother Bara used to say.

I shall stop here. I still love you more than I can say, still miss you so much it hurts. Still, forever, remain yours, and yours alone.

Love,

Magda.

*   *   *

Expenses report, from Marcel Bordchamp's effects

Expenses incurred, 7th to 12th of March:

For the dog, Garo—46 Kr. (you can take that out of my salary)

[*in the margin, black ink, wide hand*]
Don't be ridiculous.

[*all the following have check marks next to them, in black ink*]
Donation to the Diocese of Warasdin—1 T
A new axle for the coach—6 Gr.
Fee for the coachman who drove it to Topliss—1 Gr.

Total: 1T, 7 Gr.

Addendum No. 268-46 to the dispositions of the Medicinal Office

From the desk of Simon Aigner, Esq., Medicinal Office Assistant.

In accordance with Addendum No. 34-46 to the dispositions of this office, and with the reports received from Topliss (see attached file)

I hereby request the approval of the payment of the sum of 20 Taler, to be paid to one Erhard Ferdinand Pradl, for the finding and destruction of a vampire reported to pester the area of Warasdin and Topliss.

This being a total of ....20 Taler.

In Vienna, on the 2nd day of February, 1747.

[*signed, left, with seal*]
Simon Aigner,
Medicinal Office Assistant

[*signed, right, with seal*]
Count Friedrich Wilhelm von Haugwitz,
Head of Directorium

FOUR

CHILDREN OF THE NIGHT

INTERLUDE

From: Jonathan Holmwood (jwlh1947@amol.com)
To: Dani Văduvă (bornwithteeth@webmail.com)
Date: January 16, 2018
Subject: Re: Mina Harker?

Hi Dani,

Thanks for your patience. Last section!

Just one long letter, this time, this one supposedly from D—'s own hand. I can imagine you're sceptical about this—trust me, so was I—but my father swore by it all his life.

He never told me exactly *why*, mind, only that it had come to him "through work" and the source was good. He worked for the Home Office in the 'fifties and 'sixties (my father was Alastair Holmwood, if you want to look him up), so my best guess is this was either seized by the police at some point or fell into his hands in political circles in Whitehall. Neither possibility is hugely reassuring. I enquired discreetly among some of his old friends, but came up blank; either they genuinely hadn't heard of the letter or they were keeping schtum.

I've looked for "Bogdan" before, in any number of ways, and never with any luck. Whether he's still around, still in London, or still has any sort of influence—whether he ever *existed*—I can't say.

And that's a thought that's kept me awake more than once.
Jon

CHILDREN OF THE NIGHT

Emil Minchev

DEAR BOGDAN,

I hope my long overdue letter finds you in high spirits and excellent health, as befitting a true heir of our most noble race. I received your last communiqué more than a century ago and much has happened in my beautiful land since you chose to leave it for the English city of London, uprooting your entire family and substituting sacred heritage for vulgar modernity and peaceful serenity for busy cacophony. For you should know, my friend, that a single drop of noble Székely blood has more intrinsic value contained within it than the entire bloodworth of that sprawling metropolis you now call your home. You, who are a direct descendant of Bulgarian Kings and Queens, are a god among insects in the teeming streets and overcrowded squares of that accursed city. You, who fought the savage Turks alongside me at the battle of _____ and dealt a mighty blow for Christianity against the Sultan's insatiable lust for conquest, must feel like a great warrior prince mobbed by unenlightened rabble in that beehive of a city.

There were, however, certain passages in your last letter, my dear friend and brother-in-arms, which, when reread and reevaluated, piqued my interest and impressed upon me the need to rethink my hard stance against your desertion. I was impressed by certain new and exotic possibilities that you outlined with your typical prudent logic and eloquence. You claim that beings such as ourselves can live in happy abandon in a place the size and breadth of London, subsisting on its inhabitants, for what is one human drained of all life in a city as populous as an entire country? What are ten humans found dead and bloodless as compared to a famine that kills thousands, or a plague that takes tens of thousands?

Here, people know me. Here people fear, detest and even fight me. The people of London know nothing of the ways of the old world. They are ignorant of my kind, ignorant of my awesome powers and ignorant of their true place in Nature's order, which is, as you well know, under our undead feet.

I must confess that at first the idea of leaving my ancestral home seemed perfectly foreign to me, akin to sawing off my legs or setting my magnificent fortress alight. My roots and the roots of my noble kind are buried deep within the sacred earth of this most beautiful and proud country. My blood has irrigated this land for hundreds of years, the bones of my ancestors form its sturdy spine. I am as much a part of the landscape as the great black mountains that tower over my castle and the deep dark forest that surrounds it.

Notwithstanding my initial misgivings, certain unexpected events, which I will now relate to you, have forced me to reconsider the notion of joining you in England and taking full advantage of this new and richer hunting ground you so vividly describe. The prey might not be of the pedigree I am accustomed to, but my present situation requires some sacrifices. I am prepared, therefore, to live among the cattle and get fat on their blood. Principles and high ideals might be nourishing for the soul, but never the belly.

THE UNEXPECTED OCCURRENCE of which I speak happened in December of last year, during the fiercest and most prolonged snow storm to ravage my country in decades. Angry black clouds rolled in from the frozen north and swallowed up the sky as far as the eye could see. The sun, my ancient enemy, dared not show its face for weeks. Roaring gales and icy darkness ruled the land. The winds blew so keenly that they could strip the skin off your body, and at night the cold became so severe that even I, who am darkness, felt its piercing chill.

One night I went out for a stroll, as I adore violent and destructive weather and delight in Mother Nature showing her claws. After an hour or so the howling winds quieted and the storm subsided. I was walking back to the castle and admiring the sudden hush which had stilled the winter night when a cloud moved across the sky and the silver light of the moon revealed an unexpected sight by the side of the road—a shattered, overturned carriage which had obviously veered off the road and crashed into the frozen trees. Perhaps the coachman had been blinded by the snow flying in his face and had lost control of the vehicle on the narrow, treacherous road. I had known this road to claim the life of many a careless traveller and had, in the past, enjoyed its spoils in the form of maimed, helpless survivors only too glad to be rescued from the cold and accept the hospitality of my castle. The horses lay dead in the snow, their majestic bodies broken in the violence of the crash.

I approached the grim wreckage, feeling somewhat like a scavenger, and peered inside. Rather disappointingly, there were no bodies within, only blood—dark red and already frozen solid. I saw a long curved knife on the floor with a shattered ivory handle, and a length of sturdy rope soaked in blood. Most peculiar. I decided to go around the carriage, and discovered a trail of fresh blood in the snow, leading from the wreckage to the trees, presumably left by the passengers, who had apparently survived the crash and crawled away to nurse their injuries. On closer inspection of the snow, however, I came to the conclusion that the people had been dragged away from the equipage, since I could see neither handprints nor shoeprints.

The question was, who or what had dragged them away? I stared at the woods where the blood trail vanished, suddenly apprehensive. My vampire eyes penetrated the darkness, but I could see no bodies anywhere. I sensed, however, a peculiar, unfamiliar smell in the frigid air—acrid and earthy, but at the same time sickly sweet. A hot-blooded, organic smell. The storm had started to rage anew around me and the trail was fast disappearing beneath a thick layer of fresh snow.

I realized, then, that it had become unusually still and quiet, even for this time of the night. Every dark instinct told me that there was something lurking in these woods; something vile and eldritch, watching me from the gloom like an animal waiting to pounce. A creature, perhaps, of some dark and perverse origin, trespassing on land it had no right to spoil with its foreign presence, intent on savage acts it had no right to commit in my native country. A creature that had laid claim to spoils that by right belonged to me.

A rival.

Curiosity drove me forward. I ventured into the woods I considered my own, to investigate this supposed creature, presuming it to be the architect of the crash. The blood trail continued for some distance and soon I found myself deep within the quiet forest, where not even the piercing shrieks of the winds could reach me. It was pitch black and freezing cold, but my heightened senses helped me to find my way in the dark. The cold cannot hurt one who is not alive, of course, but the snow did slow me, as the drifts had grown monstrous during the long winter months. Finally the trail ended, rather abruptly and right in the middle of a clearing among the tall, majestic firs. It was as though the people had vanished into thin air! Thankfully I had enough presence of mind to look up, and what I saw shocked even one as ancient and powerful as myself.

An enormous spider's web, as big as a tent, hung from the thickest branch of the biggest fir tree, with four human shapes tightly wrapped inside it. I could see the dark outlines of their twisted bodies through the translucent tissue of the web. I must admit that in all my years on this earth I had never laid eyes upon such an otherworldly sight. Naturally I was anxious to examine the web and reveal its secrets, so I quickly climbed the tree and tore at the surprisingly thick, sturdy threads with my claws, all the while looking around for the thing that had spun it. The woods, however, continued to be deathly silent. I knew it must have been something monstrous in size and strength, in order to spin such a giant net. Some unknown—and unfamiliar— beast of the night who had caught four flies in its silken trap to feed on.

An image of a gargantuan man-eating spider appeared, unwanted, in my mind, but I dispelled it at once, for I knew no such creature existed in these lands. I examined the bodies and discovered that three of the people were dead—an elderly couple and their young son, judging by the similarity in features. The fourth victim was a girl, even younger than the boy, who also appeared dead at first, but my senses detected a thready pulse. I held my hand in front of her mouth to make certain of that and felt a weak, warm breath—probably the only source of warmth in the entire forest. Unlike the others, her thin body was neither broken nor covered in blood. She had escaped the crash with only a few superficial cuts and bruises to her cheeks, forehead and arms. I studied her features and concluded that she was the daughter of the family; her father, mother and brother were dead, but she was still alive, if only barely so. The woman and the girl were pale-skinned, fair-haired and possessed of a regal Nordic beauty, while the men were stout, short and swarthy, very much like the local mountainfolk.

Gazing at the girl and her proud, queenly features, frozen in a state between sleep and death, I felt an unfamiliar pang in my gut that had little to do with hunger. The curiosity and bloodlust that had brought me here had all but disappeared, supplanted by a most uncharacteristic concern for the well-being of a creature who I would normally drain of life without hesitation. The hunger <u>was</u> there, aroused to a fever pitch by the blood and carnage, but it seemed that something had overshadowed it, even tamed it: perhaps curiosity as to the nature of a beast capable of such hecatomb, or maybe the serene, striking beauty of the lone survivor that had transfixed me so completely.

Whatever the answer, I decided to rescue the girl from her silken tomb and bring her to my castle, rather than suck the life out of her, as I had initially intended. Perhaps I could restore her to consciousness and question her about the being that had attacked her carriage and slain her family. If indeed there was such a creature living in my woods and attacking my countrymen, I needed to know. These were my lands and my people, and I could tolerate no other monster preying on them.

I used my sharp claws to sever the strong, viscous bonds holding the girl, then carried her pale, near-weightless body down to the frozen ground. It was no easy work, wading up the steep incline with the snow flying in my eyes and the icy gusts constantly seeking to pry the limp body from my fingers. After nearly an hour I saw the jagged battlements of my fortress emerge from the squall like the skeletal remains of some ancient behemoth. I quickly crossed the dark courtyard, kicked the doors open and carried her inside my cold, empty castle. I climbed the south tower, which has always been the warmest, put her on the bed in one of the guest rooms and lit the fire. Then I gently undressed her and rubbed her chest, arms, neck and face with brandy, hoping that its warmth would thaw her back to life. I saw no signs of frostbite anywhere on her listless body. I cleaned the cuts and bruises, which were shallow and already healing. Her milky white skin was like delicate porcelain to the touch: smooth, but cold; hard, but brittle. Finally, after an hour of diligent work, her cheeks reddened, her eyes fluttered and I sensed her pulse quickening. I wrapped her in bear and wolf skins and moved the bed closer to the raging fire.

I waited. After another hour of staring, unblinking, at the arresting beauty of her face, my gaze began to wander around the vast circular room. Everything within it was covered with a thick layer of dust and was in an advanced state of disrepair. The walls were mouldy and the sideboards musty, and fat cobwebs hung from the ceiling like grey curtains. For the first time in centuries I felt shamefully conscious of the ruinous state of my ancestral home. It was as if the fair-haired maiden lying in my bed was a brilliant light, revealing the cruel truth of my surroundings—a pure white radiance against which all the jewels in the world would dim in compare.

Another uneventful hour passed before she stirred in her slumber. Her pallid countenance, so still and tranquil, began to ripple like the bright waters of a sun kissed river. Her exquisite eyelashes fluttered and her lips parted, revealing perfect white teeth, unaffected by age or decay. The movement of her breast hastened. I had to look away from her swanlike neck, for it was reddening and swelling with the blood of life.

As I stared at the wall and tried to ignore my stirring bloodlust, I heard a sharp intake of breath and when I turned, her pale blue eyes were fixed on me, wide with fear and surprise. I opened my mouth to speak, but when she saw my fangs, her eyes swelled with tears and her lips began to tremble. She was but a child; a helpless babe lost in the frozen wasteland! I moved to soothe her, but that only made her more afraid; she quivered like a dying leaf and fainted. That is how I left her for the night, sleeping by the roaring fire, her cheeks red with the heat, achingly beautiful in her serene abandon to shock and fatigue.

There was a small window outside her room and I stopped to admire the magnificent view. The tempest had subsided and the first golden rays of morning were climbing over the eastern peaks of the mountain, so that they shone like quicksilver. I could see the sky above them lightening. Praying that she would neither expire due to unseen injuries sustained in the crash nor leave the safety of the castle and perish in the harsh winter cold, I retreated to my coffin. Though I was exhausted, it took me the longest time to fall asleep. My mind constantly wandered back to the moment she had opened her eyes and looked upon me with such helplessness and horror. However hard I tried to think of something else, her angelic features would emerge from the darkness of sleep like a beacon of brilliant light, disturbing my languor and filling my head with doubts and unwanted thoughts.

At dusk I emerged from my coffin and immediately sought out my guest in the south tower. I found her wide awake and afraid, but she had not attempted to escape, perhaps because the terrible blizzard had started anew and fresh snow was blowing in earnest through the open window. She did not look as if she was in pain and the cuts and bruises had healed completely. The fire had died, and she was shivering from the cold. I quickly relit it, setting the damp wood aflame with my will.

Her eyes never left my face, not even for a moment, wide with dread and full of wonder. I approached the bed and this time she did not shrink from me, but her face became strangely blank and still. One of the wolf skins had fallen to the floor, so I picked it up and put it over her, then sat on the edge of the bed. After a while she stopped shivering and her teeth ceased to chatter.

"Who are you?" she asked in a surprisingly calm, quiet voice. She was local, judging by her accent. I noticed a heavy ring on the middle finger of her left hand: a gold serpent eating its own tail. I knew this Ancient Egyptian symbol very well—what the Greeks called the Ouroboros.

I surmised that she had judged me friend rather than foe, seeing as how I had taken care to keep her warm and snug under all those skins and firs.

"Who are you?" she repeated.

"I am... Dracula," I said, staring at her in anticipation of her reaction.

Her eyes became even wider, but then she nodded, not as affected or surprised by the answer as I had expected. She continued with the same serene voice.

"Do you intend to kill me?"

I was impressed by her icy composure. Yes, there was a fearful tremble in her tone, but her stare never wavered. Perhaps she only looked innocent and helpless...

"The reverse, in fact. I saved your life."

She frowned. "Where are my clothes?"

"I removed them. They were torn and soaking wet. They are over there, drying."

I pointed to the chair upon which I had deposited her clothes, before moving it closer to the fireplace.

"What happened?" she asked.

Suddenly there was a sharp edge to her voice, out of place in one as young and frightened as she'd appeared. Her eyes narrowed and her mouth became a thin red line.

"Your carriage was attacked," I replied. "You remember nothing?"

She shook her head. "No. Attacked by whom?"

I ignored the question. "Do you not even remember the blizzard?"

She looked out the window at the thick white curtain of snow and shivered. "No."

"What about your family? Your father, your mother and brother?"

Suddenly her face darkened and her eyes filled with tears. I assumed they were tears of sadness, but I could not have been more mistaken.

"What about them?"

There was that hard edge to her voice again, harder still. Colour rushed to her cheeks and she blinked the tears away.

"Are they here?"

She looked around, as if expecting to see them in the room.

"You remember nothing of the crash?" I inquired, trying to keep my thirst at bay, looking away from her swanlike neck and the throbbing blue veins within it. I could smell the hot blood rushing around inside her body.

She frowned and shook her head. A golden curl fell to her delicate shoulder.

"Your family is dead," I said.

For a long time she said nothing. She looked neither shaken nor sad. Her beautiful face was still, a mask. Finally her lips parted and she spoke.

"Did you kill them?"

"No. I came across the carriage by the side of the road. The horses were dead and there was blood. I found your family's corpses in the woods, suspended in a giant spider's web, spun in the branches of a tall tree. You were also caught in it, but you were still alive. I brought you here, in my home, to heal."

She swallowed. "But you are a vampire. You feast on helpless maidens such as myself. Why did you spare me?"

At first I was taken aback by this bold question. Then I leaned forward and bared my teeth. "You wish I had not?"

To my utmost surprise she did not flinch at the sight, but narrowed her eyes and pursed her lips again.

"I do not know what I wish," she said mournfully and looked away. She sighed, then wiped away a solitary tear with the back of her hand. "So you just left them there to rot?"

"Yes. They mean nothing to me. They will not rot; the cold will preserve them."

She nodded. "I see."

She shifted slightly under the covers and frowned.

"Are you in pain?" I asked.

"No," she replied. "But I am freezing."

"I shall bring you more wood for the fire," I said. "But first I need to know what caused your carriage to crash. You say you do not remember?"

I thought I saw the shadow of a sly little smile appear for a moment on her lips. "I do not. Perhaps it was the blizzard."

"Perhaps. Do you at least remember where you were heading?"

She shook her head. Her tears had dried; I was perplexed by how she was suddenly gazing at me—like a curious child examining an unexpected present.

"Your eyes are so red!" she said. "And you reek of the grave."

"I <u>am</u> of the grave!" I retorted, irritated by her fearlessness. I was used to features distorted by terror, and hands clasped in desperate prayer. "Bred in darkness and despair. Dead and yet alive, living by taking life."

"But you did not dare take mine."

I was furious. "You suggest I was <u>afraid</u> to do so?"

She blinked. "I suggest nothing. But you did spare me, for some reason. What was it?"

"You demand answers from your gaoler? You shall get none!" I shouted. I stormed angrily from the room, locking and bolting the heavy oak door behind me.

I WANDERED AROUND the castle for over an hour, angry at myself for being angry, lost in uneasy thoughts, torn by indecision. Her question echoed around inside my head, her voice strangely cold and distant, like the whisperings of ghosts. Her calm had unnerved me. I had expected terror and resignation. I was used to them; even hungered for them, in a way. But I had encountered curiosity and quiet calculation instead. Even defiance. And that was the true reason for my sudden loss of temper: my cheated expectations. After I regained my composure, I returned to her room with fresh wood for the fire and some food, but when I unbolted and opened the door, I discovered the fire red hot and blazing and all the dust and cobwebs gone. But she was still in bed and looked as though she had not moved since I had left her. Outside, the storm was raging, but there was no snow gathered on the windowsill, even though the winds had picked up speed and were howling like hungry beasts. I know my castle very well and was mystified, since there ought to have been a great pile of fresh snow on the floor.

"What do you intend to do with me?" the girl asked, with the same eerily calm voice as before. She seemed to have grown even more beautiful in the intervening hours—as pale and exquisite as a Greek statue and just as motionless.

I put the tray down on the table by the window and threw the wood on the fire. "You must eat," I said curtly, pointing at the roasted venison and sweet wine I had brought.

"I shall."

She moved to get out from under the covers, then remembered her nakedness and blushed violently. "My garments..."

I stared at her burning face, savouring her profound embarrassment, for it was, at long last, a genuine and welcome sign of vulnerability. Then I bent over the chair where her clothes were laid out to dry, picked them up and threw them on the bed.

"You are angry?" she asked with an arched eyebrow.

I remained silent.

"How have I angered you?"

I looked away.

"Please, tell me."

"Eat," I said and left her, once again bolting the door behind me.

But this time I was unsure as to the reason—because I was afraid that she would escape, or because I was afraid that she would follow me and demand an answer.

*   *   *

I MUST ADMIT, my friend, that I was at a loss as to what to do with her. I was at odds with myself and, as you might expect, shocked by my own unbecoming and indecisiveness. I lusted after her sweet young blood, but I lusted even more after her sweet young body. One could not exist without the other, but I wanted both. Her willfulness and perfect beauty made me weak and flustered. Yes, my friend. Weak! I desired her for myself, but we could not have been more dissimilar. She was the embodiment of radiance and virtue, I was darkness and depravity personified. She was but an innocent child of nature, I was ancient and immortal.

Perhaps her strength mirrored my weakness. Perhaps she drew confidence and courage from my soft indecisiveness. Perhaps she had found a chink in my armour and was exploiting it out of expedience, afraid for her life. Whatever the case might have been, the next time I entered her bedroom—for I viewed it as <u>hers</u> already—she was fully dressed and sitting in the chair by the fire, immersed in a book she had acquired I knew not how, since I recognized it as one of my own. But the library doors were locked and bolted! The food lay cold and untouched on the table. She looked up when I entered and grinned. It was the first time I had seen her smile, but it was well worth the wait. It made her look older, and even more alluring.

"Why have you not eaten?" I inquired.

She lowered the book and stared at me. I could feel the heat from her gaze on my cold dead skin. My anger melted like ice left in the sun.

"I have," was her answer. An obvious lie, issuing as sweetly as summer mead from her lips. I glanced at the book in her lap. It was one of my English books. A history of the city of London.

"How did you acquire this book? Have you left your quarters?"

"My cell, you mean."

My temper flared anew. "You are not to leave this room without my permission!"

Unmoved by my wrath, she simply stood before me, with a quizzical, almost superior expression on her face.

"Your eyes grow even redder when you are angry," she announced.

"Did you leave this room while I was away?"

"I did not."

She was used to lying; her voice did not so much as tremble as she uttered this bold untruth.

"So where did you find the book? I recognize it as one of my own. You must have taken it from the library downstairs!"

"No. I found it here on the table."

I moved closer. "You lie!" I hissed.

Her face grew very still. She did not shrink from me, but rather held her head high, stuck out her chest and said:

"I do not."

This time there <u>was</u> a flutter in her voice, but it was not a flutter of fear, but of anger. My perfectly reasonable accusation had offended her.

"How could I have left this room through the door you locked and bolted yourself?" she snapped. "I cannot pass through walls."

Her cold, hostile voice quickly cooled my anger. For the longest time we stared unblinkingly at one another, locked in a speechless, furious battle of wills. There was something of the serpent about her perfect stillness.

"Perhaps I left it here by mistake..." I muttered feebly. A craven admission, utterly unbecoming one as strong-willed as myself. She, in contrast, seemed uncharacteristically rigid and unyielding. Her penetrating, accusing gaze made me uneasy. I felt like a hunter caught in his own trap. Who was holding whom captive here? Who was questioning whom? "Did you perchance remember something more about the accident, and what might have caused it?" I continued.

She saw her chance and went on the offensive.

"No. <u>You</u> claim my equipage went off the road and my family was carried away and murdered by some strange creature of the night. I do not believe it, for I recall nothing of that nature. I do not believe you. However, I remember you bending over me with glowing red eyes and bared teeth. Are you not a creature of the night yourself? Have you not a reputation as a merciless murderer of innocent families? A reputation well deserved, as far as the people of my village are concerned."

Every single utterance of the word 'you' was like a sharp blade, hurled at me in spite. And they had all hit their mark.

"My reputation is indeed well deserved, as you will soon discover to your sorrow!" I growled and stormed out of her bedroom for the second and final time, not only bolting the door, but barricading it with a chair wedged under the door knob.

I spent the remainder of the night brooding over our tumultuous conversation, going over her responses in my mind, pacing up and down my empty halls, and all the while feeling her incandescence in the room above my head like a raging fire. There was indeed a fire— not in the south tower guestroom, but in my head, consuming my thoughts and turning my resolve into ash.

When I awoke the following evening, it was with a lighter heart than before, for I had made a decision in my sleep. I have always found that the wisest decisions are those made while the brain rests. Only in sleep, when that organ's mighty gaze is turned inward and undistracted by the outside world, is the brain truly free to think. So when I pushed open the heavy lid of my coffin, it was with a steady purpose, for I already knew what I had to do. I had decided to get rid of the girl and her uncanny influence over me once and for all! I intended to kill her by drinking her sweet blood and draining her body of life. I had little choice! I could either extinguish her radiant light or suffer to be incinerated in it. Her inexplicable power over me grew and grew, hour by hour, and I knew that it would eventually consume me, body and soul. Every time I looked upon her, I sank lower and lower beneath her feet, stupefied by her beguiling beauty. Every word she uttered was a poisonous missile aimed at my heart. The wounds she inflicted would suppurate, and the rot would spread, turning my free will into dust. She meant to make me her slave!

I, who have always been a master of men, subjugated by a simple village girl a hundred times younger! I, who have slain men uncountable and led armies undefeatable, subdued by a weak and feeble woman, wounded in a crash and half-frozen in a blizzard!

No! I was driven to action by sheer humiliation. I was prepared to extinguish her brilliant light and embrace the darkness anew; to restore my dignity by destroying this sweet, innocent child. I had to! I surrendered to the bloodlust, rushed up the tower steps like a furious wind, pushed the chair away, unbolted and unlocked the door and leapt inside the room, claws out and teeth bared, ready and eager to exsanguinate her on the spot.

To my utmost shock and disappointment, the room stood dark and empty. The bed was cold, the fire dead and under the gaping window—a mound of fresh snow!

I let out a furious scream and destroyed the room instead, growling and slavering like a wild animal on the rampage. I overturned the table, smashed the chairs to pieces, toppled the sideboard and tore the bed to shreds with my claws. Then I jumped out of the tower window and transformed, mid-fall, into a bat. I circled the castle on wings of swift rage, scanning the snow for tracks. Ere long my senses perceived a barely noticeable unevenness at the very edge of the forest. I quickly descended, transforming in flight and landing on my feet in front of a small set of footprints in the snow, undoubtedly left by her bare feet. The trail of prints led through the trees and I followed it, determined to catch up with her and exact a most terrible revenge for her betrayal. I was certain she could not escape me, least of all in my native woods, which I knew better than the back of my hand.

She had headed due south; by the depth of the impressions, and the distance between them, I deduced that she was not even running, but rather walking at a leisurely pace. What nerve! Despite the complete darkness and the extreme cold, she had not stopped or wavered even for a second, always heading south, past the Borgo pass, away from my fortress and the narrow road which had claimed the lives of her kin. Perhaps she meant to return to her native village and hide there. I pictured her walking through the trees in my mind's eye. Not wading through the snow, but rather treading lightly <u>upon</u> it, like a thing of air and mist. A weightless, disembodied spirit, shining in the dark like a torch. I felt the hunter's lust grip my heart and pour fire into my veins, and my haste and deadly resolve increased. I was determined to let nothing stand in the way of my justified wrath, even the uncommon feelings I had developed for the girl ever since I first perceived her exquisite beauty. Her tracks went higher and higher up the steep mountain, and the drifts I waded through became deeper and deeper.

Two more hours of silent ascent passed, but I was yet to see a glimpse of my prey and was beginning to feel apprehensive about the fast-approaching dawn. As yet there was no greying in the night sky, but my instincts told me that the first morning rays of deadly sunshine would be climbing over the jagged horizon in less than two hours. I knew these mountains as I knew my own castle—they were an extension of it—and I knew of no village so high up as this. I was proven spectacularly wrong, however, as you will soon find out, my friend!

After another half-hour had passed uneventfully, I took on the shape of a wolf, to grant me speed and stealth. Running on all fours, bobbing and weaving through the frozen trees, I followed her intoxicating scent higher and higher still, feeling the bloodlust even more acutely than before, surrendering to the primal instincts of a ferocious predator completely. My claws longed to tear at her flesh and my fangs were bared in anticipation of her warm, deceitful blood.

Then, to my utmost surprise, a tiny village emerged from the darkness, tucked away in a deep gorge between two pointed peaks, surrounded by tall fir trees and half-buried beneath thick snow. I counted twenty-seven dark houses, all huddled together and clinging desperately to each other, with a small empty square in their midst and a narrow steep road snaking between the trees, leading down the other side of the mountain into the valley below. Thick black smoke rose from the chimneys, and golden candlelight flickered in the windows. I quickly turned back into my human form and strolled among the houses, rapt with amazement and forgetting for a moment the bloody purpose of my journey. I was fascinated by the presence of this sleepy little village right at the heart of my hunting ground. I had been completely unaware of its existence up to now—I had no idea how the local people had managed to preserve their secret for so long. There was even a church! By far the tallest and grimmest building in the village, it was thin, black and windowless and rather looked like an etched blade driven deep into the frozen earth by a giant's hand. There was even a bell tower, though I had never heard its toll.

As I was walking among the cottages, I glimpsed black silhouettes darting inside and heard fearful whispers and the shushing of small children. Ere long all candles were extinguished and I heard the unmistakable sounds of swords being unsheathed and heavy axes being taken off walls. I sensed eyes watching me from the dark and following my progress. The houses gave out warmth and I could smell the blood of all those who resided within them, huddled together like animals. I took notice of the fact that all the doors were made of heavy reinforced oak and were locked and bolted, and all the windows had iron bars and thick iron shutters.

I could sense great fear here, simmering under the surface like an underground river of fire. Greater than I had ever known. And I was not the cause; that much I could surmise. These people were not afraid of vampires—I saw no Christian crosses painted on their doors and no garlic wreaths hung above them. They were terrified of something else. The fear was ancient and deep. These people had been living with it from time immemorial, passing it on from one generation to the next, same as a craft or a custom. A fear that was as much a part of their daily lives as the pursuit of warmth and the trapping of beasts.

I walked onto the little village square and approached the strange-looking monument which occupied its centre—a misshapen stone cross with a dozen river-polished rocks piled all around it. There was an inscription on the cross and just as I was about to bend over and read it, the thick oak doors of the church burst open and a man with a long black beard walked out onto the square to meet me. The village priest. He was tall, dark and uncommonly strong and virile for a priest. He appeared to be a warrior of men rather than a warrior of God, with his stout frame and determined features; I could picture him more easily holding a heavy sword than a dusty hymn book. As he approached, the iron cross in his clenched fist glinted in the moonlight. He hoisted it and shouted:

"Stay back! Do not corrupt this holy place with your evil influence!"

He had a deep, booming voice not unlike my own. Indeed, he was a brave and powerful man, but also a fool, for he was at my mercy, cross or no cross. Though strong, he was still a mere man: mortal and vulnerable as all the rest of them.

"What is this place?" I asked.

He ignored my question. "We are grateful for what you have done, Count, but we seek no further quarrel with you and we shall defend ourselves as best we can."

"I do not know what you mean. What have I done that deserves your gratitude? A minute ago I did not even know this place existed."

"Yes, but even so, you have delivered us from great evil. Greater even than yourself."

These words intrigued me, as unfathomable as they seemed at the time.

"What is this evil of which you speak?"

The priest lowered the cross, but only slightly; and only because his hand had started shaking with dread. His pale blue eyes had grown dark and all the blood had drained from his face. "It is an ancient evil under a modern guise," he said in a fearful whisper. "An evil that has devastated our village and terrified our people. An evil that knows neither Christian mercy nor human decency."

I took a step forward and he raised the cross again. "Stay back, I said!"

"An evil that spins webs of silver thread and devours people whole?" I asked.

He nodded darkly. "Indeed."

"Start at the beginning, then," I instructed him. "I wish to know the complete story. When did this evil first appear in your village?"

"In its present guise? Only a year ago, to the day."

"What happened?"

"A child disappeared. A young girl. On the next day we found her in the woods, high up in one of the trees, wrapped in a vast spider's web. Her body was mummified and hollowed out, her insides gone. There were no traces in the snow immediately below the tree. No traces at all! Ten days after we buried her, her little brother vanished from his crib in the night. We found him on the following day in the same condition, his little body desiccated and drained of all vital fluids the web even higher up an old spruce tree. Again, no traces of the perpetrator were discovered. We believed it to have been some wild animal unknown to us, but there were those who insisted that we were dealing with an evil intelligence, pointing to the fact that the second child had been abducted from a room with a locked door and a bolted window. The third and fourth victim were twin boys, stolen from their bedroom while their parents ate supper next door. Again, the window had been closed and its shutters bolted, and the door had been in full view of the mother and father the entire time. There had been no earthly means of ingress, yet somehow the monster had passed through a solid wall to spirit the twins away. We found them three days later, dead and half-eaten, their little faces distorted by mortal terror.

"Soon after that the mayor's nine-year-old daughter disappeared from her room in broad daylight in the presence of her mother and grandmother, who were discovered flat on their backs and out cold. Their faces were red raw and covered in blisters, as if they had been sunburnt. In the middle of January! When they regained consciousness we questioned them. They remembered blinding white light and the girl screaming... and then darkness and a terrible, blood-curdling laugh. We formed a search party of all able-bodied men in the village, armed ourselves with whatever we could find and combed the entire forest, going so far as to encroach on the lands around your castle. It took us nearly a month, but we finally discovered the mummified remains of the missing child in a hemlock tree deep inside the forest. When we returned, another little girl had been snatched. The last one. The last child in the village. She had been kept under lock and key in the basement of the mayor's cottage, which had the thickest walls and sturdiest doors. But the monster, whatever it was, had no fear of either walls or doors. The girl had once again been spirited away from a locked room in the presence of her mother and two elder sisters, who had been knocked unconscious and badly scorched. We were bereft with grief and consumed with anger. The parents were inconsolable."

The priest shook his head in sorrow and lowered the iron cross. And at that instant I knew. I knew what had happened to the girl I had rescued. She had not fled from my castle, fearing for her life, but had been abducted from her locked bedroom in the south tower by the very same creature terrorizing this village and its inhabitants! I had failed her. I had been called upon to save and protect her, but had done

213

neither. And now she was, in all probability, dead or dying, wrapped in a silvery cocoon up some tall tree deep within the forest.

"Almost nine months passed without further incident," the priest continued. It had started to snow again, but he took no heed. "Then a new baby was born. I cannot begin to describe how diligently this little boy was protected and how attentively we all watched over him. It made no difference in the end, of course. The child vanished in the same fashion as all the others, this time from the cellar of the very church you see behind me. The fiend entered my church! Even <u>you</u> cannot enter it! We were desperate to find the culprit and to rid ourselves and our village from this evil presence once and for all. We were tired of living under a pall of fear. A savage thirst for vengeance invaded our souls and bled poison into our hearts. We fell under its wicked spell, one and all. I am ashamed to admit that I joined the chorus of voices demanding bloody retribution. Even the gentle and forgiving women allowed the lust for vengeance to overcome them. Most of them joined us as we formed another search party and scoured the woods again, this time with the help of a hunter we hired from a town three valleys over, determined to find this child-murdering monster and tear him limb from limb. And again to no avail. We killed dozens of wolves, lynxes and bears, but there was no monster to be found. And when two months later we returned home, exhausted, frostbitten and despondent, we discovered that all but one of the remaining women had been abducted. Vanished without a trace, just like their children before them!"

The priest's eyes welled up with bitter tears.

"It seems to me that you were searching without for something that resided within," I said softly.

He gave me a dark look, then nodded dolefully.

"Who was the lone survivor?" I asked.

"The mayor's other daughter. A girl, no more than seventeen years of age."

I had expected as much. "What did she say had happened?"

"She said she remembered nothing. And we believed her... at first. But there was something odd about her. She seemed distant and indifferent, and not at all surprised to see us return empty-handed. By her own admission she had been living alone in the village for days, but seemed completely unperturbed by her ordeal. At first we took it for numbness from shock, but it was something else. Something much more sinister. I noticed how hungrily she stared at one of the women who had come on the trip with us. The one who had come back with child."

The priest swallowed and shook his head.

"There was something altogether unsettling about that girl: the sly smile that seemed to be constantly playing on her lips, the unnerving way she seemed to... for lack of a better word... glow..."

Suddenly I was grinning. "Glow?"

Could it be true? Was it possible? Not even in my wildest dreams...

"Yes. I was not the only one who noticed it. Other people also thought her behavior strange. All the women, in fact; at least, those that remained. The men seemed to be enchanted, even entranced by her! They all started acting like amorous boys around her, constantly showering her with gifts and following her around like faithful dogs. Even the mayor, her own father, began... looking lustfully at her. At his own daughter! I and the women attempted to convince the others that there was something wrong with the girl. At first they refused to believe us, but then we found the bones."

The priest was silent for a moment, staring solemnly at his feet.

"Bones?"

He nodded. "Yes. Piles of bones. Hundreds of them. Maybe thousands. Animal and human. Buried deep underground. You were right, Count. We should have looked inwards, rather than outwards. But we are a close-knit community. We must be, in order to survive this high up in the mountain. We are used to dangers coming from without: ravenous wolves and hungry bears, violent storms and sudden avalanches. Cold snaps and harsh winds. But we are not used to dealing with dangers from within."

"You searched the cottages," I said.

"Yes. The monster was not lurking in the woods that surrounded us, but living in plain sight in our very midst! It was the mayor's longsuffering wife who finally suggested searching the village. And we did. We found the mass grave, if you could call it that, in the cellar of an abandoned cottage belonging to a family that had perished from smallpox two winters ago. The bones were buried deep within the frozen earth of the cellar, wrapped up in the same silvery threads that made up the cocoons. And for the past several months, the mayor's daughter had used this same cottage, this very charnel house, to dry herbs and prepare ointments and potions for her ailing grandmother. She was gifted in the healing arts, you see. That should have been our first clue."

I could barely contain my excitement. "She was a witch?"

"An evil, vile witch! A child-eating murderess, hiding behind a pretty mask of purity and virtue! A child of Satan and a direct descendant of the warlock who founded this village, more than a thousand years ago."

Yes! It all made sense now: a warlock's curse had kept this village hidden from me all these years!

"Yes!" continued the priest. "The girl was a witch and a monster! A thing of unspeakable, unimaginable cruelty! Walking among us, preying on us! Spreading its repugnant influences and satanic agencies! Corrupting and contaminating our souls! Bathing in the blood of the innocent! Beguiling and depraving the men, snatching and slaughtering the women and children!"

The reverse of myself, I thought, for I have been known to beguile and deprave the women and snatch and slaughter the men. This dark and disturbing tale was becoming better by the minute. Was it really possible for such a formidable beast to inhabit my lands unbeknownst to me? My excitement quickened at the very thought.

"But what did you do?" I asked.

"We had no choice. We had to destroy her. Some of the men fought us. All of them, in fact, except her chaste, noble brother. The mayor forbade us from touching a hair on her golden head—he was under her spell. In the end the women had to take matters into their own hands. Her own mother, the mayor's wife, devised a plan. She concocted a powerful sleeping draught out of belladonna leaves and dried cloudberry skins and surreptitiously fed it to her daughter. The instant the witch lost consciousness, her magic broke and the rest of the men came to their senses. But then another problem arose. How to dispose of her? Nothing seemed to work. She was impervious to all our attempts to end her life, not matter how savage. Her body was not of this world! We tried stabbing her in the heart, burning her, drowning her, beheading her, crushing her with heavy rocks, strangling her by the neck. Even feeding her powerful poison. Nothing seemed to work."

I admit I was impressed. I had known a number of witches in my lifetime, as it were, but I had never known one so powerful. Even I, who am essentially omnipotent and immortal, am susceptible to certain holy weapons and ancient methods of extermination.

"You say she could not be killed?"

"Yes. Her body was invulnerable. The blades broke, the fire died out, the water evaporated, the rocks turned into dust. The hands burned the moment they touched her skin. The arsenic did not even slow her breathing. Finally her grandmother suggested taking her to you."

I started. "To me? Why?"

"She said that only one as powerful as the witch herself would be able to banish her back to hell. Fighting fire with fire and evil with evil, as it were. So her father, mother and brother volunteered to undertake the perilous journey to your castle—risking their own deaths at your hands, a price they were willing to pay for the good of the village. Their sacrifice will forever live in our memory and the memories of our children and our children's children. We will never forget them in our prayers as long as we live, and there will be a monument honouring their sacrifice as long as a village stands here." He pointed at the stone cross in the middle of the little square. "That is why we shall be eternally grateful to you, Count, for ridding us of this terrible evil..."

I found it difficult to contain my merriment. I suppose I must have smirked, because he flinched then, unnerved. This fool thought he could fight fire with fire and remain unscathed. He thought he could direct and deceive dark forces he could not even begin to comprehend. Such is the folly of mortal men—they know nothing, but act as if they know everything.

"The girl you speak of is alive and well, my friend," I said, very much savouring the change that suddenly came over him. His eyes widened in shock and his jaw dropped. "She must have awoken during the journey and lashed out at those who had sought to destroy her. I found her unconscious among their corpses. The equipage must have gone off the road in the struggle. She had managed to slay her treacherous relatives, but the injuries sustained in the crash had momentarily incapacitated her, exhausted as she was from the effort of fighting three people at once. I, of course, carried her to my castle and nursed her back to health."

"You nursed her back to health?" the priest shouted, his eyes bulging in terror. "But she is a monster!"

"So am I, you foolish peasant!" I roared, incensed. "You dare presume to use me as your attack dog? Unworthy worm! Kneel before me, or I shall take your head for my mantelpiece!"

He raised the cross, quaking like a leaf in a powerful gale.

"Stand back, spawn of Satan! I warn you!"

I bared my fangs, which made him blanch.

"You? Warn <u>me</u>? Who do you think you are, priest?"

"I am a man of God!" he spat, going red in the face.

At that instant something bright and heavy fell on him from above, like lightning splitting a tree. His body was crushed beneath its weight with a sickening wet crunch. His foolish head cracked open and his brains spilled out onto the snow and mixed with his ignoble blood. It was a glorious sight.

She stood on his broken corpse, terrible and beautiful, a goddess of sadistic malevolence, her eyes glowing like blue fire, her exquisite mouth curved into a rapacious grin, her angelic features assuming a predator's merciless ferocity.

"Good morning, Count," she said, in a crisp and clear voice that carried around the hushed square like the tolling of a funeral bell.

"Good morning, my dear!" I replied with a deep bow, extending my arm. She took it and stepped off the pile of broken bones and pulverized flesh. Her touch was warm and smooth, but firm. I gazed at her, mesmerized by her regal beauty and enthralled by the savage bloodlust I could see shining in her eyes.

"Forgive the interruption," she said and her lips formed a thin, vulturous smile, "but it did not seem you were getting along."

"I was just about to punish him for his insolence."

"Insolence was not the cause of my disagreement with him. He endeavoured to murder me, inciting others, more feeble-minded even than himself, to do the work in his stead. A coward to boot."

"So I gathered. Unsuccessfully, for which I am glad."

"Of course." She looked me up and down, frowning, and I saw how the flakes of snow melted the instant they touched her shiny golden head. "I hope you will forgive my abrupt departure from your tower," she said loftily. "I am indeed grateful for your hospitality and care."

Her icy, superior tone struck me as insincere and affected; there was heat bubbling underneath. "Then why did you jump out of the window?" I asked, trying to keep the reproach out of my voice.

"I did not. I flew out. But I should have thought the reason for my leaving perfectly obvious. I did not know whether I could trust you. You were part of the plot to get rid of me, after all. The crux of it, in fact. Those hungry looks you gave me did not go unnoticed, dear Count. And the way you licked your chops whenever your sombre gaze found my neck."

My gaze inadvertently found her neck again. I simply could not resist its charms. The scent of her hot young blood was overwhelming.

"But if you feared me—"

"Mistrusted, never feared."

I smiled. "Then why did you stay in my castle beyond the first night? Your injuries were not that grave. You could have easily escaped the very same night I brought you in to recuperate."

She narrowed her luminous eyes. "Recuperate? You brought me in to question me and then to satisfy your thirst for blood!"

"True," I admitted. "But my question remains. Why stay?"

She blinked and that sly smile made another fleeting appearance. "I was curious about you."

"Curious?"

"Yes. I wished to know more about you. I wished to... find out what sort of creature you were."

"I thought my reputation..."

"Your reputation is well deserved, dear Count, but does you great injustice."

"I do not follow."

"You are not the scarecrow people make of you. Your legend has turned you into a monument. A monument to evil, yes, but a thing of stone and mortar nevertheless. Immovable: grand and threatening, but stiff and languid. However, the truth I discovered was different. You are so much more! Not a statue at all, but alive with anger and lust and craving and pride. You are an elemental force. A storm, full of evil purpose, raging and rampaging, ravishing and ravaging the land. A wicked intellect the likes of which the world has never known. A creature of dark beauty and awesome power. A thing of the grave and proud of it!" She looked over her shoulder. "And now, if you would excuse me, I have some unfinished business to attend to here."

She turned away, leaving me speechless, and strode towards the closest cottage, with bloody-minded purpose. After a moment, I found my tongue and asked:

"May I help you finish it?"

She answered without stopping or turning.

"You can accompany me, but you must not interfere. They are mine to punish."

She rapped on the heavy door and waited.

"They will never open willingly," I said, thinking of the priest and his dramatic demise not minutes ago.

"They shall. People are sheep. And now that I have killed their shepherd, the flock is leaderless. They will not know what to do. See?"

The door was slowly unlocked and unbolted. The man who came out to greet us was big and strong; he hoisted a heavy double-edged axe in his meaty hands.

"Stand back, witch, or you shall feel the swing of my axe!" he bellowed, but his voice shook with fear and his eyes were bulging. "You will not desecrate my house with your vile presence!"

"Foolish peasant!" she snapped, raising her left arm. A string of silver thread shot out from her open palm, wrapped itself around the man's mouth and nose and brought him forcefully to his knees. He dropped the axe and began desperately pulling and clawing at the thing with his fingers, but to no avail. Smothered, he died in a matter of seconds, writhing on the ground, kicking and moaning in pain. When it was over, the witch bent over his corpse, which began to decompose before my very eyes. The skin darkened and withered, the hair fell out, the arms and legs shriveled and the chest sank. I moved closer and saw a long semitransparent leathery tube, not much larger than a finger, driven into his neck. The other end of the tube disappeared somewhere beneath her clothes. After she had drained him, she stepped over his wilted remains and went inside the house, rubbing her hands together with evident glee; but emerged a minute later, disappointment writ large on her face.

"Only his ailing father," she sighed, then looked over to the next house and licked her lips.

"If you kill them all now, what will you eat come next winter?" I asked her. "Leave some alive, so they can procreate and supply you with fresh food later on."

She pondered this.

"Wise words, Count. But there are far too many of them still breathing. Do not forget that they tried to murder me. Maybe I shall leave ten or fifteen of them. Or perhaps one from each family. But the rest will pay."

She set about her task with a greedy, hungry air, going from cottage to cottage like the plague itself. I noticed no change in her appearance and had to wonder what became of all the flesh and viscera she consumed. After the seventh murderous visit I began to feel apprehensive. The sun was slowly creeping up the peak under whose shadow the village was nestled, and would soon emerge to scorch me with its pernicious rays. I estimated that if I started immediately, I would barely have enough time, even downhill, even as a wolf, to run the distance to my castle.

I finally stood before her and said mournfully:

"Unfortunately I must now leave you."

She stopped dead in her tracks and stared at me, her eyes alive with feeling. "Leave me?"

"The dawn will break soon and I must flee."

"You? Flee?"

"Yes. Even I."

She lowered her eyes and smiled. "Why go all the way to your castle to sleep?" she whispered softly. "Why not sleep here with me?"

My mouth went dry. I dared not believe my ears. Her smile became wider and she raised her head. She met my transfixed gaze and blushed, but did not look away. My head exploded with the sound of a thousand bells tolling in unison. I could sense her tender pulse quickening. The scent of her blood became unbearable. It was like a trumpet call to battle.

"Am I correct in thinking that it is native soil and darkness that you require?" she asked quietly, reveling in the blush like a maiden in love.

"That is so," I replied, hardly recognizing the voice as my own.

She extended her arm, all thoughts of deadly retribution clearly forgotten.

"Then I know the perfect place. Follow me... my love."

I took her delicate hand, burning with desire, and followed her to a dark cottage at the very edge of the village. I surmised it was the one she had used to dry herbs and prepare remedies. She led me to the cellar and showed me a great black fissure in the very rock upon which the village stood: a cave as old as time itself and as deep as the oceans. The air smelled of damp earth and ancient stone, iron ore and black magic. We trod on bones that reeked of death and putrefaction and whispered lovingly to each other. That is where we consummated our union, in the stygian darkness, in the cold stone belly of the mountain, knee-deep in bones, surrounded by the restless spirits of all the people she had slain. She undressed before me, slowly, majestically, never taking her shining eyes from mine. Despite the utter darkness, I saw every detail of her exquisite white body; her silver skin glowed like the moonlight had assumed human form.

"This will be the first and only time, dear Count," she uttered softly as she stood before me, proud and unabashed.

I frowned, barely containing my excitement. Inside my body, a storm was raging.

"Why?"

"That is my destiny. I cannot escape it."

I took her naked body in my arms. "Then it will be my destiny also."

I kissed her, and she smiled inside my kiss. "Beware that you do not burn yourself playing with this fire, dear Count."

"If self-immolation is the price, I am more than willing to pay it," I replied.

And then it happened. She transformed into the marvelous monster that she was. I was dumbstruck with awe and adoration. She was even more gruesome and magnificent that I had imagined! Mere words cannot convey her savage, inhuman beauty! A creature of dark potency and immense power. A Druid queen, born to rule the living, as I was a vampire king destined to reign over the dead. A match made in Hell!

Afterwards we lay together on a bed of fine silk thread, breathing as one and thinking as one, wallowing in wordless bliss deep within the mountain's dark bosom. I could feel the great Carpathian forest silently watching over us, and the entire underworld of beasts and monsters sharing in our moment of marital harmony. It was as if all the creatures of the night had paused to welcome their new King and Queen, and Nature herself was standing attendance upon us, savouring our morbid union.

"I am with child," she proclaimed at last, shattering the perfect silence into pieces. She took my hand and placed it over her belly, which was so warm and hard I pictured hot coals inside it rather than a baby.

"I am glad," I said, which was the truth. It had never occurred to me before that I could father children, but now I had, the thought was strangely pleasing. "But how do you know?"

"A mother always knows. In three days I shall bear three children. All of them girls."

"I am glad. It will be an honour to be their father."

"And then I shall die."

A long, terrible silence followed this pronouncement. I was speechless again and, for the first time since I could remember, overcome by dread. The thought of losing her caused me physical pain.

"That cannot be!" I protested, my voice shaking with emotion.

She stiffened in my arms. "But it <u>shall</u> be! It is my destiny and my nature, dear Count. You cannot change your destiny any more than you can change your nature."

"Neither is set in stone!" I said. "Nature changes all the time! And men have always striven to usurp their fate and escape the shackles of destiny!"

"Mortal men!" she spat with disdain and indignation. "Mortal men are foolish. We are not."

"You will perish giving birth to them?" I asked, choking on the words as if they were stones.

"No. I will perish giving life to them."

I took her hand in mine and squeezed. "I do not understand, my love. Why must you die?"

"So they can live. One life in exchange for three. I think it a good bargain."

"Do not speak so cavalierly about your life!" I said with a trembling voice. "It is much too precious to be bargained away!"

She laughed. "My life is but a link in a chain, as is yours. We are all of us expendable, as long as the chain remains unbroken. The dance of life must continue."

"There must be another way!"

"There is no other. I have seen into the future and I have decided."

"It cannot be your destiny if it is a choice!"

"It is my destiny to make that choice. When you fled the approaching dawn, was that a decision you made? No, it was your destiny to flee! We cannot escape our nature and we must obey its rules."

"But our very nature is unnatural!"

"Only in the eyes of mortal men. But they are ignorant and do not realize that we, who are creatures of the night, are just as much a part of Nature as they are. We simply occupy a position above them in Nature's order. We are the predators and they our prey."

"But..."

"You are the living-dead proof, my love. You are the proof that death is natural. You are the proof that death is destiny. And I shall embrace both in three days' time."

"No! I am the proof that death can be deceived and conquered! I am the proof that death is not destiny, only a stepping stone towards a different kind of life. I am the proof that you can change your destiny and escape the tyranny of the laws of Nature! Why must you die, my love? Why must you sacrifice yourself? Why must you succumb to the vulgar weaknesses of the flesh?"

She sighed and caressed my cheek. Her hand was warm and soft. I relished her heavenly touch, trying not to think of a future time when I would have to exist without it.

"Because I am ready," she said softly. "And I prefer it. And I know that you will be a wonderful father, my love."

"You prefer it? You prefer death and oblivion to eternity with me in our castle?"

She put her hand over my mouth.

"Quiet, my love. I know that it hurts, but you must be strong. Let us savour this moment and not spoil it with futile regrets. It is as it should be. You know as well as I do that death does not mean oblivion. I will continue living in our children, in their hearts and minds. My blood will flow through their veins. My magic will flow through their blood. Flesh is fleeting; blood is eternal. My memory will live on. Forever."

My eyes welled up with hot tears. Yes, my friend. Tears! I was weeping for the first time since I could remember, and my black heart was breaking.

"Indeed it will," I said. "But I will miss you."

She lovingly caressed my cheek again. "And I you, my dark prince."

We kissed. And it was magical in more ways than one.

IT HAPPENED EXACTLY as she had foretold. Three days hence she laid three gigantic eggs, as big as beehives, one black and two white, in a nest she made for herself in the bowels of my castle, out of silver silk and human skin. After three more days of brooding, during which time she only drank fresh blood and warm honey, the eggs hatched. Three beautiful babies emerged from their leathery sacs, mewling and squinting at the blinding light radiating from their mother.

The two white eggs produced two identical dark-haired girls with glowing black eyes, while the dark egg contained a fair-haired little babe with pale blue eyes and translucent skin. The witch bathed them, licking them clean with her own tongue, then called me over to claim and admire them. She looked drowsy and tired, but joyous and content. I knelt before her, my face a mask of dumb delight, reached into the nest and held the triplets. They were warm and squirming in my trembling arms, tiny morsels of tender flesh with big heads and luminous eyes. Perfect in every way! I was speechless with joy, unable to express the warm feeling of happy pride swelling in my bosom. They ceased bawling when I held them and met my gaze as an adult would. They instantly knew me as their father and protector. They were so beautiful! And so strong! Each one had the iron grip of an eagle and the steady gaze of a ravenous wolf preparing to strike. And their newborn scent! They smelled of fresh snow, cold rock, moist earth and warm blood.

I could not take my eyes off their puffy little faces. I felt immediate love for them, profound and unquestionable. At that moment I knew I would do anything for them, even sacrifice my own life for theirs. I embraced them, for they were mine. The little darlings certainly knew their father, for I could swear they embraced me back! Then I looked upon their mother, my loving bride, who was beaming next to me.

"They are perfect," I whispered.

"Of course."

"They will rule the night!"

"Yes."

I embraced her. "Our children. Children of the night!"

"Yes."

By the time I had finished marveling at our offspring, she was fast asleep in my arms, with a placid smile on her beautiful face. She slept for three hours, during which time the triplets became more and more restless and unhappy. Finally they began shaking their tiny fists at me, thrashing about and crying out as if in pain. I was at a complete loss as to what to do. In the end I had to shake their mother awake. When she opened her eyes and saw them in their distress, her smile vanished and she looked upon me with such sadness I nearly choked.

"It is time," she uttered and sighed.

"Time for what, my love?"

"My time to die; theirs to feed. They are hungry and I must be their first meal. You must kill me and they shall do the rest. They might be only hours old, but their instincts will guide them even better than I could."

I was aghast at this.

"I cannot take your life! It is precious to me!"

"You must. Otherwise you risk theirs. The only nourishment they can tolerate is their mother's flesh."

"No!"

"It is the truth. They must consume my body and absorb my magic. But I cannot take my own life. I am not strong enough. You must do it."

"I refuse. I cannot harm you."

"Then you will harm them!"

She pointed at the three little darlings mewling at her breast.

The thought of killing her appalled me, sent paroxysms of grief throughout my body. In my despair I turned to her and begged:

"Please. There must be some other way! Why can't we feed them peasants?"

"So they should grow up to become peasants?" she spat at me. "Is that what you want for your children? To be common peasants?"

"No!"

"To be sheep and not wolves? Weak and not strong? Gutless and not fearless?"

"No! A thousand times no!"

"Then you must do it! They must eat of me to become like me! To absorb my powers and inherit my sorcery."

"But why me? Why should I commit the deed? I am your beloved!"

Her eyes flashed.

"Exactly for that reason, my love! Murder forges a sacred bond between victim and slayer. A bond as strong as love and twice as enduring. If you kill me, our union will be doubly cursed—it will outlast time itself! Our love will live forever!"

I hung my head in dark dejection. "Killing you will devastate me," I whispered. "I will never be the same."

She moved a little closer, reached up and raised my chin.

"Only if you fight it. Only if you resist it. If you embrace it, if you open your heart to it, you might even take pleasure in it."

"Pleasure? Take pleasure in destroying my one and true love? Never!"

"But you must! Open your heart, my love. Think about the children. Think about your offspring. Think about your legacy!"

I thought long and hard, but nothing could make the idea of ending her life seem even remotely tolerable. Losing her was terrible enough, but the thought of slaying her with my own hands was akin to torture. I felt pain, true physical pain, imagining a life without her. I felt weak and cowardly enough to beg for mercy. To plead with her to reconsider, and relieve me of this great burden. My thoughts grew more and more desperate and my resolve began to waver, but finally the hungry cries of my children became too much for me to bear. I sighed and said:

"I see that I have no choice. There is nothing I can say that would dissuade you. What do you require me to do?"

She nodded, pleased. "Killing me would be difficult, even for you. My body is cursed; it will fight you back, even if my soul is willing. There are only three ways of killing me that guarantee my death. Three ways to bring about my lasting extinction, each more difficult and hazardous than the next. The first way is to destroy me with magic more powerful than my own. For you, that would be impossible, for you are not a sorcerer. The second is to drown me in the blood of seventy-seven young virgins. But that requires time and effort we cannot spare. You must therefore take the third way, which is the most dangerous and arduous. You must pierce my still-beating heart with the living bone of my one true love."

"Living bone?"

"Still attached to the living body. The index finger would be quickest; you must skin it and strip the flesh. Perhaps sharpen it, because the heart is a tough and hardy muscle. Then you must stab me in the chest with it and pierce the heart. I can make it so you feel no pain."

"No. I will welcome the pain. It will distract me from the horror of what I have to do. Will it hurt you?"

"I shall cherish the pain, my love. Are you ready? Shall I fetch you a sharp knife?"

"No need," I said and smiled, the crooked, hopeless smile of the condemned. "I can do it with the claws of my other hand."

"Then do it, my love. Do it and be done with it!"

I proceeded to cut the skin of my index finger and peel it back, revealing the crimson flesh underneath. Then I started stripping the bloody meat off with my claws. The pain was exquisite, like an ever-rising crescendo that muffled my doubts and numbed my sorrow. Finally the bone was bare and I sharpened it with a whetstone, turning it more or less into a stabbing weapon.

After I had finished, my radiant bride crawled towards me and embraced me as I knelt, spattered with blood and viscera. She was freezing cold to the touch; so cold, in fact, that she burned. Her eyes were alight with feeling, and when she kissed me, I felt hot tears on her cheeks. They were tears of joy rather than sorrow—that knowledge sustained me. I shall always remember the look she gave me as she lay on her back and opened her breast for me. A look of unconditional love and utter devotion. She was as still as a statue, but her eyes stayed open and never left my face, even as I raised my arm, ready to strike. I saw not a tremor in those bright, adoring eyes. Not a shadow of doubt, nor a shudder of fear. Just loving care and absolute devotion.

I bent down and kissed her burning lips for the last time, then said, my voice creaking under the weight of my grief:

"I shall always love you, my queen."

And I struck.

Her lips parted and her eyes widened. Her body heaved and dark blood poured from the hole I had opened in her breast. Her arms and legs thrashed violently and the angry wound grew in size and depth. She opened her mouth and tried to speak, but no sound escaped her lips. The white flesh of her bosom hardened, withered and split with a terrible sound, revealing the ribcage underneath. The pierced heart beat faster and faster, gushing hot, dark blood: an ugly, cruel sight. A powerful scent of burning flowers rose in the air, and thick white smoke billowed out of her mouth.

Then, suddenly, she was still. Her eyes glazed over, the thrashing ceased and the beating of the heart stopped. The blood quickly clotted around my hand, turning black and viscous.

It was over. My queen was dead.

Then it was the children's turn. They immediately descended upon the corpse and started tearing it to shreds with tiny claws I hadn't known they had. Their eyes shone with glee and their bellies rumbled with hungry anticipation. They were terribly efficient, working together rather than squabbling as other children would. It was a grisly sight to see them wolf down the raw flesh of their mother, tearing away chunks of flesh and cramming them down their tiny throats. Grisly, but oddly satisfying.

While they were so engaged, I looked upon the face of my dead wife and saw that she was smiling.

When the feast was finally over, all that remained of her was her skeleton. The babies crawled away, engorged and covered in blood, then started burping, licking one another and purring. Ere long they fell asleep in a heap of pudgy white flesh, sated and content. I took her perfectly preserved skeleton in my arms and wept. It was my last time. Then I buried it beneath the nest, in my native soil, deep within the bowels of my castle, in a beautiful marble sarcophagus I had specially made and shipped from Greece. It was just as smooth and white as her precious skin had been.

PARENTHOOD IS NOT for everyone, my friend. Raising my wonderful daughters has been difficult, but gratifying. They are growing so fast! Only yesterday I had to teach them how to hunt woodland creatures and drink their blood, and today they are exsanguinating whole families and decimating entire villages. They have voracious appetites and absolutely no mercy for the people of my land. Nor should they have. They are particularly partial to babies, who they sometimes gobble up whole.

At first I thought they would grow up to be vampires like me, but their nature is far more exotic. And more savage! Despite their tender age, they are already quicker and more perceptive than me and have better hearing and eyesight, which makes them formidable hunters. They spin webs of silver thread just like their mother and even travel in that fashion, in ways I cannot even begin to comprehend, becoming silvery threads on the wind.

When they hunt, they sometimes bite their victims on the neck and suck their blood out just like a vampire, but other times they would take them up a tree, encase them in a cocoon and slowly drain them, leaving only a mummified husk behind. And they always hunt together; always. They do everything together. They are inseparable, and unstoppable, sharing an understanding which dooms any person, no matter how strong or skilled in combat, attempting to escape their clutches. They absorb and master everything I teach them about the craft of hunting and killing, but they improvise and improve upon techniques I have been perfecting for centuries. They are truly their mother's children in dark intellect and inventive cruelty. It took them just a few short years to claim their dominance over the whole of Transylvania—to make the locals fear them even more than they fear me, their infamous father!

They do not have control over the meaner creatures of the night as I have—rats, bats, owls, moths, foxes and wolves fear and avoid them, rather than serve them, as they do me—but this is hardly a crucial omission in their formidable arsenal, which seems to be growing by the day. They are, unfortunately, as vulnerable to daylight as their father, but are not as dependent on native soil; they can sleep in any dark corner of the castle, wrapped in their webs.

As far as I can tell, only the fair-haired one is a proper witch and a true heir to her mother. Her black magic is strong and will grow stronger yet, I am sure. She is different from her sisters not only in abilities and appearance. She is more resourceful, more ferocious and more willful than her siblings; whenever they misbehave and disobey me, I invariably discover that she has been the architect. She is, in fact, their unspoken leader.

I named the dark-haired ones Persephone and Nyx, after the ancient Greek goddesses of the underworld. They are true twins, extremely alike in both character and appearance and prone to complete each other's sentences. They are spiteful, quick-tempered and proud and take after me in many other aspects of their personality. Perhaps that is why they worship and adore me, but also fear and respect me. They are skilled in the art of necromancy, as am I, but they are no witches.

The fair-haired one will grow up to be the image of her mother; and that is why I named her after her. My little Yaga's notoriety spreads by the day and she is fast becoming a living legend. There is not a child alive in Transylvania today who has not heard of her and woken screaming in terror at the very thought of her. She populates the nightmares and stokes the fears of the entire population of my native land.

For some time I was the proudest and happiest father in the world, but then a new challenge presented itself—with my three darlings rampaging throughout the land, snatching and slaying its inhabitants and satisfying their primal urges to the utmost, food was becoming more and more scarce. And even worse, the terrified mountain people began fighting back against our kind. They started hunting us, armed with torches, crucifixes, garlic and clever weapons. One time they nearly managed to capture Nyx, wounding her in the leg with a silver arrow dipped in poison. I needed all my skills as a necromancer to save her leg and preserve her life, sucking the poison out and summoning the spirit of her mother, who told me how to treat the wound with herbs and spices and stop the infection from spreading. Yaga became so angry that she tracked the vulgar men responsible for this outrage and cursed their village, which was consumed by an unholy fire that very night. The men died in unspeakable agony as their bodies were turned into pungent black ash by the merciless flames of Yaga's wrath.

Nevertheless, in recent months the situation has become so dire that each time we go out hunting, we must climb further and further down the mountain in order to find a village still untouched by my daughters' appetites. We must take special care to avoid the cruel traps set by devious hunters. And every time it becomes more dangerous, because the sheep have grown cunning in their desperation; and although powerful, my darlings have neither the experience nor the stamina to survive on their own.

AND NOW WE come to the grim conclusion of my tale. I have accepted the fact that I can no longer afford the luxury of putting sacred heritage and ancestral pride before the wellbeing and survival of my children. I can no longer sustain my precious daughters as they should be sustained. We have drained this land of its noble blood and forced its people to take up arms against us. There is not enough food here for my children to grow strong and happy, and this new hostility puts their very existence in jeopardy. It is intolerable.

I have, alas, yet another reason for seeking my family's fortunes elsewhere. I had always intended to send off my three little darlings, when they come of age, to be taught by the Devil himself at Scholomance, where I studied myself, mastering the art of necromancy and so much other dark arcana. That plan, however, came to naught when I learned that the ten-pupil quota had been filled the previous year with the admission of a Hungarian warlock. There is the world-renowned Cueva de Salamanca, of course, where Pope Sylvester himself studied magic; but I cannot in all good conscience send my darlings to live in that sun-drenched and garlic-infested peninsula. Domdaniel, near Tunis, is little better. That leaves only one other option for the dark education of my noble daughters—the Invisible College, situated in the very same overcrowded metropolis you now reside in.

So it has come to this, my friend! I, the proud and direct descendent of Attila the Hun, am forced by evil circumstance and changing times to abandon my native land and seek a new home on the other side of the world, amid uncultured and uncivilized barbarians who neither know nor fear me. But even the most common blood is better than no blood at all, and I shall endeavour to translate the local people's contemptible ignorance into tranquility and bliss for me and my hungry offspring. Furthermore, my daughters shall receive an excellent education in your city, taught by some of the most learned witches left in the world after the demise of my precious Yaga.

I have already set events in motion, dear Bogdan. I have called upon my loyal Szgany to help me with the arduous task of transporting my coffin, my most valued possessions and my daughters from beautiful Transylvania to grim London. I ask you, my trusted friend and companion, to supply me with the names of one or two discreet English lawyers who could arrange matters on the English side. I would also value your help and advice in choosing a suitable house in London with a suitably deep basement, preferably in a private area near a spacious public park.

I look forward to reading your next letter and maybe even seeing you in the flesh.

Your friend,

Dracula

FIVE

THE WOMEN

INTERLUDE

From: Jonathan Holmwood (jwlh1947@amol.com)
To: Dani Văduvă (bornwithteeth@webmail.com)
Date: January 18, 2018
Subject: Re: Fw: For the blog.zip

Hi Dani,

Thank you for the files! I've added these to my own, including the copies of everything I've kept safely lodged in several places—including with my solicitors in London—since the early '80s.

Again, good luck. I'm too old to be getting involved with all that sort of thing, but if there's anything I can do to help from here, let me know.

Thank you,

Jon xx

THE WOMEN

Caren Gussoff Sumption

I.

Report to The Gipsy Lore Society: The Transylvanian Gipsy, Keeper of Blood-Oaths, as told to Professor Doctor Octavius Maxwell Fogg by Mera Szgany, Wallachia

DESPAIR NOT AT the state of Orientalism, gentlemen: I send this dispatch from a true heart of Gipsyland in the Carpathian Mountains, and there, at this remote *vatra*, exists no better place to make my study of Romany charms, craft, and lore of the Vampyre.

Lo, our century is of science, and we are men of reason! Being men of reason, we grasp that the cultivation of knowledge in its lowest forms does not, by nature, pollute the higher forms. I reach back to our shared primitive antiquities, to converse with the naivety of the natural world, and, therefore, to the Gipsy. Gipsies, the humble priests of the religion of the peasant and the poor, for their lore as concerns the Dark Immortals, both primitive and innocent as it is, demands inquiry.

We are called, as men of this century, to advance in the science of man himself as well as the evolution of reason.

There is an old belief among Gipsies that Vampyres walk among them. Across all former Lands of Saint Stephen's Crown, Vampyre presences appear as man-eating Pricolitsh wolves, as over-ripened ground fruits made animate during full moons, and as cloven-footed, nocturnal suitors offering no more than ill-repute for any sweetheart accepting their affections.

The *mullo dudia* appears here as well, as it does in farther-flung Gipsy settlements. These maleficent lights drive men to madness with a vampyrrhic draining of any Godly connections. It is a horrible fate, to be sure, and a story persistent to keep the Gipsies of this land observing specific and prescribed death rituals and propriety, as the *mullo dudia* haunts violators of these rituals.

In fact, these death rituals figure largely into Gipsy history in Transylvania. Wallachia alone reports stories of the Vampyre as recounted by Sir Jonathan Harker, et al: the blood-draining immortal as found in England and modern Europe. It will be clear later in this report that the survival of these peoples depended on these death rituals in practice, and was instrumental in their connection to the Wallachia Vampyre himself.

Interestingly, gentlemen, as Harker experienced, I firsthand found the superstitions rampant among the Roomanian peasants of the Borgo Pass region. They recount these stories in whispered tones, and over spice their dishes with garlic.

In the villages, Mister Harker, his wife Mina, the physician Seward, the American, and Professor Van Helsing are well-remembered. Notwithstanding Harker's definitive report on the final death of the Vampyre, I found a surprising number of the villagers remaining unwilling to travel the pass through the Carpathians; instead choosing long, circuitous journeys to traverse the mountains.

All this I was told at Bistrita, by the dowager proprietress of the Frumoasa Han. The inn is most historic and picturesque, and has been owned by the same family since the time of our first Tudor King. The lady proprietor—Zsófia, as she is called—has been most helpful and informative, to prepare for my final leg and encampment. Though my Roomanian and her English are elementary, we quickly established excellent rapport.

The town is picturesque with medieval charm. Narrow alleys open to well-trod squares. The structures are primarily thatch and wood, with touches of remarkable flair: uncanny visages, of excellent masonry, peer at visitors from unexpected perches atop homes and shoppes.

Mistress Zsófia confirmed the location of the castle ruins, described by Sir Harker, and that it is still tended by camps of Gipsies. I gathered the ancestors of this Gipsy tribe were sworn to the former Voivode, Vlad Țepeș Drăculești III, and loyal ever since.

If true, *sui generis*. This tribe has upheld their duty an unprecedented length of time. With no more restraint than a word given centuries past, these Gipsies have fought their very nature to sustain a blood-oath.

Why not roam, as they are wont to do? It is the way of the Romany. This set me to work with renewed zeal.

In my sparse and comfortable room at the inn, I reviewed the writings of Harker and others. The good woman Zsófia contributed to the framing narrative of Bistrita, which I've documented separately in my notebooks. Further study is warranted on the Roomanian village tales of missing girls and domestics, mutilated livestock, and waylaid travelers never heard again. Of the state of the Gipsies, however, Zsófia knows little except to confirm their presence, and cross herself—not from lack of generosity, dear colleagues.

Zsófia herself kindly oversaw the refitting of my carriage, and a supply of goods I had never considered. She insists the sturdier wheels are necessary for the last leg of the climb, and the supplies of garlick, blackthorn, juniper berry, and dried rose petal tea will save my life. Dear lady. She cooked a breakfast the morning of my leave, eggs seasoned to an inch with the customary garlick and pepper, and saw me off, with the requisite gestures against the evil eye and the devil, a waving handkerchief, and crosses to protect me from daemons.

The Borgo Pass road is rugged, uncared for. Though I am a seasoned horseman, as a coachman on this terrain, I am amateur. I therefore kept slow and steady, and—grateful for the new wheels—enjoyed my time and the scenery.

Early on, there are farms and farming families, but the rolling agriculture soon gives way to more foreign views, no less breathtaking. The Carpathians appear of indigo rock, collared with snow and clouds. The foliage is of the deepest green, but in the thickest forest, pines and fir stand shoulder to shoulder and swallow the sun; they are patches of dense black, inky smudge in the far distance.

The air grows thinner, but remains richly perfumed. I am remiss in my botanies, but strains of pink oleander, and some celadon and viridian blossoms I cannot name (samples enclosed) stand up to the cold and flourish.

The excitement and intoxication exhausted me, and I thought it prudent to retire at dusk. I covered myself well in fur blankets, and slept at the helm of my carriage.

Gentlemen, I was under stars clear and close, dozing to a lullaby sung by a waterfall somewhere in the crags. I was only disturbed once, by the howls of distant wolves celebrating a successful hunt.

I started again at dawn, and the day proceeded much as the first. At the top of the afternoon, I reached the pronounced ascent described so feverishly in the diaries of Mister Harker. Gentlemen, his consternation is to be understood. This rise is remarkable. To the eye, it measures the same gentle angle as the road already traveled; but to the stomach, and to the strain suffered by the horses, the climb is abrupt, precipitous, and entirely unexpected. I cannot describe it in sensible terms. It is a terrain that nearly reduces a man to belief in magic, to decipher the experience. All I could do was slow the horses, and stay true.

Up, up, up I inched, until in the afternoon, unsettled, I arrived. It is most jarring. But, as promised, I was at my destination.

I pulled gently into the massive courtyard, enclosed by the ruins of a once-magnificent castle.

Truly, one could imagine the estate at its prime, comparable to the majesty of any in England and Europe. At one time, its stone battlements reached to the sky, with windows taller and wider than the mightiest of men. Now, it is a ravaged skeleton, home to only wind, ravens, and decayed finery. I stood, dwarfed by its size and possibility, only disrupted by ribbons of campfire smoke from the far side of the courtyard. That I missed the *vatra* of *vardos* and tents, I can only attribute to the size of the ruins and my relief at flat ground.

I setup my encampment in the center of the yard, close enough to force familiarity, but not so close to frighten. Children, as they most often do, first approached me, with the bravery of the uncorrupt. Soon after came Romany with warmly suspicious welcomes, and then women, with hospitality of fruited tea and a spot of rich stew.

The Gipsies were excellent specimens of their race: strong and stout, but well-proportioned, with heart-shaped visages and skin bronzed by exposure and roughened by industry.

I established quickly that I *rokkered Romanes* and local argot. There was immediate rejoicing, and soon, I was moved closer to camp, and invited to a feast in my honour.

Dinner was fine meat and winter vegetables, followed by walnut cake drowned in cream worthy of Devon. As the children toddled to bed, there was plum brandy, passed freely. The men drew their fiddles, and toasting and singing and dancing lasted well into the night.

My rapport found its boundary, however, when I set to my task the next day. At breakfast, over leftover cake and the customary tea, I asked directly of the Wallachia Vampyre and their extraordinary oath.

I was politely put off, at first, and given tours and visits and other activities designed to busy me. When I asked again, it was requested I lead prayers, and afterward, met each time with appeals for ceremonial duties, which could not be refused.

When it became apparent to my hosts that I would not tire of my inquest, nor honour their polite rejections, the older men sat me down to recount their folklore. It was a queer thing, as we know it is the Gipsy women who trade in the mysteries and magic, and who are the tellers of these tales. But I did not wish to offend, and there is value in collecting provincial versions of familiar tales, and how they would differ told by men. I heard them through: the colorful mischief of pumpkins given life; dog-men hungry for the virtue of vulnerable *rakli*; and the *mullo dudia*, who in this region appear not as lights, but as faceless men who walk sideways (I have also documented this in my notes, as well as the protections mentioned: turning garments inside-out, carrying stones with naturally-worn holes through them, sprinkling thresholds with iron filings).

These stories were excellently told, and I offered my admiration and appreciation. When it was apparent they were finished, I asked my questions again, as directly as before: "Good sirs, I thank you for this knowledge, but there is more I wish to know. Please tell me of the immortals tied to this land, the dark gentry, the never-dead. I wish to know the family to which you are sworn, of this castle, the Drăculeşti, loyally all these many years."

"Do not ask us this thing, *Rye*," the old men said. They did not look angered; simply tired, in a way beyond age, beyond even a hard day's work.

I did not immediately press further.

If this inquiry were to only satisfy a personal curiosity, or even to simply legitimise Harker, I would not have continued. But I steeled myself with our higher purpose, and pushed my query into each interaction.

I deployed strategies ordinarily successful with Gipsies, offering pay, trade of goods. Each time, the doors to knowledge were firmly shuttered.

I remained a welcomed guest; there were no reprisals for my insistence. But, gentleman, I admit, I began to despair none would ever speak of the Vampyre to me.

I had been with them a fortnight—a failure—when I was approached by a *chavvy*.

"Why do you want to know of the Devil?" he asked. His eyes were bright, wise, and I briefly wondered him a dwarf, but his smooth, unmarked skin verified he was but a child, if a remarkable one.

"*Chavvy*," I said. "For generations, your people have shouldered a terrible burden. I wish to understand its effects fully."

"Can you help us?" he asked.

How does a just man give a child hope that is not false, but neither defeats their spirit? I answered him with honesty. "I do not know."

That seemed to satisfy; moreover, I credit the *chavvy* with deft persuasion, because on the fifteenth evening, I was greeted at my carriage by a *doykitso* of indeterminate age: over fifty or so. The fire played off the black shine in her plaited hair, the shadows in her cheekbones, and her quick smile full of small, tight teeth. She introduced herself as Mera Szgany, a Hungarian name—I remarked on it, and she answered, "He gave us that name, when we struck the abominable bargain."

She seemed a woman of fair education, and she explained, in a pure dialect, that she was schooled as a young girl in Roomanian, Saxon German, and a little English, under the tutelage of the Bishop of Satu Mare. This assertion was hard to believe, but proven by her articulacy—equal to or beyond any English commoner.

"What do you know of the Vampyre?" she asked.

"I have read the accounts of Jonathan Harker, his wife, and the doctor and professor that aided them." I answered.

"Ah," she said. "Yes. The *Inglezítska* and the *Ivropáno*. I remember them." Mera Szgany studied me with flashing black eyes. "What did they say of us?"

"Little," I answered. "The same as the villagers: that you serve the Vampyre and his interests. That you served him well."

"It is *klaviya*. Slavery." Mera Szgany spat on the ground. "Do slaves serve? Or are they forced?"

"Slaves are forced," I agreed.

"And slaves of a Vampyre are chained in thrall." Mera Szgany pushed her fingertips together. "Though we were desperate, though we were hungry and frightened and dying, we came to him of free will. We struck the bargain that gave us our name and our curse." She watched me carefully for a reaction. "But those were the last choices we Szgany ever made."

I kept my face neutral, though my fingers itched to take notes, and questions rose in my throat. My respectful silence pleased her, and she continued. "I will tell you what you want to know of the Vampyre, on one condition."

Victory, gentlemen! "I will meet this condition."

"You will hear what I say, you will write it down, you will keep it true."

"*Phenav chachimos*," I agreed. "Only the truth, Mera Szgany."

Mera Szgany spat again, but this time into her palm. I copied the gesture and we clasped hands.

We had our own unbreakable bargain.

Mera Szgany gestured for me to sit back, and then, sirs, the floodgates opened in earnest.

What follows is transcribed from her tellings.

Night Fifteen-th

"My people were promised many gifts from the prince that ruled this land. He told my people that his palms were open, that the land yielded iron and the water glinted with its gold. We would be welcomed here. So my people crossed the Danube onto this land.

"We were deceived.

"This prince gave not my people gifts, but instead gave my people *as* gifts, boons for lords and priests from whom he wished favor. My family was presented to monks of Făgăraș.

"We were slaves for the first time. *Klave cigani mănăstirești.*

"And so we lived. We were slapped by those open palms. Iron and gold? We worked it and washed it until the metals held the smell of our blood.

"Our equals were dogs; and that is how our monks treated us. They chained us up, bred us, beat us. They sought to train us, like dogs loyal to their master, to obey them, even to love them.

"But we could never be like the dog. We would never submit, not truly. If they looked, they would see we are like the wild horse or the forest stag: fierce, magnificent, unbroken.

"So it went for five lifetimes: we worked, we loved, we suffered, grew old and died, all inside their cages. But we never called them master. And so they despised us."

The sky lightened to dramatic tones of orange and blue. I had not realised we'd passed the entire night. A lovely *chej* maiden set me down a breakfast of walnut cake and jam-laced tea. One bite and one sip, gentlemen, and Mera Szgany was gone.

I climbed into my bedroll, exhausted. But sleep was fitful, in stops and starts, punctuated by the sounds of the caravan life. My dreams were strange, febrile, full of things half unseen and remembered.

I was awakened by a different *chej,* with food, at dusk. My chagrin at missing the day was soothed by a hearty supper of spiced lamb, delectable, along with a side of riced turnips. And in front of my little fire, stoked back to life by my lovely server, sat Mera Szgany.

"Good evening, *Rye*," she said. "I can talk whilst you eat."

I agreed, and Mera Szgany poured me a bit of sweet red brandy to accompany my plate, sat back on her heels, and continued her tale.

* * *

Night Sixteen-th

"For five lifetimes, we lived, the best that we could. *Klave* outside. But inside, free." She beat her chest, over her heart, in emphasis. "And for five lifetimes, this, we did.

"But then came the Black Sickness. You know of this sickness?" she asked.

I swallowed and nodded. "It affected much of Europe," I said. "Many, many, many people died."

Mera Szgany continued. "We had seen other terrible illness. Some of my own *vitsi* perished from the Great Sweat and of Pox. But the Black Sickness was beyond compare.

"The Sickness came as tumors, big as onions and filled with cream and blood. First, they grew beneath the arms, and then, around the sex. They ruptured, and the sick tanned blue and purple, as if they bruised all at once. It was devil-ugly, and as deadly. It took almost all in the villages. Children, too.

"And it took the entirety of our monks.

"But it spared my people. It little touched any *kalve cigani mănăstireşti*. Even when we took pity and nursed *gadjin*, when we cared for the men who treated us like dogs. No day ended without death, but we were healthy.

"*Nais tuke, Devlesa*! It's what we thought. Oh, thank you, sweet God. You free us finally, your children. We could afford to be kind. Things would be made right.

"We tended the monks like they were fellow Gipsies. We fed the fires so it was never dark, one of us was always with the monks. We kept watch, *vartováni*, like they were our own. When they left this world, we closed their eyes with stones. We had no gifts to give them, except handfuls of the land to which they tied us. We ate *pomona* in their honour. We killed and buried our hate."

Mera Szgany laughed, an angry, ragged sound. She refilled my cup with the red brandy, and then overfilled her own. It was so full of spirit, gentlemen, that she leaned down to the glass for the first sip to avoid spilling it. Then she emptied the remainder in a haste one hates to see in a woman. She wiped her mouth on the edge of her shawl and continued.

"When the last monk died, we looked over our inheritances. We were free, but needed supplies. *Vardos*, horses, quilts. We took down the gilt crosses and the silver urns. We poured out the water from the great jewelled bowl, unhooked the tapestries that covered the altar and the walls.

"There was no disrespect. We worshipped *Devlesa* with no such trappings. He did not require them; we did, to trade for goods.

"The men carried the goods to town. The women and the children, we rested.

"Our men were robbed of our goods, and chased away. The villagers swarmed the monastery grounds with torches and with ropes. They meant to hang us, then burn us, kill the witches. They thought us evil, fraught with magics and spells. They said we cursed them with the Black Sickness.

"They said we were devils, and held our trade as proofs.

"My people argued otherwise: if it were our doing, with witchery, why would we wait for five generations to strike down our captors? Why wait so many years to punish the villages who allowed it?

"We were to the monks as their children; the gold and the silver were our right. We had nothing. No horses, no *vardos*, not even an iron pot. We were no longer slaves, but we were not to be free.

"We ran for our lives. If we were caught, we were whipped, and hanged. Our women violated, our children sliced and mutilated.

"We could not run forever. Because we were clever, we went to the quietest place, to the safest place, the one place we could air our bleeding feet.

"In the times of so many dead, the graveyards were fallow. Too many to bury, not enough to do the digging.

"This is how we lived. We made our first bargain, to bury the dead. We would live in peace, only if we treated their dead as we treated our monks. They would all be buried like Gipsies.

"Some of my people wished to run, take our chances in the hands of *Devla*. And if we died, we would return to Him.

"Most of us were too like the forest stag. The mighty stag is wise; he knows when to run and when to be still.

"So we lived among the dead. No one sought to kill us, but no one saw fit to let us be alive.

"The peace was brutal. It was also brief. When the Sickness waned, the *gadje* looked to us for other ills, naturally caused: stillborn babies, curdled milk, too much rain, too little rain, accidents and tragedies. For all, we were suspect. They're dark witches, they said. They eat the dead."

This is where she stopped her story, this night. I passed the day as I had previously, in fitful sleep though to supper. It occurs to me to note that this situation struck as apt: should one seek knowledge of Vampyres, one should live as one.

DEAR SIRS, IT also behooves me to interject some thoughts I had at the time. There should be no doubt that at the beginning of our acquaintance, I undervalued Mera Szgany. She is, obviously, a remarkable woman of any race. Well-spoken, an excellent narrator of history, if not guilty of the natural Gipsy proclivity for exaggeration for the sake of a hearty tale (for the woman's account to be strictly first-hand, as she presented it, she would be no less than 400 years of age; as I stated, her exact age is difficult to ascertain, but I estimate in her late 40s, perhaps 50s). I admit that I was and am troubled by only one attribute of my capable guide: she is, almost, without emotions.

She recounts nearly unspeakable horrors with no grief. Her eyes are lively, but her smile feels insincere, as if it is a mere courtesy, and delivered as an afterthought. It pains me to write this. I feel I am denigrating the humanity of one gracious enough to educate me, and repaying this generosity with judgment. Perhaps she quells her emotions with the red brandy she sips through our evenings (and as noted, occasionally gulps). I have but a glass out of politeness, but she nurses several. This may be the cause—alcohol affects each differently—though I remain uneasy.

After the *chej* for the evening cleared away my dishes (another traditional stew, this one flavoured well with cinnamon), my guide approached, settled in, poured us brandies, and began.

Night Seventeen-th

"We first met the Székely and his man when it was dark. The two of them strolled inside the graveyard, lost in their deep conversation. We hid, in fright, thinking the villagers finally came to murder us in our sleep. We lay face down, in silent horror, praying to Devla to save and protect us.

"The men passed between us. So closely, I could see their expressions: not of kindness, exactly, but neither unkind.

"They did not acknowledge us, even as they stepped over us, as if we were boulders or cairns, instead of people trembling in submission. Their boots were excellent leather, pantaloons velvet and fine wool. I was inexplicably ashamed and angry at their indifference.

"I sat up, defiant, and stared, bare-faced and bare-headed, at the interlopers, until they left us, and the cemetery.

"My father rightfully rebuked me for my carelessness and indolence. I have always had a well-deserved reputation for brazen curiosity and strong will, not admired in women.

"The men returned the next evening. Though there were but two of them, and they dressed as men unaccustomed to work, they led horses laden with food and supplies, laid a table with their hands, and then invited us through gestures to rise, to rise and to eat.

"It was... unexpected."

Mera Szgany laughed then. Perhaps it was the hypnotic effects of her storytelling, or the dancing campfire, or perhaps the warming effect of the sweet fruit brandy; but I was captivated at that moment by the mouth of Mera Szgany. I've written of her small, white teeth, which shone whiter against the berry-stain on her drunken lips. I laughed too, gentlemen, for a most curious reason: not because the story was funny, but because at that time, I wished nothing more plainly than to see that mouth laugh again.

It was an innocent moment, lest I suggest otherwise. It was such a singular, immediate desire that I feel compelled to document it, if only for further study.

Regardless, the moment passed, and Mera Szgany continued.

"My people rose, and ate. First with trepidation, then confidence. It was as one befriends wild beasts. Our hosts stood back and watched; they did not speak, to us or one another, nor did they partake.

"The food was fine! But I hardly remember it. After plates were scraped clean and bowls emptied and licked, the Székely and his man summoned me to approach.

"When I came close, I realised: never before have I seen such men. The Székely was *long*, though average height. His face was long, his nose, fingers, feet, all long. His brows and beard formed a circlet around his face, and his lips were red like a maid's.

"His man was less drawn, but still remarkable. Orange curls framed a man's face, which was pale and pretty as a girl's, though his nose drew to a beaky point. A tame raven which sat atop his shoulder, ruffling occasionally, but otherwise placid.

"The Székely greeted me in Magyar. I do not know it, but recognised it. I answered in Roomanian, which he refused; then in German, which was acceptable.

"He asked me, in good German, 'You stood to face us, girl. But it was not courage, but *shame* that emboldened you. Why?'

"'That is true, sir. I am tired of our weakness,' I answered plainly. 'We are a people much reduced.' I spoke to both the Székely and his man, but only the Székely answered.

"'There is no ignominy in survival.'

"'Perhaps,' I agreed. 'But one needs a reason to continue to survive.'

"'And you have none?'

"I continued with simple truth. 'None that is clear to me.'

"The Székely considered this in silence. I felt my people's eyes on me, but did not falter until the Székely gave answer.

"'I can restore your people, I believe,' he said. 'I would like to discuss a covenant to benefit us all.'

"Then I turned to the eyes of my men: my grandfather, father, and husband stood at the front, knees trembling but suspicious now. After all, what would these strange *gadje* want with a mere woman?

"Yes, I was judged, even by those closest to me, by my sex. Though educated and known for my will, a woman was not a comfortable choice as mouthpiece for my people.

"The Székely read the proceedings. 'Stand down your men. I admire adherence to traditions, but I shall only strike this agreement with you.'

"We were thus dismissed. My grandfather and husband quickly formed a *kris* to hear out the strangers, but I explained that while men wished to contract with us a bargain, they would only take me as delegate.

"Their indignation was as expected. Accusations flew of trade in my virtue, at which my husband bristled: 'The men are rich. They laid us a fine table, and wish to enter into a contract. They are not Romany; their ways are different than ours. That does not stand in the way of gain. My wife is educated, well-spoken, and known for her audaciousness, but her faithfulness is true. Let her deal.'

"He was persuasive, my husband."

Mera Szgany stopped. Her eyes were tearful, and she dabbed at them with her shawl. It was the most show of emotion I had seen, and I felt keenly her loss. She filled our glasses and we toasted.

"To the memory of your husband," I offered. "May he rest in eternal peace."

Mera Szgany drank. "My husband is not dead, *Rye*."

"I see." I was confused.

She set down her glass. "No one here truly dies."

I followed again. "Of course not," I said. As we know, gentlemen, much of Gipsy culture is still rooted in its eastern and Hindoo roots, in that ancestors are ever-present, if not re-incarnated. I saw firsthand the comfort they found in that, as Mera Szgany regained composure and continued.

"The *kris* granted me authority to deal with the Székely and his man on their behalf. It was an unprecedented call, but when you are starving, every food is sweet as cake."

At this point, my hostess paused. Dawn was touching her classical rosy fingers, and I admit to feeling queasy and grateful to retire even into poor sleep.

As had become our ritual, my supper was set out for me upon awakening, and Mera Szgany indulged me whilst I ate. She started:

Night Eighteen-th

"The Székely and his man returned the following dusk. It was a night much like tonight, foggy but still. Their horses were burdened. Another table was set, but for us, a rug was unrolled and three plush chairs set upon it.

"He asked many questions about my people: how many, which relations, health and custom, strength and talent. His man took many notes, unperturbed as his raven made a nest in his firey orange curls.

"The Székely tested what I knew of history, which was limited. He launched into grand stories of the Ottoman Empire, wars and revolts, complicated lineages of succession. My people fell to sleep, but I listened politely, and soon it was dawn. As the sky turned orange, the Székely and his man excused themselves, promising to continue negotiations the next evening."

The comparison between the business described and that between Mera and myself was not lost to me; however, it seemed inappropriate to interrupt.

"I was confused, but unused to business. Perhaps this was the way of men.

"The next evening, as planned, the men returned, set a table and meeting parlour for us. The Székely continued his talk of history and into politics, and I contained myself as the low moon illuminated the fog.

"My reputation is as much for impatience as brazenness. I interrupted the Székely when the moon rose above the fog. 'Sir, this is all for my betterment, and I thank you. But I will be restless until we settle our business.'

"At this, the Székely smiled, quite horribly, pointed teeth white against his unnatural lips. 'This *is* our business, child. I wish to employ you to my house, and you need know the house to which you swear. I am Vlad Drăculeşti, Voivode of Wallachia. I offer you and yours free rein in my home, use of all holdings, and safe passage anywhere in the lands you travel.'

"'That is most generous,' I replied. 'And for this, we only need only swear allegiance?'

"The Székely smiled again with his terrible mouth, and held up three long fingers. 'You need only swear allegiance to my house, and bear an oath to attend me when I need, and to perform simple errands without question.'

"I looked at the Székely and his man. Though I was uneasy with them, I attributed that to status and tradition. There was no way to refuse, so I nodded assent.

"'Excellent,' the Székely said. 'Let us go home.'

"I roused my people from their sleep, and by the time we'd gathered the little we had and the *bori* wrapped their babies, the Székely and his man had their horses packed, lanterns lit to shepherd us through the mist.

"This castle, back then, was a marvel, worthy of royalty. My people had only seen it from a distance, looming down from on high. It was in a glorious state, not the rubble we sit among now."

Mera Szgany gestured around us.

I nodded, struck again by the grandeur of the ruins. "It must have been truly a spectacle."

Mera Szgany nodded. "The castle, she was already an old woman, but still capable of rendering men speechless.

"So, we were. Too speechless.

"Before our eyes, the fog parted like a great curtain. The castle stood, imposing, breathtaking, and on this courtyard, then tended and covered in inviting grasses and flowers, stood *vardos* the likes of which were found in dreams. Exquisitely painted, in colours to shame even nature, and supplied with copper pots and warm quilts. Horses culled from the voivode's own stables—silver mares, large-footed stallions—grazed calmly on the rich pickings. And then, as we stood agape, beautiful woolly dogs trotted out to greet us, nuzzle our hands, each one sweet-natured, or trained to be so.

"Surely we all understood this bargain was not as it seemed. We are not *dilo*, fools. We were overwhelmed, hungry, reduced. And the Székely, he is a hunter and know when to strike. 'My house is your house. Forever.'

"I nodded, unable to find words for the first and last time in my life.

"A small desk was set down, and the Székely's man unrolled a parchment. I am an educated woman, but the contract was of florid words too ornate to be but illustrations. Symbols. It was dizzying.

"'Can you write?' the Székely asked me.

"I nodded again, took the quill and signed my mark. The Székely's man examined my name carefully, then spoke for the first time. 'Surname?' he asked, in a voice deep and musical.

"'There has never been need,' I answered.

"The Székely's man gave the contract over to the Székely. He took the quill from me, and next to my name mark, added Szgany.

"And so, we were bound together with the house of Drăculeşti, Vlad Ţepeş, Voivode of Wallachia and the Raven King, for eternity."

Mera Szgany stopped then, and closed her eyes. I saw the wear our nights had taken on her. Though she expressed little emotions, besides a tear here and there or a brittle laugh, the story had emptied her.

I had more questions, and vowed this night would be the last I imposed on her. "How long, madam, before you knew what he was?" I asked.

Mera Szgany opened her eyes again. In her exhaustion, they'd taken on a certain redness. I wondered, colleagues, if I had misjudged placing her at fifty years of age.

"Quickly," she said. "He did not hide his butchery." Mera Szgany began to straighten her shawl, and snapped for a *chej* to collect our empty glasses. "I bid you goodnight, *Rye*. You have your story." She stood up and gave a tight curtsey of finality.

I could not let that be all I delivered forth to mankind. There were now more questions than answers.

"Madam, you have been a most accomplished and generous storyteller. But I must insist you grant me but another hour. There are things not yet clear." But she would not heed my appeals.

Mera Szgany spoke again, clearly, into the night. "*Rye*, we are done. I promised our truth, and I delivered it. That was half our agreement. Now, you are obliged to fulfill the other half."

My next action I nearly omit, for it is so out of character for myself. But I must relate this, in all its truth, not just to meet our higher purpose, but to, indeed, honour my oath here. (Perhaps I also suffered under poor sleep and the weight of sweet brandies clouding my judgments.) I pushed myself up, and though I felt, again, queasy, I easily overtook and grabbed Mera Szgany's arm.

I meant to entreat her one last time. I thought only to eke the last bits from her—salient points she may not value as a scholar would—but instead, gentlemen, I had a horrible shock!

Sirs, it may seem fantastic, but it was as if I had been burned, only by ice itself; and the ice the good lady's flesh.

I cried out in pain and confusion, stumbling backwards through the dying embers of the fire before collapsing into my rightful seat. And though I now understood her to be no lady, I summoned her thusly, "Dear lady Mera, please."

Mera Szgany took pity on me, I believe, in that moment—if she was capable of such a thing. Perhaps she understood I would take this so far as I could, regardless of circumstances. Or she had developed a feeling for me during our time. Whatever it was, she humored me, and set herself down again. She sat prettily, albeit in a different form, haunches up, a beast, waiting patiently for me to collect myself.

"Ma'am," I said. "Pray tell me, what are you?"

"I'm damned to live out my name," she said. "Mera-pen Szgany."

"*Mera-pen*?" I asked, though rhetorically. Sirs, you and I and anyone with elementary Romany know the word, which means 'to die.'

"I am so punished until my people are free from the oath I swore." Though she had no eyes in her sockets, I could swear I saw angst there. And that I did not understand.

"*Mera-pen*, your people are free of your oath. Your man was murdered. Your men tried to defend him, but goodness prevailed. Dracula was laid to rest, and so you, his enthralled, should be discharged."

Death laughed her coarse laugh. "The *Inglezítska* and the *Ivropáno* thought they knew all. But they never once asked the Szgany."

A cold sweat started on me. I was growing cold, quickly. "Tell me."

"The Szgany belong to the house, and the house belongs to the one that raised Drăculeşti to power. Drăculeşti is at rest, but the Raven King lives still."

"Drăculeşti's man," I said. "The Raven King."

Death stood up again; I would not stop her this time. "His man," she agreed. "Goodbye, *Rye*." And she was gone.

Gentlemen, I have more commentary, but I am feeling quite weak, and fever is stupefying. The Szgany have brought me some broth and some extra coverlets to make me comfortable, and a nice *chej* lays a cold cloth to my temple.

Sirs: this is where my father's article cuts off, barring a final note scrawled at the bottom: *Hungary Bohemia king, house Hunyadi. Matthias Corvinus, corvus genus raven, library black army war for Austria.* I have only these papers, none other of his possessions or artifacts, nor the notebooks to which he refers.

I have corresponded back to a Madam Zsófia Sala, at Frumoasa Han in Bistrita, Romania, who it was that sent me these sheets, at great effort and expense. She is the self-same woman mentioned in the article, and was very fond of my father during their brief acquaintance. She has agreed to seek rumours or answer to his whereabouts, and to send any personal goods or effects, should they be located.

She seems an honest and simple woman, though she claims this article was delivered to her in the middle of the night, by a great black bird.

My humble appreciations,

Olivia Fogg Cruthers

Manchester

December 1899

* * *

II.

Letters Home: London to Bucharest

23 January

Gulo Mamo,

I really hope Káko Ray came by already to tell you I called and am fine and every mailman in the whole kingdom is striking, It's something to do with a pay rise, and there are plans to authorise private posts, but not yet. So, this letter may be quite long, writing on it until I can send it.

Anyway, Káko told me you can use the telephone any time you want, even to call me in England, and no charge, no problem. Only it means you and Nena Domino have to be in the same room with no yelling.

Do this for me? For your most vestacha and only chej? Otherwise, you will hear nothing of me until the when and if of this strike ends, or private posts open for business, and even then, who knows how long this will take to reach you? The best and fastest mail to Bucureşti takes a week, even inside Europe.

And yes, Mamo, I know how excited you were to have me stay with family, but amaro vitsi lives in the White City Estates—it is far west London, not near the university. London is so much bigger than we could imagine. I would have to take the train after dark to get to and from. I know that would worry you.

The London Szgany would have moved me right in, if I asked. You are right—familia si familia, no matter what. Blood is blood, even on just meeting. But I am a grown up woman now, whether you like it or not, and I'm going to university in i bari luma, the big world. I am going to only study and practise, practise and study, and I need some space and some privacy, and there's none of that in a good Rom household, full of bustle and nosing.

(I am sworn, though, to never miss a single Sunday lunch there. On my honour, as a Szgany.)

Instead, I found a room in Hoxton with three other university students. The flat is very close to school, and I have my very own room with a door that closes and shuts out and in my music.

Mamo, I love this little flat. The windows face east, and there are two water closets (yes! two!). We share a television and a telephone, in the flat, not the building. Know that my flatmates might answer when you do call, so be friendly, Mamo! They are nice, and they are close to their families, too. I think you would like them when you meet.

Emily is also studying music—she is studying operatic voice. We have a lot of classes together, even though I am officially now studying "Composing and Composition." She's a fan of Gypsy jazz, especially Django Reinhardt (you remember, that Belgian Manouche famous for guitar).

Nance and Sookie are my other two flatmates. They are studying at the art college, and have been friends since they were in nappies, as they say. They dress in so many colours, I would think them Gypsy, except that they wear trousers, instead of ankle-length tsóxa like good romni.

Sookie's family hired me part-time, too, to help sell flowers and jam at their arcade stall in Covent Garden. Their people have held the same stall for 75 years! It's just a little money, and it won't interfere with my schoolwork or Kurko lunch at the Estate. I will only work on Friday and Saturday, and my classes are Monday, Tuesday, and Wednesday.

My flatmates tell me this weather is as cold as we will get, and I almost laughed! It is nothing compared to how it is right now at home. January with so little snow, it is almost none. I will miss crunching through fresh falls of real snow, and how nice it is to come inside afterward to a hot bowl of ciorba. The way you make it, of course, lemon and meatball. Even if the postmen settled the strike tomorrow, I will always be sad you cannot mail soup (or even better, pišota with sweet cheese... ahhh! I want).

I like London. There is more that I have not seen than what I have, yet. It is busy, and so flat. If the buildings were not tall, I bet I could see straight across the city. I like the parks, nature in the city, and the big, black ravens and crows, and stone grey pigeons who grew up with people and nearly tame. I like the pieces of wall that were built by the Romans a thousand years ago, ruined bits you just come across between buildings here and there that still survive. This place is like a quilt made of scraps and bits stitched together.

I am learning so much. But do not worry, Mamo. Learning more does not push other things out of my head. I know who and what I am, and living in London, and living with white girls will not change me. It will only add more and more. Please try not to worry. Please try to be proud.

I am going to pause here. Today is Thursday and so it is my study day. I have to write down for my composition teacher the notes that make up one of the scales I am used to. Our music uses different ways of ordering higher and lower notes than most Western classical music. My teacher wants me to pull these apart and present on Monday.

So, for now, me kamav tu, and I will write more later.

Yours,

Lolo

23 January

Dearest Kezia,

You baro moy!!!

You can't tell miri Mamo what I told you about Nico. Now she knows I am going to give him back his ring at Saintes-Maries, and she is going to worry more. I have not heard from her, but muro Káko asked, which means miri Mamo told him. And she could only have heard it from you. Unless you only told muro Káko or Nena... and miri Mamo would never believe it from them.

No. You had to tell my mother. She forced it from you. She could always get what we were up to from your mouth. And she is going to worry more, living with English girls, rather than Szgany, that I'll toss all my modesty away! She is going to imagine I have my legs behind my head, wiggle walking around the big city on my buttocks, like some sort of lubn'i! Ha ha ha!

I miss you, i amalni. I like my gazhya flatmates, but they are no Kezia. Why do you not have a telephone yet? Even the Szgany here have their own, in their house. You cannot see my face, but I am pouting.

(We even have a television! But I truly have not had any minutes to sit and look at it.)

How are you? And... how is Peti? Have you ridden in a wagon together yet, with someone's Baba (bet she had fuller beard than his!) to chaperone? I am only teasing. I am jealous of how you feel for Peti. If I felt a tenth of that, I'd happily marry Nico and be a good bori and have ten chavvies and take care of lesi Mamo and live happily ever after. I imagine it's almost torture courting at turn of the century speed, like we're all living back in Ardeal vardos, travelling up and down the Borgo Pass.

But once you are married and have your own house... I will hope it comes soon. But not so soon that I am not home to dance at your wedding and drink all your wine. Ha ha ha!

I am doing well. I love London, I think. I wish I could show you. It's more than we imagined. London is every colour, every smell, every sound, all at once. Budapest is like a village compared. I could sit in one spot all day and all night for a week, and maybe never see the same person twice, or more than that. I try to not be overwhelmed. I have people. The London Szgany took me in right away, and I am to visit and eat with them every Sunday, without fail. I will write more about them in a bit. Something about them is strange to me, even for family, and I cannot seem to quite name what it is. I wish I could talk it out with you. You always help me untie my thoughts when they are in knots. My dear, sweet bigmouth Kezia.

Let me see. I said I like my gazhya flatmates. They are nice to me, though they call me a "country mouse." I think it is teasing; there is no meanness in their faces when they say it, and they worry over me getting taken advantage of when I am on my own (they don't yet understand that I am Romany!).

I do not think I understand anymore the fear of gazhe like we have back home. My gazhya flatmates are like you and me.

If there are differences, it's that they do not seem to know shortage or hard times. They throw away things in the rubbish we would never at home, and I have to stop myself from pulling back out good things. They throw away empty tins and bags, bones and apple cores still with meat! They also tease me over this. Nance told me I am "just like me gran, who lived thru the war, wit' rations an' all." But then she said I am the "fittest gran ever," which means I'm too pretty to be a granny, and so I know she means it with sweetness. I am pretty sure.

They also tease me because I feed birds. Here in England, it is actually a pastime for old people! But it makes me less homesick and I talk Rumanian and Romany and they cock their heads and listen to me, so long as I have bread.

(Oh! On a different note, the girls envy my hair. My hair! All that pravo bal that I wished would curl is in fashion here on me, "fit gran.")

I have to study today, soon, so I will write more later. I am not rushing, anyway. All the postmen are on strike everywhere in England. And since you do not have a telephone...

When I come back, I will tell you all about school, and if anything interesting happens in the meantime.

Peace,

Lolo

*   *   *

24 January

Salutări Profesor Văduvă,

Many warm greetings from London, sir. I am enjoying classes, very much; London and the University are much like you described. I hope this short note finds you well.

I have already completed a short work to present to my classmates in Music Theory. Our instructor was interested immediately in my "Gypsy idiom," and how the early/late tempo and unusual pitch sequencing developed my ear. I have enclosed a draft of my presentation on the double harmonic scale, fifth mode of Hungarian minor for you. I hope you enjoy.

I accompanied the presentation by playing a selection from one of the few examples I could find in classical Western music: Debussy's "La Soirée dans Grenade." If you have other suggestions, please do let me know.

As always, your grateful student,

Lolo Szgany

PS: Pardon the untimeliness of this letter. I am not sure if the news reached Romania, but there is a country-wide postal strike, and mail is being routed to the continent in a circuitous way. We all hope it is resolved soon. Again, my fondest regards.

27 January

Mamo,

It is now Sunday evening, and I have returned from Sunday lunch with the entire Szgany kumpania (so it feels). I am overfull, in every way: this, Mamo, is exactly why it is good that I can visit the estate, and then can come home to a small and quiet piece of the world that is mine. To recover!

Anyway, I think I met fifty uncles, fifty cousins, fifty bari phenya, fifty phure, fifty borya. I must have met some twice. And some, they tell me, were not even here!

You are laughing now. I can hear it all the way here! "You should be happy to have so many people, when we thought most dead." It is baxtali to have our family close by, and I do know I am lucky not just for me, or for you, but for all our familia buried at the Borgo Pass and lost in the Porajmos. The Szgany are many.

And most overwhelming!

It isn't as cold, like I said, as home, but it is cold enough. So there isn't enough space inside for all the people and all the food at Kurko lunch. The tables sit outside, ringed with fires in steel cans to keep us warm.

No one sits, though. We eat and talk. And eat some more. They fed me until I had to push my jaw up and down with my hands to chew.

Then, there was boxing, not on the television, but every man and boy, age seven and over. Beating each other.

Men are the same everywhere, I guess.

And since I bring up men... you know, by now, that I am going to give back Nico's ring... and I know you have been waiting all letter for me to mention it.

I have not even told Nico yet, but I am sure that he knows. I will see him in May, at the processions for the Maries and kali Sarah, and I want to do this in person. Nico is a dear sweet boy; I like him very much. But I do not love him.

Gulo Mamo, please trust in me. You did not raise me to be any simple chej. When you took us to Bucharest, you did this so that I would have chances. You were lucky to go to school, and you made sure I had more than luck behind me. You suffered without, to buy me a concertina, then a fiddle and a guitar, so I could learn to play better than a man. You did so much. And now here I am, at a university in one of the greatest cities in the world.

Trust you did a good job.

And when you can't, remember Del tut dukhel. God sees all, right?

Right now, Mamo, I do not want to marry anybody. And when I do, I will marry for love.

This is not the last I will hear of this, and it is not the last I have to say. In the meanwhile, I will be good, behave, practise and study, and work very hard.

So, about that. I finished the homework I told you of earlier, and presented it. I mailed a copy to Profesor Văduvă, so he can keep up with my progress. I worked at the flower stall with Sookie, her mother, father, two brothers, grandmother, and other flatmate Emily. The market is like a Christmas market, but all year round. I smiled a lot, wrapping flowers for buyers that grow wild at home, violets and oleander, and some dark roses, and all that smiling did well for sales, Mrs. Ridgeway said. They are happy to have me, and I pull my weight (again, said Mrs. Ridgeway).

It is time I gather together for tomorrow, and sleep. Class is early, and I present to my class on scales.

Again and still, me kamav tu, and will write more soon.

Your Lolo

28 January

Sar'shan, Kezia,

I have to tell you about Sunday. I am bursting apart wanting to talk to you. I both have so many thoughts and have no idea what I think.

Imagine the biggest wedding and imagine the biggest saint's day, then put them together over foldable tables set with enough Sunday lunch to feed all of them, plus fifty other people not yet arrived. Now, imagine, all those people are related to you, by blood, somehow, and it is dizzying to try and figure out how, because it can't be possible... and yet, here we are. There are fifty, I think, of everybody—fifty uncles, fifty aunts, fifty cousins. Fifty babies, fifty grandmothers, on and on until I am dizzy.

Remember in maths when we learned that everyone in the whole world, anyone, anywhere, Romany and gazhe, are all sixteenth cousins?

Anyway, keep imagining how each one of these fifty relatives ask you the same question, and the answer is always unmarried chej should be in their mother's house, and not at university because all chej are too delicate and too pure, like flowers, to be exposed to the wicked world of gazhikanes without withering under the weight of evil and pollution. We need to be protected by the familia, by a husband. You know.

Now, keep thinking of this as the same fifty refill your plate with more food, more food until you are almost nodding in agreement that romni girls are i luludyi, innocent and corruptible, and you do not even realise you are nodding along, worn down like the record grooves of your favorite song (only this is your least favorite song). But you nod, worn, and you hate it. And you hate that you hate it because your mother wants you to love it, and I am a terrible daughter, maybe, but I am not a flower.

The lunch was over, and the men gathered, and the old women lit cigars. I expected music. But here, the old women puffed their cigars and the borya carried dishes inside. And I was left with all the other unmarried fragile, shukari cousins to mind the babies and littlest chavvies.

That was okay, but disappointing. But then the men filled the courtyard, replacing the tables with a boxing ring. And all the men and the cikno romni, 7 or 8 years old, stripped down to short pants and shirt sleeves, and set to beating on each other to prove their manhood.

I left soon after, slipping out to catch the train. And on the ride, I started thinking thoughts, and grew angry. First at myself, then at everyone.

No one asked about my school or my music, and there was no place made for me to mention it. I was welcomed, but as another worn down romni nodding her head, which made me angrier still.

Who raises these boys and these men? Women. Who spoils these boys and these men, so much that they can act like beasts and make the decisions? Women.

You think I'm talking shesti, but will Peti let you keep studying? You are smarter than he is. And he won't, so you won't, and he is still a kind and forward-thinking Romany, and you love him very much. I know this.

Here is a thought I keep thinking: do we teach the men to hate us? Do we hate ourselves?

I am not going crazy. And I am not ashamed of being Romany. But I have to tell you, and swear you to secrecy, that I like living with these English girls and I like that they are not ashamed of being girls. At first, I was shocked. They keep their pads and cloths right in the bathroom, and if a man came to visit, he would see them, along with stockings drip drying in the bathtub and maybe even brassieres.

But then, why not? Is it such a surprise to a man that women bleed? Is it such a surprise that we wear stockings and panties and something to hold up those breasts they love so well, and that feed their sons? Do you think Peti does not know, that he thinks you are pushed up and in and out by magic and innocence? Does he really think he will be polluted if you cook during your time, or you brush him with the hem of your skirt? No. I think not. I think not, or you, my dear friend, would not love him so well, and he would not be worthy of your love.

But. And. I do not know what comes after these words now, for me, at least tonight.

Now I AM talking shesti. I feel the distance between us today. I am tired, so will pause this where I can say good night and that I miss you, with a smile, and not sad schoolgirl tear stains on my midnight note.

More soon.

Your shesti Lolo

30 January

Kezia,

There is a private post that is going to carry these pages to France, then into the mail from there. It is frightfully expensive per letter, so I have stuffed miri Mamo's letter in with yours. Please bring to her. But press your lips tight together, baro moy, promise me! Ha ha!

Nais tuke, amalni.

Lolo

6 Feb

Mamo!

I am still shocked at how quick my letters arrived. Perhaps it is good for Romania that England's postmen strike. The private post is expensive, but efficient!

I'm still emotional from hearing your voice. I did not expect to hear from you so soon, and I am grateful and happy.

I will answer as many questions as I can remember that I did not get to in our call. You quizzed me, and I was too soft and slippery with joy to have everything stuck. It will be a reason for you to call me again (see how cunning your most vestacha and only chej is?)!

I did not describe London or my room, yes. You always pushed me with words. When I talk with music, you see through my eyes, but the connection is too poor, too expensive (like the post, like food, like the train, like London!).

My days are simple. Here, I wake early (early compared to the other girls). I make tea, strong, and mix in jam and sugar and milk (I don't get English tea. It's weak, and thin, and everyone drinks it all day long), I sit with my tea as long as I can make it last, and eat bread with butter, or cheese and leftovers. If I am good or I am lonely or I am tired, I will eat biscuits too. Store bought, from a tube, lacquered in chocolate. I miss the fruits at home, but I eat well. School days, I dress and walk if I can. Seeing the same sights at the same times makes me feel more at home, and there are even a few faces I see at the same sights and same times, and we say hello. Classes go until 3 o'clock, then we break for tea, and I rehearse until 6, and take the train home because it is dusk. My flatmates and I chat, and eat a cold supper, and then retire to study and read and study. And read. My flatmates watch the telly—television. But I am happier to read and practise. And write my letters, of course!

Work days I rise and I breakfast, and we are at the stall by 6 am. I started bundling flowers, but I made good sales, so Sookie's family keeps me at the front. I handle money, answer questions. It makes me smile all the time because we sell flowers that I picked all over for nothing, thinking nothing, of them even popping up in the cracks of stones in Bucharest. And here, we sell them, tied bunches of oleander and violets, aster and bellflower. English people pay extra and I get to keep that. Even I feel the cold by the time we close the stall, and I always treat myself to a cup of hot chocolate from another vendor who gives us a low price. Then, home, to practice, reading, studying. Reading.

I am not a movie star!

Kurko lunch starts at 11, on time, so Sundays, I am on the train by 9:30. This way, I am early, and avoid the scoldings of fifty aunties (ha ha ha!). In fact, right now, it is growing dark, and I have pages to read and sleep to get so I can make that morning train tomorrow.

Me kerav miri Mamo,

Loliya

7 February

Mamo, where are you? Where are you? I hung up the telephone with Káko Ray ages ago, and he said he was going to fetch you right away.

He does not know anything, I could tell, and I did not tell him anything except that this is an emergency and to please get you. I cried at the end. I could not help it.

Mamo, where are you? I am scared, Mamo. Ke dar mánge.

Saint Sarah, protector of the Romany and mother of travellers, to you I come to confide my sorrows and joys and offer my heart. I pray for myself in my hour of need. Gulo Sarah, come to me.

I am freezing cold. My hands, feet. Ke dar mánge. Ke dar mánge.

Oh, Mamo. Please call. Please call. Call.

7-8 February

Kezia,

My dear friend. Forgive me. My hands are so cold and I cannot get warm.

Ke dar mánge. I cried myself asleep waiting for miri Mamo. But she has not called and I woke up again. Ke dar mánge.

Ke dar mánge. Though I am safe. I am safe. I am in my flat and my girls are asleep and I am safe.

Why am I still so afraid?

You will not believe. I do not believe, sitting now, cold hands, scared like a child. But phenav chachimos. Every word is true.

I went to Kurko lunch, just as I have, the past two Sundays.

Today was not lunch at all. It was a wedding.

"I did not know!" I said. "I brought no gift." Prikaza, bad luck!

But no gift is expected, at your own wedding.

My wedding.

Two big cousins took me by the hands to present me to some moosh, dragged up from muck. With a big bowl face, filled with soft pudding, and with a voice like a growl. His hands, cratered like the moon, and his eyes. Oh, his eyes. I knew his insides were even uglier then.

But there he stood, licking his lips like I were a dish, and a Grandfather Szgany promising him my price.

If I were frozen in place before, I burned then. I yelled, "Nashti! No, I will not!" I yelled and I screamed. Aunties giggled—a "nervous bride"—as the cousins now held back my arms, and grandfather came close to my face, whispering, "Dear one, be calm, have joy! This match is baxtali, dear little one."

Joy? Calm? Luck? So what did I do? I spit.

I spit in the face of a Grandfather Szgany, who blinked and let it drip. "All little girls are nervous on their wedding day," he said, part to me, part to the crowd, fifty of everyone, and one beast.

"I am not getting married!" I yelled and yelled.

A familia of boxers forgets the strength to hold up a violin for hours, and I pulled free. A familia of boxers, and no one expects me to throw a good punch.

And I threw a good punch. Right across the nose of a Grandfather Szgany.

Blood and blood. I spilled blood. I froze still again, I thought for shock myself of what I had just done. But it was not just that.

I froze and time froze, because in all of one single second, the Grandfather Szgany did more than was possible. Inside of one moment, one alone, he held back his blood with one hand and held out the other, clenched in a fist. I waited for his blow, but none came. Instead, he opened his fist where he held a mound of dirt. It was my dirt, I took a handful from home, silly me, sentimental me, so I would always be able to rest in Romania, even far away. How did he have it? My dirt is in a jar, in my room, across the city. My mind spun and spun.

Then he said these words, clear as day, even holding back his blood, holding my dirt:

"Listen to me, girl. You were born Szgany, and you will be Szgany. A horse may buck and a horse may kick, but if it has been bought and paid for, being broken is its fate."

We looked at one other, and I broke the state. I yanked and ran. If I am a horse, then I bucked and I kicked, and I ran.

Cousins and uncles and boriya reached for me, but I shook them off. I do not know how. I was running for my life.

I ran and ran. I lost a shoe, kicked off the other. I ran out of the estate. I ran hard and fast, but I could not get free. I ran and passed cousins, aunties, Szgany everywhere! I passed them on the street, driving in automobiles, looking down from rooftops. I ran past Shepherd's Bush station, I ran clear to the next. And my family, they were already there, for me... but just looking, looking. I thought they would grab for me, but they did not. They just watched. They just looked.

Everywhere, like the eyes of monsters.

I jumped onto the first train that arrived. I sat down, small and compact, and I tucked my bare feet underneath me. I rode one train after another until I got home.

When I looked the door, my knees gave. My flatmates picked me up, and asked what was wrong. My feet were black and frozen through.

I told them nothing, only "I am unwell," and "Good night," and I went to my room and I closed the door.

I wrapped myself in my blanket and I waited until the sun went down, and my flatmates went out or to bed, and I crawled out and called Káko Ray. It took me a few tries to dial all the numbers in the right order. And I begged him to wake up, and to get my mother.

But she has not called. I am waiting and waiting, and it is growing early. I fear now something has happened. Something terrible. She should have called by now. Even if muro Káko dressed for a Saint's day, he would have reached Mamo by now, and even if she was asleep, then woke up, washed, dressed, cooked everyone a grand breakfast and did the dishes straight after, she would have called by now.

Ke dar mánge. Something is wrong.

At first light, I am sending one of the English girls to mail this. If something has happened... dear amalni, you have always been like a sister to me, and I thank you forever. I love you, my friend. I love you.

Lolo

15 February

My dear Kezia,

I am so sorry that I worried you, amal, and thank you for calling me as soon as you read my letter. The fever made me lose my mind, no?

When I try and remember the night I fell sick (and wrote that shesti!) I can only remember here and there—scenes, like photographs, and nothing in order. And when I try and set things in order, it becomes even less clear.

It was a terrible, horrible flu. I have never been so sick. I was too cold and too hot and trapped in dreams.

I am the most baxtali rakli in the world. I have flatmates who love me, who got me to bed, brought in the doctor, and sat by my side through my fever until it broke. And I have you, almani, worried for me, and my mother and uncle and auntie, and now family here too, bringing me ciorba and nettle tea and sweet cakes, enough to share with my English friends (because no Szgany will admit my English girls grew in esteem as they cared for me, but oh, they have!).

I am feeling much better and stronger, but on doctors' orders (both gazhe and Romany!), I am to rest at least one more day. I've made a bed on the sofa, where I can watch birds (visiting the windowsill) and the telly all day long (though every show is on Decimal Day— we have changed currencies here, official today, and you'd think we invaded Czechoslovakia, how heated it gets).

More soon,

Your recovering Lolo

16 February

Muri vestacha Mamo,

I have convalesced well—in fact, I may be one of the only people ever to have gained weight recovering from the flu. And I am quite embarrassed... everyone made such a fuss over me. I am touched, and baxtali to have been so taken care of. But Mamo, somehow... it has also made me more lonely, somehow. During my fever, my flatmates could not understand the Romany (and Romanian) that I spoke in stupor, and the familia was by daily to check on me and bring soup and sweets and medicine, but would not come inside, no matter how sincerely invited. And you and Kezia, and even Ray and Domino, sounding so far away by telephone...

Bah. I am being a brat. Being ill makes me more sentimental. Tomorrow evening, if I am well enough, I will venture out for the first time since my fever broke. Quite by chance, I read there will be a showing of Mihai Viteazu at a small cinema nearby. Kezia has seen it ten times, not a joke, and you, even you, Mamo—two times yourself, correct? I am thrilled like a child to see it, and thankful for the timing. See? Baxtali Lolo, no?

17 February

   PS: Aye, Mamo! You were right. What a film! I could not be prouder to be an Ardeal Szgany. Opre Romania!
   I had a truly wonderful evening. I love you very much!
   Love,
   Lolo

18 February

Kezia, Kezia, Kezia,
   I have asked of you so much these past few months; can I ask more? It is irresistible to know secrets, but then, once you do, you are weighed down by the responsibility. Do I throw an anchor around your neck?
   I will give you a second to decide. Meanwhile, I saw Mihai Viteazu last night, and I cried and cheered... and swooned. Yes. I understand now! I would have seen it with you all those dozen times too!
   All right. Now you decide! If you do not want to carry this, I understand, my sweet friend. And so, burn the rest of this letter without reading it.
   ...
   ...
   ...
   ...
   ...

You did not burn it, did you? Ha ha ha!

I met someone. At the cinema! I saw Mihai Viteazu (finally) and this someone was the one who paid to rent the theatre and show the film in Romanian.

Oh, ho ho! You say. That is good news: you met a rich big spender friend. Where is the secret?

He is not Romany.

He! I know! And even beyond that, he would not be my type if he were: he is older, and not quite handsome. But he is sophisticated and well-read, enjoys music and art... a gentleman! He is of Hungarian heritage, and speaks Hungarian, Romanian, German, English, French, and I think more even, that we did not discuss.

At the end of the film, I was bawling, happy and sad, proud and moved, all those things. As the lights came up, a hand patted my shoulder, offering me a handkerchief. I dabbed my eyes and nose and then he said, "That is a tremendous film. When I first viewed it, I felt as you do, now."

(Do we give back wet handkerchiefs to their owners, by the way?)

I introduced myself, and he introduced himself ("Matthew Corbin," he said, and I think he would have kissed my hand if I let him). Then he asked if I wanted to discuss the film further over tea, since he'd yet found anyone else with as strong a reaction. I nearly said no, but his bird (he has a tame raven! True! On his shoulder) cawed at me in a way that sounded pleading... and you know how I am about birds.

In the lobby, I got my first look at him: medium height, medium build, with beautiful orange red curls (almost too pretty for a man). He is obviously older than I, but I can't tell by how much, and it has not yet come up. His face is not masculine, but neither is it feminine... with elegant features and an aquiline nose. His skin is exquisite, though, so smooth that it seems blurry... as if he is going fast, or I am going very slow.

We talked of music, and history, and Bucharest and Sibiu, and so many other things I cannot even remember all we covered. Tea turned to brandy and Napoleons, and only once did I feel out of place or strange, and only when I realised that Matthew had barely touched his cake, except what he fed to his bird (whose name is Katona, and sweet as a kitten)... meanwhile I nearly licked the plate free of all leftover cream.

"You are so enchanting," he said, "I forgot to eat." And we both blushed and laughed like idiots. But then he said, "I must be bold. I would like very much to see you again." And I blushed like a maiden or, maybe, still an idiot.

Of course I agreed. Thursday, we will go out. On a date? Oh my. Ha ha ha!

He is full of manners and respect, and tried nothing fresh, and sent me home in a private car. And I woke up this morning to a delivery of six dozen red roses. My flatmates went crazy wanting details, but you my best friend get the details first, always.

Oh, the flat smells wonderful. The roses are deep and rich, almost like wine. There are other things I could say, but I will not, yet. It is so lovely having some secrets. Do not worry, amal! When I am ready to share, your ears—well, eyes—will be the first.

Peace,

Lolo

25 February

Salutări Profesor Văduvă,

Thank you, sir, for your kind comments on my presentation and suggestions on researching the use of Romany/Byzantine modal scales, and the article on heterophonic counterpointing as an interpretive device used by the first violin in Gypsy orchestration. You are right, sir, the musical idiom is more than just the scales with augmented seconds.

Our Winter holiday starts next week, and I must admit, as much as I relish the hard work I do here, I am grateful for a brief rest... a rest that includes deeply reading this article and sketching out ideas for my composition final project (of course).

I hope this note finds you well.

My best wishes,

Lolo Szgany

Note left for Lolo's flatmates, 28 February:

Dear girls,

I don't think my family remembers that I'm in rehearsal all day today (I know! I am NO FUN!) so if they call, remind them I won't be over for lunch today? Thank you, loves.

Gran-gran Lolo

4 March

Ah, Kez! Kushti! Your letter was so beautiful. You know I would never miss your day in a hundred years, and I will be there. May is the most beautiful month, too. I agree, and a traditional celebration at the pass will be wonderful... there will nothing but green, young leaves and wildflowers to compete with your beauty, and bright sun to warm the guests almost as warm as your love. Te aves baxtali!

And I am beyond happy, beyond pleased to hear that you are finishing your schooling even after the ceremony. I am humbled that my rambles inspired you to talk frankly with Peti, and thankful that he is as rational a man as you foresaw.

I wish more Romany men were as Peti... I wish more gadje men were as Peti! As unrestricted as it seems for gazhya, some struggles are the same. Saturday, I am going with my flatmates to a march of women calling for rights. Can you imagine? There are such gatherings in England often. I am excited and a small bit frightened. But mostly eager.

I take to heart your reservations about Matthew. But you are now playing the fit gran, warning me of the temptations of the devil! Ha ha ha!

I am being careful, dear granny, I promise. I have committed no sin—not even lying. I am not mentioning to miri Mamo... yet, and Sunday, I took my violin on our date so telling the vitsi I missed Kurko lunch to practise was, strictly, true.

Also, I agree that Katona was an attraction. He is a sweet-natured bird and now comes to me and sits on my head when I call him!

But Matthew is tender and respectful, and honours our Romany ways. He is made of more than money (but he has so much of it! And no fear of spending!). There's depth there, something older than his years, and some mystery I have not yet even approached.

More soon, amalni. Sookie has returned with takeaway suppers and the four of us are painting signs with slogans to carry at the march.

—Tjiri Lolo

6 March

PS: Kez, the march was incredible. I am overwhelmed and exhausted, but had to write now, while I still hold the feelings... there were thousands, yes! Thousands of women. Old, young, white, brown (but no other Romany I saw), Grannies (not joke Gran) with canes, mothers with tiny chavvies, other students... all dancing and walking and singing for justice through Hyde Park and Oxford Circus. The weather was misery, snow and rain, and we gave up our signs once they turned to mush. But no one went home, we stood and walked all together with joy even as we fought against injustice.

There is so much possibility, Kezia. So much we can be. I hope you feel these words vibrating when you read them, because I am buzzing as I write them. Opre, raklya!

10 March

Mamo, I send you a postcard because... I can! The strike is ended, and the Royal Mail restored. So, a quick note is within the budget (and schedule! Classes have started again) of your poor, hardworking chej. Ha ha ha! The front is the Museum at the Royal Academy. One day, they will own my fiddle and my guitar. Ha ha ha! I love you! Lolo

10 March

Kez,

The enclosed postcard is Regent's Park, pretty eh? I came often to feed birds here before Katona stole my heart. I came today on a whim, and the strangest thing happened (too long to fit on the card so...) I brought my lunch to share with the birds, and had a crowd of them, when a madwoman came to me from nowhere. She was thin and matted, unfortunate, and I had nothing but the other half of my sandwich. I was about to offer her when she ran my birds off with some yells and stomps, and told me to never feed them again. She said, "Pikey, them birds are not ya mates, they mean to do you ill." When I asked why, she sang a strange little song I had never heard (but was caught in my head) and would not go until I agreed to leave at once. Ah, city life.

I stopped at the library on my way home and looked up the song. It's an old English rhyme for chavvies, "A Farmer Went Trotting." It starts with a farmer and his daughter who ride their horses together, and then, "A raven cried caww and they all tumbled down / bumpity bumpity bump! / The mare broke her knees and the farmer his crown / lumpity lumpity lump!" It goes on that the raven laughed and vowed to do this everyday to the farmer, too. Horrible! Why do people want to frighten children? Ha ha ha! I thought you would appreciate, since you say London sounds so boring.

    Love,

    Lolo

Note left for Lolo's flatmates, 11 March:

E, B, and N,

    I am off to my weekend holiday with Matthew. If anyone calls for me (my mother, the extended fam, or Kezia), please just tell them I am so busy studying and you will give me a message! Thanks! Lolo

11 March

Kezia, my dearest,

    I am off on a holiday now. Matthew wanted to show me the English countryside. It's lovely, but not Romania's equal. We stopped at a small pub for lunch, a real English lunch of little pies filled with potatoes and pickles and dark malty beer. Well, I ate, and fed bits to Katona when Matthew was not looking (he gets so cross with me when I feed Katona treats, but I know a raven's stomach can take anything I can, and he and I have become such good friends. Yes, maybe because I feed him treats!).

    Matthew has had stomach trouble for a while now. I'm starting to worry because he says he can't keep much down and it's been going on for... almost as long as I have known him, a month? He refuses to see a doctor, however, and I will not nag him like a wife... yet. Ha ha ha!

Aside from his delicate stomach, he sunburns easily, and he takes such care to protect his face and hands.

You would never know if he was suffering because he is in excellent spirits. He hides his discomfort to not ruin my time. He is thoughtful. More soon.

2pm

Our grandmothers always told us to be careful what we say, lest we pull it into being. Right?

So, Matthew deceived me a bit. But no, I'm not angry. I do not yet know what my true feelings are. But I will return to that.

I thought we were visiting a historic inn in a particularly beautiful part of the English countryside.

But it turns out that Matthew has taken me to Ravenswood, an enormous estate he purchased. It is both opulent and peculiar, as well as terribly old-fashioned, though I am sure that is just a reflection of good aristocratic tastes. You know my peasant aesthetics, ha ha ha!

It is the biggest house I have ever been in, as big as my university.

Maybe not that big... but it is big, and feels bigger because it is so empty. Not of things: it's full of furniture and art and quite a lot of books. It's empty of people.

As far as I can tell, Matthew has not hired any staff or he has dismissed them for the weekend because he has romantic inclinations (he has not overstepped his bounds in any way. He has shown me to my room, which is as far away from his room as one can be while still remaining in the same wing!).

I expected there to be a lot of servants for a house this size (I guess), but no one greeted us, and Matthew cooked our dinner (yes! he cooked—an unexpectedly tasty meal—and the kitchen is as large as my whole flat!).

So, it seems to only be the three of us, Matthew, me, and Katona as chaperone (ha ha ha!), though there are strange echoes and thuds. I know all houses make noise, so a large house must make large noises, right?

I am in my room (large!) trying to relax and consider what I feel. Coming here must have been important to Matthew. He must have been afraid that I would refuse him if he told me outright where we were going. Perhaps I'm being presumptuous, but I wonder if invoking "wife" pulled something into being, like our grannies say. Maybe he wanted to show me the house that he bought to live in as a married couple?

Oh my. My, my, my, my. I do not know how I feel about that. And I do not exactly like this house, I mean, to live in myself.

The location is odd. It's in neither village nor country, exactly. Just remote. And you know I love the countryside, so it's not that we are too far from of a city. It's just as if the house is nowhere. I mean, of course, it is somewhere, but I don't think I could tell you where.

There are no landmarks, just land.

3:15pm

I just went to ask Matthew about where we are. He seemed to think that a stupid question (I think his pains must be worsening). He said they are moorlands, quite well known even, in the West Midlands. Shesti. I do not know what they would be known for except being horrible, and West Midlands only confuses me more... west of middle? Perhaps I am stupid. But I will tell you, these are not the moors of Wuthering Heights, though, amal, at all (not that I am any sort of Cathy, nor Matthew a Heathcliff).

6pm

Matthew has closed his door. I think he is feeling more unwell. I can hear him inside, though moving things, as loudly as if the door were open. I can hear Katona cawing, as well. The acoustics of this house are interesting. I do not wish to disturb him now, but I am excited to play my violin here and see how the sounds travel.

I walked around the halls some. The furnishings are old but remarkably kept (Matthew mentioned at dinner that they are all heirloom pieces and have been in his family for many years).

There is a recurring motif throughout the house... a black bird—a raven, I presume—carrying a jewelled ring in its beak. I understand Matthew's love of birds, then. I grew up surrounded by flocks in Bucharest, he grew up seeing their image everywhere...

This design really is everywhere, carved into chairs and the sides of tables, stitched in embroidery on linens and tapestries. Something irks me, though. The motif is so familiar (and not just because I have now seen it a hundred times, ha ha ha!). I have seen it somewhere, in a book, maybe, or? I recognise it. But from where?

10pm

Kezia, things are wrong. Very wrong. I heard voices and out my window, I see... Kezia, my relatives are here. Kezia, my mother is here. Kezia, my flatmates, in chains, severed, on the table where hours before I thought of... now, Matthew feeding, eating and drinking. The Raven King Hunyadi, sire of Dracula. And we, his slaves.

Monsters, monsters, everywhere.

Kezia, I was not dreaming. I was not ill. Miro Devla, I was not dreaming.

11:30pm

Kezia,

Twice I have escaped.

There will be no third, though they do not want to hurt me, they said, because I am the daughter of Death. They want to protect me, because I will have a daughter and my daughter, it is fated, will strengthen the Szgany.

But I do not trust them and you should not either. I walked out, agreeing, but it will never be.

Hide, miri amal. Take your Peti and never again go home. Take what you can and walk into the night.

That's what I am going to do, though it breaks my heart. I will not tell you where I am going. We will never speak again. It will be easier to be dead.

I love you, my friend. Always.

Lolo

III.

BornWithTeeth.Com

Welcome to the world of Dani V.
Roustabout, dreamer, work-in-progress.

"We will stomp to the top with the wind in our teeth."
George Leigh Mallory

About me • Popular posts • Archive • Posts by tag
Latest posts • Contact • Home

Follow me!
Facebook | Instagram | Twitter

All content ©2017, unless otherwise stated. All opinions my own.
Click links at your own risk.
Powered by WordPress

*   *   *

August 10 (Public)

BRITISH COLUMBIA'S ON fire. There's 123(!) fires right now, and some have been burning since JULY. For real. Look at the <u>BC emergency page</u>. Some are just marked "<u>out of control</u>." Like, they are burning, yeah, we know, and there's not much we can do about that.

We're getting the smoke down here, now. It's making the sky really strange: the sun's a dull orange coin you can look at, straight on, just about. It's a sci-fi sky.

And if today's anything like yesterday, the haze will hold in the heat so it's going to be a bad one again.

Bad one. Meh. We're lucky here, actually. All we've had is a hot summer made a little hotter by someone else's misfortune, and a <u>record 53 days without rain</u>. Sure, it looks like the end of the world, but it isn't. It's another day, a perfectly fine, perfectly uncomfortable Seattle summer day.

And another perfectly fine, perfectly uncomfortable summer day in which I haven't told my mother yet.

Dani Văduvă's a big chicken, dear readers. Bawk, bawk, bawk.

I had chances, too. Just this morning, I brought us two iced coffees and sat while my mother reads the paper. Bless her, she still gets the paper-paper. She's a voracious, but slow reader, smart, but painfully slow (English is, like, her third language!). And she defends her dead trees in the cutest way: "Paper feels more patient, waiting for me to finish, copilul meu." Screens stress her out.

Anyway, I brought us coffees, sat down, and asked what she was reading.

"They're speculating whether the smoke will interfere with the eclipse," she reported. "I hope it clears out."

My mother's been trying to get me to care about this stupid eclipse for months. She bought THREE pairs of approved viewing glasses (in case one breaks). She never spends frivolously. Woman is eclipse serious.

I should be thankful she isn't obsessing over the fires, though. Usually, it's the kind of thing she would focus in on, read some pattern or omen in it.

"I'm sure it'll be fine, Mamă," I said, or something which maybe sounded dismissive because she set down her coffee, pulled down her eyebrows in the middle like she does, and looked at me over her glasses. "Your hair is getting long, copil."

And there was my first chance. *I agree, mother. And there is a reason why... you know that photo of you at my age? The one you said was right before you left Romania? You're wearing two braids and a headscarf, but also a The Who shirt and that pair of giant sunglasses, like a fucking rockstar. I wanna look like that because...*

(Check the scan of that pic on Instagram. 1970, baby.)

Instead, I said, "I like it long."

My mother picked up her hair and held it away from her neck. "It is so hot to be growing your hair, copil. Grow it in the winter, if you want to."

Second chance. *Well, mother. Hair may be hot, but wigs are hotter, and I want to start my life as soon as possible already,*

Instead, I said, "Cut *your* hair, if you are uncomfortable. I'm fine."

She dropped her hair. It fell like a heavy curtain. "Maybe," she said, "we should both cut our hair."

Damn it. I couldn't tell, still can't tell, if she's bluffing. She's got a stone cold poker face.

"Maybe," was the best I could say. "Maybe we should."

Bawk, bawk, bawk.

August 11 (Public)

MY MOTHER WAS not bluffing, people. ZOMG.

This morning, I bring out our ritual iced coffees for us, and instead of reading her paper, she looks at me and says, "Get dressed, copil. It is mamă și copilul ei haircut time."

Sidebar: my mother has to suspect, right? She's called me "copil" since I was, I don't know, 6 or 7. Never "son." Always "copil." Child, or "copilul meu/ei," my/her child. Never "băiat," little boy, or "fiu," son. Always copil, non-gender-specific copil.

Anyway, OK. My hair is pretty scruffy, and I could get a good cut that would look good now, and then grow out with some shape. "We need to go to a good place," I say. "Vain, or Scream or Libertas."

My mother sits up to argue, she has her cheapskate face on, but she changes her mind and agrees. "Anyplace you want."

So, hold tight, my people. Pictures to come. We're going to Vain!

Mamă și copilul ei haircut time FTW.

ETA: Check us out. I know mine looks pretty basic, but it's got good bones. And Mom! I was floored she went straight for a Rosemary's Baby-era Mia Farrow pixie cut. There was SO MUCH hair on the floor. I don't think she's ever had hair this short.

It changed her whole look. I mean, I knew we Văduvăs had serious eyebrow action, but this put them up front on Mom. Ba-bam!

When we got home, I supervised her tweezing a few of the strays (she's never been a shaper), and now, those brows are ON POINT. Here's a close-up.

Can you even believe this woman is 65? Please, please, please let me have gotten those genes. Lord knows, I missed out on the music talent, but if I got this, then no complaints, at all, ever.

OK, I hear you. DID YOU TELL HER?

What do you think?

Bawkity, bawk.

Let's review my missed chances today:

- When Mom said, "That cut is a bit feminine on you, copil." No shit! *Mother, that's totally what I'm going for.* Nope. I must have just looked worried while I was screwing up my courage, because she quickly went on to tell me how nice it looked, and then onto whispering to me for advice on tipping.

- After the cuts, at Chipotle, because we were both starving, when the guy behind the counter asked me, "Miss, do you want guacamole for $1.25 extra?" and I did not correct him, and my mother afterward assured me that I don't look like a girl. *That's too bad, Mom, because I am a girl.* But instead I just smiled and ate my burrito.

- Later, waiting for the bus on Third Avenue, I got checked out by a sort of handsome chickenhawk. At first, I wondered if I'd been clocked, but his look was so deep and interested, and, well, I have to say it, enthralling, it could not have been anything but. He was totally not my type, and, you know, feminism! and standing with my mom, inappropriate! My mom totally picked up the vibe, followed it to the source, and then killed his line-of-sight like a mildly horrified mama bear.

Are we making a betting pool yet, dear readers? Like guessing the date of a baby or something? How many more times can I chicken out before I grow a waddle and wings? Post your bets in the comments. Closest wins a prize. A gift card to KFC or something, LOL.

August 12 (Public)

THE AIR'S STILL pretty bad. And now some fires near Twisp and Omak, and a few places in eastern Washington have joined the party. And my mother casually drops that she wants to pack up, take the RV down to Oregon, so we can "see the full eclipse," then move on somewhere, maybe east again.

FUCK.

She hasn't really talked to me about why I took a leave of absence from school. It's been the room elephant (not including, yanno, the other stuff). I thought she was giving me some time—one of the things I know I scored on the parent front is that my mom trusts me and my judgement (she's always been good about that). But, fuck. She's had her own agenda, and didn't say anything because she's selfishly relieved. Something's spooked her. Some something (the fires? Some tragedy on the news? A coincidental happenstance of some bullshit variety?)

Maybe it's the actual eclipse. I fell for it that she's interested in it, but instead she sees it as some literal harbinger of doom.

This is what she does.

And I'm home, for a year, whatever my reason, so she can indulge this crap (again, always, my whole life) pull up stakes, cut bait, and go. With me. Convenient.

Only not.

All I can think is, *dammit woman, I'm approved for HRT and starting next week... do you know how hard that was? and Holy shit, I need an address to get my license mailed when I change the damn thing We can't just leave.*

I probably am looking at her with some sort of hateful disbelief while I think all this, because she sets her face stony, ready for a fight. It looks even more set than usual, but that's because of her haircut and those excellent eyebrows.

But there's no way to fight this. You can't fight madness.

I've tried, believe me. I've used every trick, strategy, beggary in the book to ask, wheedle, cajole, force, embarrass, compromise, and beg her to get help. And she won't. She doesn't think there's anything wrong with her, nor believes there's anything anyone can do to help.

Because, hard truth time: I think my mother has undiagnosed, untreated paranoid schizophrenia (the <u>DSM-IV code 295.30</u> says it's the most common illness that causes the sort of psychosis she has). And she's had it my whole life.

My dear, smart, loving, mother sincerely and thoroughly believes someone—well, really more a someTHING, with the powers she claims it has—is stalking us and wants to kill us.

I could write so much on this, but I don't know where to start ATM. I could write a memoir about it (life w/my cray mom). Needless to say, she believes this. No, KNOWS it, like we know the sky is blue, fire is hot, and water is wet. She knows someone is out for us. And there is no fighting that.

Best I can do is stall it for awhile.

We go back and forth, back and forth ("we need to stay," "it's not safe," "I don't want to go," "we have to") and keep throwing out reasons (I have friends, opportunities, she has good job), escalating until I hit one that finally hit pause.

"Mamă," I say. "I got a full scholarship to UW."

You'd think that was an obvious lie, I mean, why would I not have started with that, right? But my grades were good, and she so wants me to do well, have a good university education and a career, that she is willing to overlook these little red flags.

(Could I, should I have told her the real news? Yes, probably.)

My mother stops. She's obviously pleased and proud, but also worried, now. She considers things. "You are not giving up on school, then?"

(Is that really what she thought? That I was just a complete dropout? A+ parenting for waiting this long, mom!).

"No way," I answer.

"Giving up was never your style, Danior," she says, and in a second, I've moved from pissed to weepy. I can't wait to see what kind of dumpster fire of emotion I'll be on hormones.

But we stay. We're staying. And for today, that's a victory.

* * *

August 13 (Private, draft)

I WOKE TO music. My mother plays classical when she is working something out. It's a nice piece that I've never heard before, When I ask her about it, she just says it's Debussy and slams away her violin.

She'd been up awhile. She's already made and drunk her coffee, and as I poured some for myself, I saw two smashed cig butts in the sink.

She hasn't smoked—well, in front of me—in a long time.

"Good morning, draga mea Danior," she says, and then sees that I see the butts in the sink. "I was thinking, that's all."

I ask her what about. She looks sad, and I kind of feel guilty, but also... not.

"I have made a difficult life for you, I think," she said.

Crap.

"You've made a great life for us, Mamă."

And in her way, she has. I know I was unexpected, and she is older than most mothers, and raised me all on her own.

More to say. Finish this later. Ugh. There's more going on because now she is looking at her jar of Romania (a quart of dirt, for real) and I know that means she is really sad, and I'm going to be a good child and drag her to the mall or something, a movie. To be continued.

August 14 (Public)

HAPPY HRT DAY.

Today is the first day of the rest of my life (I know, honk!)

I'm going full speed ahead: hormones, starting today. I'm going to name change on Wednesday, then file the new gender designation Friday. I've got the paperwork, I've got the signatures. And I've got the time.

I also decided I'm going to stop pushing myself so hard to do some Hollywood reveal to my mom. It's silly and unnecessary. It's not as if I just "came out" as female; I was born female (why can none of us say "born this way" now without silently adding "baby" at the end? Damn you, Gaga). Figuring out who I am and what to do about it is emergent; why on earth do I think it should be different for anyone else, especially those closest to me?

I'm not a chicken, dearhearts. I'm sensitive.

Yes, sensitive.

My mother knows. She has to know. She's known me my whole life, and she's a brilliant, worldly woman. Maybe at first, she thought I was gay (I did weep over some boys in my time).

But I'm not gay, honey. I'm queer. I'm strălucitor (that means shining, sparkly, luminescent, for all ya non-Romanians in the room).

Also... I'm super nervous. A lot's about to change: my body, my brain. Even though I've waited a long time, there's still fear. There's always fear when there's any "what-ifs."

And that is life.

Off I go. Sparkle, sparkle.

ETA: OMG thank you Ivy and Ruthie! All, they gifted me a Groupon for, like, a TON of electrolysis. I don't even know what to say. Thank you, thank you... by the hairs of my chinny chin chin.

ETA pt 2: Girl hormones are go. I am imagining these tiny little ladies, dressed to kill, streaming through my body, kung fu fighting all the testosterones they encounter. Bam, kapow. Rounding up all surrendered boymones in tiny golden lassos, and... um, forcing them to serve all the ladymones cool drinks and foot massages (yes, my hormones have mouths and feets, LOL)

* * *

August 15 (Public)

WAYLAID AT MIGRAINE City, population me.

Ugh, I was warned. I'm OK if I don't move, smell or try and eat anything. Ha.

Screen's starting to make me ill. I'm off again.

Love ya!

August 16 (Public)

MIGRAINE SETTLED SOMETIME in the night, and I got some sleep. So I was able to get up and get going (nothing's gonna stop me now!).

The name change went fine (it maybe helps that I'm just dropping a few letters from my first name, and adding a middle name? The clerk kind of gave me a look like "why are you even bothering?" But whatever, lady. My life, my name, my $200 bucks).

So, yeah, I'm now Dani* Văduvă, and I can do my Change of Gender Designation Requests all in one swoop (or, at least, start with driver's license).

Something bothering me, though. At first I thought it was my imagination, but I'm starting to get creeped out. Last week, when mom and I got our hair done, I told you all about that chickenhawk checking me at the bus stop?

Well, since then, I have seen him twice. Once, downtown again, outside the Medical Dental Building on Olive, when I was getting my hormones. That didn't strike me as weird—it's downtown, there's a ton of offices in that building, and it's right across from Westlake Center, etc., etc.—but today, he was at the courthouse, just sitting there, like he was waiting for someone (me? Yikes!). It just seemed too-too, you know? It could be coincidence, but. Yeah.

It is totally the same guy, I'm sure of it. He's pretty distinctive looking: red hair, really pale, old fashioned style, kinda steampunky but less kitsch. Anyway, I'm not sure what to do.

He hasn't approached me or anything. What you think, dear hearts? Am I that fabulous, or fab-loon-us?

Am I turning into my mother ALREADY? (Getting those ta-tas isn't going to come cheap, eh?)

*I will miss Danior, in a way. In Romanian, it means "gift." In Tamil, it means "one." In Urdu, it means "otherwise." In Latin, it means "Denmark" (LOL). But my favorite is in Romany Gypsy: it means "born with teeth" (where I got my URL, yes!).

August 19 (Public)

FIRST OF ALL, I am so sorry I've been absent! I've been hit a little hard by some side effects, lucky me. I had another migraine, which has subsided, though the nausea continues.

Just over here, a-burping and a-farting. Nothing ladylike about being a lady.

August 21 (Public)

MY MOTHER GOT her eclipse. It was a clear day with a little wind even. We climbed up on the roof around 9, and sat through the whole thing.

It was fine. Very interesting, sort of. It got dark-ish, not pitch black or anything... dusky, kinda. I thought the crows were more interesting—two of them, swear to God, landed next to us in the roof and stood there with us, hanging out, waiting for it to be over. Then they squawked goodbye and took off. I guess there were lots of reports of animals and plants acting strangely.

(My mother swore they were ravens, not crows, but whatever. It was cool. Do we even *have* ravens in the Pacific Northwest? <u>Wikipedia says yes</u>, but I still think they were crows.)

Check out <u>NASA's shots of the eclipse</u>. The ones from the Space Station are really cool, even I admit.

August 22 (Private)

THAT MAN, AGAIN. I'm not imagining things. Why would he be at the department of licensing? He has to be following me.

Fucking asshole. For real, either do something or leave me alone. God damn it.

<u>I got his picture</u>. My phone usually takes better pics. You can just make him out to the left of the sign. And I swear there's a bird sitting on his shoulder. Maybe that's a smudge.

August 23 (Public)

STOOD ON THE line, submitted my documents, paid my fee... and now my license says female.

I'd celebrate harder, but getting a little paper temporary that looks like someone could have made with intermediate Photoshop is a bit of a let down.

Still. Yes!

Next up, social security. But not today, my stomach is really bugging out (which, now that I say that, is probably responsible for quite a bit of my lack of festive spirit here). I'm so queasy it's making my heart race.

Ugh. While I recuperate, check this out: <u>Twenty Animals Who Aren't Photogenic</u>. Thank you BoredPanda.com for getting me through some nasty side effects with the bestest meds (at least best legal meds, har).

* * *

August 25 (Public)

HI FROM SWEDISH Medical Center...

I'm OK now, promise! So, my stomach pain got worse and worse, really bad... like food poisoning plus gas pains plus digesting a cheese grater bad. After I got home from the DoL, it got to the point where I could barely walk and had a serious fever.

Anyway, I pretty much passed out. My mother called an ambulance and it turns out it's my gallbladder popping out some ungodly number of horrible little stones of whateverthefuck (actually crystallised cholesterol). It's a less common, but not wholly uncommon side effect (as many of y'all know) of spiro (and other testosterone blockers, too).

My dudemones aren't going down without a fight, I guess.

The good news is the lovely people at the hospital immediately dosed me with morphine, which made all the rest, including the surgeon explaining he was just going to pop out my gallbladder right quick, like a beautiful dream.

And if that did not make it exciting enough... my mother, uh, well, she knows now.

Yup.

I was either unconscious or drugged (or finally, blissfully, both), so mom has my wallet and does the admission paperwork. Of course, she pulls out my new paper driver's license, my court order, all sorts of stuff. Surprise!

Telling my mom. Nailed it.

Sigh.

Anyway, she's taking it as well as expected. Actually, better. I have to giver her credit.

I wake up this morning, groggy and confused. I can't sit up, I learn quick, because when I try, I almost barf, and I touch my stomach and there's a long incision, like someone tried to filet me (ick and also ouch).

Turns out they had to go in and take out my gallbladder the old-fashioned way (sometimes the old ways are not best, y'all!). And my mom is there, of course, exactly as I would expect, sobby and relieved that I'm all right, but also a little distant, like she is both sad and relieved truly, but also waiting for the requisite sad and relieved part to be over so she can move onto something else.

And the something else is my wallet. Which she went into for my intake papers. And contains... my temporary license (gender F!), my name change order, clinic card, etc., etc.

Not exactly how I hoped, but it's done, which is a relief. No stopping me now. Roar.

More soon. Rumor is I get ice cream whenever I want (no silly, I know that's for tonsils. I'm just joking. Though I do want ice cream).

August 26 (Private, draft)

WRITING THIS DOWN so I don't forget any of it.

Mom is there when I wake up.

"Oh, Danior," is all she says at first. Then she says, "I was hoping... this would pass. You'd grow out of it."

My cheeks flush. "Like a *phase?*" I ask, pouring all the anxiety and hurt and anger into 'phase,' so she'd feel it like the insult it was.

"Yes," she says, then, "No. Not like a phase. I do not know." She won't look at me: she looks down at the tiled floor.

I'd sit up, if it didn't hurt so much. I'm so upset, and I'm starting to cry, which makes me madder. "You don't know because you don't want to know. You never want to know what's real. You never want to know the truth."

My mother finally looks at me. She's tearing, too, but her words come clear and pointed; she's angry, too. "No child. It is *you* who does not know the truth." That 'you' has all the power of my 'phase.' Whatever expression I make, she sits down at the edge of the hospital bed and softens her tone. "It is not your fault. I have never told you. But I have never lied to you," she says, and reaches for my arm, like I should immediately forgive her, and issue a certificate of commendation and a parade in her honor, yanno, for not lying to her child.

"All right, *Mamă*. Let's lay it all out, once and for all. I am a woman. I was born and assigned the wrong gender. I intend to fix that." I don't know if what I actually say is so dignified, but it is close. And feels good.

Until my mother starts shaking her head. "You cannot," she says. "I will not allow you. I forbid it."

I laugh now, not because it's funny, but because it's the only sound I can make. It sounds mean. It *is* mean. I'm sick with it. This is the woman I was sure would always love me, no matter what. And now? And this? *Fuck you, mom.* "You can't stop me." *Nothing's gonna stop me.*

At that, tears flow. "You need to listen to me," she says.

I don't even have to say it out loud. *No.*

"Just listen. What you are, it is dangerous." She feels along the blanket for my arm. "You do not know what you're up against."

Oh, Mamă. I'm hit by a wave of sadness, anger ebbing away. I can't let fear stand in my way. "I can't be scared and I can't run from myself. And if people want to hurt me, if people want to kill me for that, then..." I don't know how to finish that sentence. How do you finish a sentence like that? "I have to live, Mamă. I'll be smart. I'll take self defense."

She shakes my arm, frustrated. "You think learning to punch is going to protect you? You think I do not know self defense? Hiding is what keep us safe. Hiding who we are and what we are..."

I jerk back my arm. Now the sadness ebbs, anger back on shore. "Oh, God! Here we go. Into the crazy."

"Danior, Dani. I may be crazy, but that doesn't mean you do not have to listen." She wrenches my arm from my chest. "I know what you are. I knew when you were 2 years old. I have done my best to protect you, keep you hidden. It is my fault."

"Mom, I'm not a woman because of a fault," I say.

"Dani, I need you to shut up."

"I'm a wo—"

"Dani, would you please *fucking* listen to me?"

I skidded quiet. She just cursed. My mother never curses.

"Dani, that man you keep seeing... the one at the bus stop, at the court, at the driver's license... he's here because of me. Because of something that happened long ago. He is very dangerous."

"You read my blog?" I ask.

"I am your mother," she says. "Of course I read your computer. It is part of my job." She drops my arm, puts her palms on my cheeks. "My vestacha chej, I have so much to tell you." She keeps her hands on my face. "Vestasha chej means 'beloved daughter' in Romany."

"Like Gypsy?" I ask, as she sits back.

She nods.

"You speak Romany?"

My mother nods. "We *are* Romany."

"We're Romanian," I say. I'm definitely, already not following, and it gets worse, very soon.

"We are both," my mother says. "We are Szgany."

"I don't know what that means."

"Szgany. Our last name, our family. Văduvă is not our name. That was the name of my first music teacher. And my first name is Lolo, not Lola."

"What the fuck?" I'm actually not sure if I say that aloud or just express it with my face.

"I know you think I am... what did you say, 'schizophrenic,'" my mother says, and I wince. "It is all right, child. What I am going to tell you will sounds like delusions. But you need to hear me."

I love her so much and I am such a shitbag. "Of course."

"The man chasing you is called Hunyadi Corvinus Mátyás, the Raven King. Or, as I knew him, Matthew Corbin. He ruled Hungary in the fifteenth century... he helped Vlad Drăculeşti take power in Transylvania—"

I already have, like, 50 questions, all at once, and I am so overwhelmed, I ask the stupidest of all. "Drăculeşti? Like Dracula? I vant to suck your blood Dracula?" *When did you know him? In the 1400s?*

"Many years ago, our people... my mother... we were enslaved to the house of Drăculeşti. When Drăculeşti was killed, Corvinus claimed his rights to the Szgany."

This is the craziest shit yet to come from my mother's mouth. Is it the drugs in my system? Her mother? Vampires, slaves. Why am I... believing her?

"The Szgany served Corvinus for many years. But in the 20th century... he lost us. The First World War and the Second World War, and the Szgany died or took the opportunity to disappear. Corvinus vowed to have us back." My mother studies my face to see my reaction, and god damn it if I'm not all in. "When I went to university, I met some of the extended family. I did not know Corvinus had them back in his power."

At this, we both startle. A nurse comes in to check on me. It's time to order lunch and to stop accidentally sitting on the call button. I have no idea if the nurse heard anything; if she has, she acts as if she hasn't. Knowing Seattle, it's probably far from the craziest shit *she* has ever overheard.

When she leaves, my mother continues. "I met him there, in London. To me, like I said, he was Matt. My... boyfriend." My mother laugh-chokes in her hand, embarrassed. She pushes on. "I was very naive. I did not know better. My mother—she sent me to him, in a way."

"I don't understand the timeline, Mamă. The fifteenth century? You went to school in the 'seventies." At least I'm going for better questions, now.

My mother nods. "My mother, your grandmother, she swore the oath that enslaved all Szgany. For that, she was punished, too. When my mother had me, she was almost 500 years old."

Yeah. I wrote that correctly. Grandma's 500 years old. No wonder my mother looks great at 65.

My mother pours a dixie cup of water from the pitcher by my bed. "This does sound crazy. Nonsense—'shesti' was the word I used to use with my best friend. Bull shit." She hands the cup of water to me, then pours herself one. Then she continues.

"Anyway, to make a long, shesti story shorter, make sense, I do not know. The Raven King had me, and let me go. He tells me that it's written, that I am fated... he tells me it does not matter if I stay or if I go, because it is not me who is important. No matter where I go, no matter what I do, one day, he will come for my daughter."

Aides with lunch trays come in then. They make a big show of moving things off my table, and I want them to just leave, and the food smells sort of horrible. My mother makes me take some apple juice then, and she refills her water. When we are alone again, she continues.

"I decided to disappear, Then, I made it so I could never have children."

I almost drop my water. "But—"

She does not let me finish. "Danior, Dani. You are mine, but I did not have you. I wanted you, desperately. I had a chance to take you, to help out someone, and I thought—"

"It would be OK because I was a boy."

"Yes," she said. "A boy would be safe. I named you Danior for the reasons you found out, all on your own. I was so proud when I saw that. You were a gift. And you would need to be strong. With teeth." My mother gulps down water like it is a shot of something, and I don't blame her. "But I knew you were a little girl soon after you came to me. I hoped because I didn't birth you, you would be... free. But I did not want to chance you.

"So, we traveled." She held open her arms. "We lived like Romany, and you did not even know. I raised you Romany, after all. We traveled like Gypsies have done for thousands of years. We travel to stay free, we travel to be ahead of monsters. War, famine, oppression, slavery, vampires. Monsters."

I'm sure I missed parts. I'll try to add them as I remember. But at this point, my mother stopped. We were both exhausted. My mother held my hand, and we shared my hospital lunch, and we watched the news as Hurricane Harvey landed in Texas. There was comfort losing ourselves in the suffering of others, strength in feeling for someone else, in watching them run from their own monsters.

August 27 (Public)

I'M HOME! IN one piece (though a gallbladder short) and sore all over (but I have a week's worth of happy pills to help with that). I am going to have one bad-ass scar, and you bet I'll show it off, someday, in a bikini.

I'm not supposed to sit up for too long, so this is just a quick update. Things are great here. I'm so happy my mother knows everything. In fact, she's been telling me stories about the past, about her life, and we're closer than ever. She even gave me things to read about women in our family, and one day, she says, I will take my rightful place.

You can't fight nature, my mother always said. You can only rise to meet her or you can run away.

And I am wayyyyy too sore to run (grin).

*   *   *

August 27 (Private)

MY MOTHER GAVE me a leather portfolio. "It's our history," she said.

Where she'd kept it hidden in this RV, I'll never know. I was sure I'd searched every square inch of this thing at one time or another.

The pages are delicate—a journal article, handwritten letters— and I'm scanning them in to protect them:

- ftp://TheGypsyLoreSociety_Grandma_Mera.pdf
- ftp:///Lolo_Letters.pdf

My mother's introduced me to something actually quite nice: tea with jam, and "Django Reinhardt—*Pêche à la Mouche: The Great Blue Star Sessions* 1947/1953." I'm showing her how to use the computer to find her best friend, cousin Kezia Szgany. They haven't spoken in 46 years.

We're getting to know one another, no more secrets.

WELL, MAYBE JUST one secret, and it is mine to keep.

I was born a girl, the granddaughter of death. Fated to bring together again a clan, sworn in blood to serve the devil. I will fulfill my destiny, but not how Hunyadi Corvinus Mátyás believes.

He's thinks he's coming for me, but I will be waiting.

Someday, I, Dani Szgany, will bring my people to the light. I, Dani Szgany, am going to kill the so-called Raven King.

Sparkle!

ABOUT THE AUTHORS

Milena Benini started writing when she was 12, and simply never stopped. She has written five novels in Croatian and one in English, as well as numerous short stories, some of which have been translated into several languages, including Spanish and Polish. She is also the winner of five SFera awards, as well as a number of other local awards. She lives in Zagreb with her family.

Emil Minchev was born in Sofia, Bulgaria, on the 26th of October 1984. He has a master's degree in International Relations from Sofia University and has translated more than 40 books, including Bram Stoker's *Dracula* and *Dracula's Guest*, Oscar Wilde's *De Profundis* and many others. He has also written for various Bulgarian magazines and published three novels of his own—*Towers of Stone and Bone* (a fantasy novel), *Unlimited Access* (an epistolary anti-utopian novel) and *Nose for Crime* (a sci-fi detective novel).

Caren Gussoff Sumption is a SF writer living in Seattle, WA. The author of *Homecoming* (2000) and *The Wave and Other Stories* (2003), first published by Serpent's Tail/High Risk Books and *The Birthday Problem* (2014) by Pink Narcissus Press, Gussoff Sumption's been published in anthologies by Seal Press and Prime Books. She received her MFA from the School of the Art Institute of Chicago, and in 2008, was the Carl Brandon Society's Octavia E. Butler Scholar at Clarion West.

Bogi Takács is a Hungarian Jewish agender trans person currently living in the US as a resident alien. E writes both speculative fiction and poetry, and eir work has been published in a variety of venues like *Clarkesworld*, *Lightspeed*, *Apex* and *Strange Horizons*, among others. You can find visit eir website at www.prezzey.net and find em on Twitter as @bogiperson. E also reviews books focusing on marginalized authors at www.bogireadstheworld.com.

Adrian Tchaikovsky was born in Woodhall Spa, Lincolnshire before heading off to Reading to study psychology and zoology. For reasons unclear even to himself he subsequently ended up in law and has worked as a legal executive in both Reading and Leeds, where he now lives. Married, he is a keen live role-player and occasional amateur actor, has trained in stage-fighting, and keeps no exotic or dangerous pets of any kind, possibly excepting his son. He's the author of the critically acclaimed series *Shadows of the Apt* and *Echoes of the Fall*, of the standalone works *Guns of the Dawn* and *Children of Time*, and numerous short stories and novellas.

FIND US ONLINE!

www.rebellionpublishing.com

/rebellionpub   /rebellionpublishing   /rebellionpub

SIGN UP TO OUR NEWSLETTER!

rebellionpublishing.com/sign-up

YOUR REVIEWS MATTER!

Enjoy this book? Got something to say?

Leave a review on Amazon, GoodReads or with your
favourite bookseller and let the world know!